# THE PORCELAIN MASK

# THE PORCELAIN MASK

## JOHNSTON McCULLEY

**(writing as John Jay Chichester)**

*To my Aunts,*
**ELLA** *and* **ANNA**
*who once told a very small boy that*
*he would some day grow up and write*
*a book.*

Originally published in 1924.
Published by Wildside Press, LLC.
Visit us online at wildsidepress.com.

# CHAPTER 1

## JOAN SHERIDAN RETURNS

One of the village taxis, a sorry, disreputable affair, with noisily clattering fenders, dashed bumpily along the rural highway and turned with precarious suddenness into the driveway, lined on either side by great walnut trees that formed a leafy tunnel to the big house at the far end. It was, despite considerable age, a magnificent house, and it had been modernized with green-striped awnings and sun rooms. The taxi was heavily loaded with luggage. There was one passenger, a girl of twenty-one or two, with an attractive face and expressive dark eyes, now shining with a light of eagerness, as she leaned toward the door of the jouncing vehicle. One slim, gloved hand rested upon the catch.

The little car came to a skidding halt beneath the old-fashioned portico, as the driver jammed the brakes with a suddenness that pitched his fare violently forward, knocking her hat awry. But even this failed to dim her happy, expectant smile; she did not so much as bother to straighten the hat. She had the door open and was out before the driver could double as footman.

"Hope I didn't jar you up, lady, but y' said hurry, an' I fed 'er the gas," he said with a wide grin that revealed two prominently missing teeth. "She's a great li'le car, ain't she, fer goin' on the fifth season?"

The girl nodded and gave him a dollar bill.

"Don't bother about the bags," she told him. "Just leave them anywhere, and I'll have Bates carry them in."

She ran briskly up the brief rise of steps from the driveway to the wide porch that semicircled the house on two sides. The entrance was around the turn; she paused suddenly at sight of the strange young woman who reclined in the couch hammock, asleep. For a moment she stared in surprise, wondering who she was. Women visitors were unusual at Greenacres.

"How beautiful she is!" murmured the girl, letting her eyes linger on the soft, oval face of the sleeper, crowned with bronze hair. "I wonder who she can be?" She softened her step and continued across the porch to the entrance.

Hardly had she entered the reception hall when Bates spied her and came rushing toward her, with that peculiar, shambling gait of his, a broad smile crinkling his thin, leathery face.

"Heaven bless us, it's Miss Joan!" he exclaimed.

"Oh, 'Daddy' Bates!" she cried. "It's so wonderful to get home again! The finest thing about going away is coming back. Only bit over a month, and it's seemed a year!"

Bates was the Gilmore butler, but he had been in the family since the time Joan was a child, and, in this moment of home-coming exuberance, it was only natural that she should use the old affectionate address. Bates, his hands clasped in front of his chest, continued to smile fondly and proudly.

"Well! Well!" he chuckled. "Won't Mrs. Gilmore be happy to see you again, Miss Joan! Surprised, too; she wasn't expecting you until tomorrow."

"The boat docked a day ahead of time," she explained, "and I didn't telegraph. Where is mother?"

"She went upstairs less than half an hour since. Your bags, Miss Joan?"

"Outside, Bates; I told the taxi man to dump them out any old place. Take them right up, if you please, Bates; there are some little things I bought on the other side, and I didn't forget you, either."

Bates sobered.

"Your room—" he began, but broke off suddenly, looking decidedly uncomfortable.

Joan, in her excitement, did not notice. "Why, of course, my room!" she cried gayly, making for the stairs and taking the steps, two at a time. Bates stared after her, wagging his head sadly, and his thin shoulders moved with a lugubrious sigh.

"Poor Miss Joan!" he murmured. "It's going to be an awful shock to her; I didn't have the heart to tell her. And her room, too!" He shambled out to the porch for the luggage.

Reaching the upper hall, Joan went swiftly to the left wing of the house, where her mother had her private sitting room, bedroom, and bath. With a quick gesture she flung open the door and, arms reaching out eagerly, fairly leaped at the little gray-haired woman who sat by the window, reading.

"Mumsey!"

Before Mrs. Gilmore could get to her feet, the girl had swooped down on her in a cyclone of joy, smothering her with kisses and leaving her almost breathless with hugs.

"I—I didn't expect you until tomorrow, dear," gasped Mrs. Gilmore. "Why didn't you wire and let us meet you at the station? Goodness, child, give me air!"

"Oh, it's so much nicer to surprise people," laughed Joan. "How are you?"

"We've all been well."

Joan sat on the arm of the chair and cuddled her mother close.

"It's so wonderful to be home again," she murmured happily. "It was a wonderful trip, my first sea voyage, and the Sharps were perfectly wonderful to me—all through southern France by motor—but there's no place in all the world like Greenacres. How is Kirk getting along with the new novel? Has he missed his severest critic?"

An anxious, half-frightened look came into Mrs. Gilmore's face. "Kirklan," she answered slowly, an ominous note creeping into her voice, "hasn't been writing much during—during the past three weeks. He couldn't really be expected to, since—"

Joan's fingers tightened about her mother's hand.

"Mother! Something—something has happened to Kirk! Is he ill?"

"No, dear, Kirklan is perfectly well, but he—" Again Mrs. Gilmore's voice came to a halting stop.

"Why don't you tell me? The tone of your voice frightens me. What has happened to Kirk?"

"An author can't be expected to do much writing, Joan, when—when he is on his honeymoon," Mrs. Gilmore finished faintly. She felt the girl's fingers, still resting across her own, tremble and become cold.

Joan's face had turned ghastly pale and there was a stunned dullness in her dark eyes. "His—his honeymoon?" she whispered. "You mean— Oh, you can't mean that Kirk has married?"

Mrs. Gilmore nodded.

"Yes, he married—about ten days after you sailed. It was a surprise—a shock—to all of us. The first we knew of it was when he brought her home with him."

Joan was making an ineffectual attempt to keep her emotions in check, to conceal the evidence that the news had been a terrible blow to her.

"Why—why, I had no idea that Kirk was even interested in any one."

"Neither did any of us. It seems that he fell madly in love with her almost at first sight; they were married, I believe, a week after their first meeting. I can't understand how a man would rush headlong into marriage like that, although she is pretty."

Joan's mind reverted to the beautiful woman she had seen asleep in the porch hammock.

"She—she is here now? Then that—that woman I saw downstairs is Kirk's wife? Kirk's wife?" She laughed unsteadily. "It's so hard for me to believe—coming so suddenly like this. Yes, she is pretty; not only pretty— beautiful."

She walked slowly to the window and stood there, her back to the room, trying to keep her face from her mother's eyes. But Mrs. Gilmore was not deceived; she had known for a long time and had feared that the situation would bring only unhappiness.

Although Joan was Mrs. Gilmore's daughter, she still bore her father's name of Sheridan. Her mother, left a widow, had married Peyton Gilmore, a childhood sweetheart, who had himself been previously married. Peyton Gilmore had been a well-known New York lawyer. Those with long memories may remember that he had dropped dead in a crowded courtroom, during a famous murder trial, while pleading for the life of his client. There was a son, Kirklan Gilmore, only twelve years old at the time of his father's death, and Kirklan's rearing had fallen to his stepmother. The two families, merged into one, had long occupied the picturesque, rural New York estate of Greenacres, without friction or discord.

Joan and Kirklan had always hit it off well together, and when, after a try at law, Kirklan had turned to writing, it was Joan who sympathized the most over his failures and rejoiced the most over his successes. Realizing that Joan's deft touches had helped the tremendous success of his novel, "Rogue's Paradise," Kirklan had given his stepsister a trip abroad.

The silence became so long, so painful that Mrs. Gilmore felt that something had to be said.

"Her name," she murmured, "is Helen—Helen Banton before she married Kirklan."

"Does—does he seem to be—very much in love with her, mother?"

"Very much in love with her," Mrs. Gilmore answered, and Joan winced.

"I—I hope he will be very happy," the latter said with a muffled voice.

Mrs. Gilmore shook her head slowly. "I'm afraid that he won't be, my dear. A pretty face is not sufficient to make a man happy. 'Marry in haste, repent at leisure.' It's an old saying, but it's true—as most of the old sayings are. Kirklan has made a mistake, a terrible mistake."

"I don't believe you like her, mother."

"My likes or dislikes have nothing to do with it. They have few tastes in common; already she is sick and tired of Greenacres, and you know how Kirklan loves it out here. She has no interest in his work, and you know how much he needs sympathy, encouragement. He's not the kind that can forge on alone; the kind of wife he should have—"

"Mother, don't! Who was she—how did he happen to meet her?"

"She was employed in some minor capacity by Kirklan's publishers," Mrs. Gilmore replied. "As to who she is—I wonder. Yes, I wonder. I don't think even Kirklan knows anything about her. I don't consider it a good sign when a girl is reticent about her family. Kirklan says, 'I've married a girl I love, not a family tree.'"

Joan winced again, for that was a line she had written into Kirklan's successful novel.

"If—if they're in love with each other, mother, I suppose that's all that matters."

"He's in love with her, but they're not in love with each other, and those one-sided romances always end in disaster. I can't help but feel that she is going to smash his life."

"She—she'd better not!" whispered Joan, her hands clenched. "We won't talk about it any more—please. I'm going to my room and unpack. I'll—I'll come back in a little while, mother." Her tone was weary, lifeless.

Mrs Gilmore gave her daughter another quick glance, as she prepared to deliver the second blow.

"I—I guess you'll miss your old room, Joan; you've always loved it so, with its view of the river."

Startled, bewildered, the girl turned away from the window. "Miss my old room? Why, mother, what—what do you mean?"

"Kirklan had your things moved to the east wing, dear. He tried to make her understand, but—"

"The things moved—from my room!" cried Joan. "Kirklan did that? He —he tried to make her understand? You mean that woman—"

"It wasn't Kirklan's fault, Joan; he tried hard enough to reason with her, but his wife is so headstrong. It is the best room in the house, of course, and I suppose she felt that she had a right, as the new mistress of Greenacres, to it. The place is Kirklan's property."

"That—that woman—in my room!" There was a catching sob in Joan's voice. "Oh, how dare she? And Kirk let her do it."

"You don't understand how headstrong she is," Mrs. Gilmore explained hastily. "She's the sort who demands, who takes what she wants. Kirklan tried to avert it, but I suppose it's hard for a man to deny his bride any-thing. Kirklan has the adjoining room, a separate sleeping chamber. It's the modern thing, I believe, these days. She's had a doorway cut through; the carpenters finished their work yesterday. I knew you would resent giving up your room."

"Of course I resent it!" flared Joan. "She has no right—" She paused and then added bitterly, "No, I suppose I'm wrong; the house is Kirk's, and she did have a right—to everything. I'm going to unpack now, there are some little souvenirs I brought back with me—"

This was but an excuse to get away, to be alone. Leaving the sentence unfinished, she fled. A moment later she was in the east wing, where her personal belongings had been banished by the usurper. Some one—Kirk,

no doubt—had tried to hang her pictures in the same position they had occupied in the beloved room that had been hers for so long. An effort had
been made to make things appear the same, but they were not the same;
they would never be the same. Here she felt a stranger, almost like a guest
in a transient hotel. Nothing would ever be the same—now.

Bates had already brought up her bags, and they were stacked in an or-
derly pile on the floor, but Joan made no move to unpack. That had been
but an excuse. She stumbled toward her bed and flung herself across it,
giving way to a torrent of tears.

"I love him so!" she sobbed. "It never would have happened—if I
hadn't gone away. I know it wouldn't have happened. No other woman has
a right to him when I love him so much."

Presently she got herself in check and went listlessly to the window and,
lifting back the curtains, looked out. From here she had not so much as a
glimpse of the Tappan Zee, where the Hudson broadens a good three miles
wide. In her old room, curled up in the window seat, with soft pillows at
her back, she had been able to look out across the water to the rugged rise
of the Palisades looming up picturesquely from the New Jersey shore—and
dream.

And now in that other room—her room—would be Kirklan's wife! Perhaps the other woman and Kirklan would sit in her beloved window seat,
his arm about her; the thought of it made the blood pound in Joan's brain,
made a red mist swim before her eyes.

Below her a figure moved across the lawn, a graceful figure in a white
sport skirt. Even from that distance the woman's bronze hair glinted in the
strong sunlight. Joan stared down, her hands clenching until the nails bit
deep into her palms.

"She has taken two of the things I have loved best!" she whispered
fiercely. "I hate her! I can't help it, I hate her!"

10

# CHAPTER 2

## THE SQUALID HOUSE

Relic of the horse-and-carriage days was the Gilmore stable, with living quarters for the now obsolete coachman and footman. Kirklan Gilmore, that he might have more detachment and quiet than the house afforded, had remodeled the stable into a studio, and here it was that he did his writing. Success in anything means hard work, and authorship is no exception. Being a successful novelist, he was a hard worker, but for weeks now, except for a mildly curious visit by Helen, who had been frankly disappointed in the unpretentiousness of her husband's workshop, the place had been locked. The manuscript of the new novel, for which his publishers waited fretfully, lay untouched and uncompleted.

It was two days after Joan's home-coming. As had been customary since her arrival at Greenacres as a bride, the new Mrs. Gilmore was having a breakfast tray in her room, and she sat at a small table by the window which commanded Joan Sheridan's beloved view of the Tappan Zee.

Frilly, lacy things were becoming to the new mistress of Greenacres, and she was an alluring picture, with the loose, flowing sleeves of her morning gown falling back from shapely arms, as she lifted her coffee cup. Morning is the severest test of a woman's beauty, and, only twenty minutes out of bed, although it was half an hour past nine, Helen Gilmore was undeniably a beautiful woman. Her age might have been twenty-three; it may have been even twenty-seven, for she was of the type that clings long to youth. Just now, however, there was in her blue eyes a look of brooding discontent that does not become a bride of three brief, honeymooning weeks.

At the hallway door there sounded the rap of knuckles against wood, and in answer to the petulant, "Yes, come," Bates, the butler, crossed the threshold with his shambling gait.

"Mail for you, madam," said Bates, holding a silver tray toward her. The topmost envelope was patently an advertising circular, which completely concealed the one beneath, and Helen with a contemptuous glance waved the tray aside.

11

"You should know better than bothering me with things like that," she said shortly; "take it away."

"There is also a letter—a personal letter," Bates answered stiffly, as he moved aside the offending advertisement, and revealed a small, cheap envelope, rather smudgy and addressed with a lead pencil in a ragged, scrawling script, as if the hand that wrote it was not far advanced beyond illiteracy. The postmark was New York City.

Rather a strange, disreputable-looking missive, one might have thought, to be received by the mistress of Greenacres. Bates stared sharply, as he saw the startling effect that the sight of the letter had on Mrs. Gilmore. Her coffee cup, poised for a moment in mid-air, clattered down to the saucer, and her fingers, reaching swiftly for the envelope, trembled noticeably. Her face had gone white, and into her eyes there came a look that was unquestionably apprehension, perhaps fear. With an effort she controlled herself.

"Probably from my little nephew," she said, evidently thinking to explain the smudgy appearance, the crudity of the handwriting. But Bates, moving toward the door with the perfunctory murmur, was not misled.

"Huh, little nephew!" he grunted, as he went down the hall. "That was a man's handwritin'. Poor Mr. Kirklan! I'm afraid he's been fooled—fooled bad."

When the butler had gone, Helen Gilmore relaxed self-restraint, and there returned to her face that haunted look of fear. Several times she turned the envelope over in her unsteady hands, delaying the opening of it.

"He's traced me here!" she whispered. "He knows."

After another moment of hesitation she opened the envelope and drew forth a sheet of paper. Quickly her eyes went over the scrawl. It began with the address, "Dear Mrs. Gilmore," and the last two words of that were underscored, as if there was a concealed gibe in the "Mrs. Gilmore."

I want to talk with you on some business. If you don't want me to come there, you better come to see me. Phone Joe's place & he'll tell you where I am.

It was unsigned, but no signature was needed for her to know the identity of the sender; she knew that all too well. Her hands clenched, crushing the paper between her fingers.

"Oh, what a fool I've been to take this chance!" she exclaimed bitterly. "He'll hound me, as he hounded me before. I—I thought I'd got away from him for good. I thought he was—"

A step sounded down the hall, a quick step that she had learned to know during the past three weeks. Hastily she thrust the crumpled letter and its envelope into the bodice of her morning gown and, as the door opened, forced a smile to her lips.

"Good morning, my dear," she greeted her husband. "Your indolent wife is just finishing her breakfast. You look as if you had been up for hours, and you must be going somewhere!"

Kirklan Gilmore, clad in a gray business suit, instead of white flannels, blazer coat, and canvas Oxfords that he wore for his mornings at home, crossed the room eagerly and bent to kiss the lips raised dutifully to him.

Gilmore was dark, while his wife was fair. He was slender, and his eyes had something of a poet's dreaminess in them—black eyes, with an intense light when he felt any strong emotion, either personally or through the characters that he put down on paper and breathed the breath of life into. He sat down beside the narrow table and touched his fingers in a gentle caress to the back of his wife's hand, as his eyes devoured her fondly.

"You don't know how wonderful you are, Helen! If I could only put you into a book—as you are. But I'm afraid it would turn out to be a volume of poetry, and poetry doesn't make a best seller. You—you are the most beautiful thing that ever lived!"

Despite an agitation that she could hardly keep from being observed, Helen flushed, and her eyes lighted with pleasure. She liked being told she was beautiful. It was the one story that never grew old to her.

"Thanks, Kirklan; it's nice of you to say that—especially in the morning. Why the street clothes? Are you going somewhere?"

"Yes, I am, worse luck. That slave-driving publisher of mine has called a halt to our honeymoon. A wire came from him this morning, commanding me to come in town and see him. I know what that means; he's going to pep me and send me back to my knitting. Well, we can't blame Atchinson for that; I've promised him the new book for winter publication. Thank Heaven, it's two thirds finished. I thought we might run into New York together; make the trip in the car, you know. There'll be lunch with Atchinson."

Helen managed to look languid and bored. "Lunch with that old pill, Atchinson? It doesn't appeal to me; but don't you think we might go away while you are finishing the book? It will take you weeks upon weeks, and that means I've got to stick around this poky hole, mooning around by myself, while you're locked in that old stable for endless hours. I'd like to go away, Kirklan."

Kirklan patted his wife's hand.

"I'd like to, Helen, but I'm used to things out here, and a change usually upsets my work very badly. I've got to dig in now for all I'm worth. Poky old hole? I thought you liked Greenacres."

"I don't; I hate it. Oh, don't start harping about 'the scenery;' the scenery's all right for a change, but I'm fed up on it. Outside of gawking around the country, there's nothing to do but get up, eat, and then go to bed

13

again. I don't know why we couldn't go down to—well, Atlantic City, while you're finishing the book."

"Oh, tut!" Gilmore reproved mildly. "You've just got out on the wrong side of the bed this morning. It's quite impossible for us to go away. It won't be lonesome for you now that Joan is back. She's no end of good fun, Joan. Greatest little pal in the world. And that reminds me that I must ask her to help me straighten out the sixteenth chapter. There's a little something it lacks, and I can always depend on Joan to supply just the right touch."

Helen laughed, but not pleasantly. "Yes," she said with an edge of sarcasm, "that stepsister of yours and I would make great pals—not! It's all that she can do to be civil. Sometimes I feel that she actually hates me!"

"That's nonsense, Helen. Joan hate you? How ridiculous! Joan never hated any one in her life."

"It's not ridiculous!" flared Helen; she was one of those persons who always flared when contradicted. She could not brook opposition, even verbal opposition. "I tell you, Miss Sheridan dislikes me intensely."

"She might be a little hurt—temporarily," admitted Gilmore. "I'm sorry we didn't leave the room alone until she got back. Perhaps it doesn't seem quite right, moving her out while she was away."

"Every one in the house looks upon me as—as an interloper," Helen rushed on. "Even the servants—I can feel their antagonism toward me. I don't know why I should be asked to—to tolerate such treatment."

"Try and look at things more calmly," soothed Gilmore. "Naturally, everything seems strange to you at first. Both my stepmother and Joan are wonderful, Helen—real mother and sister to me. You'll learn to love them very much; please, Helen, for my sake, you'll try."

"And you expect to let them make their home with us permanently?" she demanded bitterly.

Kirklan Gilmore looked uncomfortable, unhappy; this was the first rift in the lute. He was discovering that his wife, after all, was not quite the perfect woman. It is a painful realization for a new husband.

"W-well," he said slowly, "I hadn't thought of that. This has been my stepmother's home for almost twenty years, and, while it belongs to me legally, I wouldn't think for a moment of pitching her out." He paused for a moment, and his tone had a touch of wistfulness in it. "It's always been my home, too, Helen. To me there is no place quite like Greenacres; I—I wish you'd really try to be happy here."

Helen did not respond with that sympathetic understanding he had hoped for, and Kirklan, of course, could not know that the receipt of the letter only a few minutes before had filled her with a desperate anxiety to flee from the thing that threatened her.

"You—you won't—take me away?" she persisted.

"Helen, you don't know how hard it is for me to deny you any wish. Heaven knows I want to make you happy, but can't you understand that we've got to be practical? My studio is here; my library is here; and it's here that I've always done my best work. At least wait until the book is finished, and then, if you still do not like Greenacres, we—we will see what we can do." There was, despite his conciliatory tone, a note of firmness, and Helen, with a shrug of her pretty shoulders, dismissed the subject temporarily.

"You won't go into town with me?" asked Gilmore. "It will be a change, and I think you'll find it a pleasant trip in the car."

Helen thought swiftly and came to a decision. She did want to go to New York, but certainly not with her husband; she must forestall any effort of the unsigned sender of that letter to see her at Greenacres. The sooner the better.

"Why don't you use the train, Kirklan, and let me have the car?" she suggested. "I'd like to take the ferry across the river to Nyack and drive out toward Tuxedo."

Gilmore agreed promptly. "Suppose you take Joan along," he suggested. "You can't help liking her after the first strangeness wears off; really you've no idea what a perfect little brick she is."

Helen shook her head. "No," she refused, "I'd rather be alone today." And that much was true.

Gilmore looked at his watch and moved toward his wife for a parting embrace; it was the first time he had left her, even for a trip to New York, and, madly in love with Helen as he was, the prospect was depressing.

"You'll be careful about driving," he warned. "Stay on the country roads and out of the traffic; you're still a bit new at it, you know. I've just time to get the ten-thirty train."

There was no thought in Helen's mind, despite her decision to make a secret trip into the city, of risking the heavy and perilous traffic of New York. Her plan was to run the car across country to White Plains, and there board the Boston & Westchester interurban electric. In this way, she reasoned, she would avoid the Grand Central Station and the possibility of getting back on the same train with her husband.

How the most cunning of plans go astray!

After a reluctant leave-taking—reluctant on Kirklan's part—he went downstairs with the idea of getting Joan to drive him down to the station and bring the car home, but Joan was nowhere in evidence, so he had to call on Billings, who looked after the grounds and who could drive in an emergency. Billings was a silent, taciturn sort of fellow, and this silence suited Gilmore's mood exactly.

Helen's attitude worried him; her discontent alarmed him. Suddenly it occurred to him that in the two days since Joan's return he had seen his stepsister only at dinner and a few minutes afterward. Thinking it over, he wondered if Joan had been quite her usual, jolly self; if she had purposely avoided him.

Gilmore felt guilty about taking Joan's room, but it is hard to deny a wife of a few days, and Helen had actually demanded it. It never entered his mind that there might be some other reason, a deeper, more vital reason for Joan's attitude—that she feared, until the first shock of it had passed, she might unwittingly let him see into her heart. He made up his mind that on his return he would have a talk with Joan and let her know how sorry he was about the room.

A few minutes after Billings let him off at the station, the train rushed in from the north, and Gilmore got aboard. During the forty-five-minute run to New York he remained depressingly thoughtful.

"I guess, at that, it's a bit dull for Helen at Greenacres—and will be even more dull when I've got to lock myself in with my work. I ought to have some company down, I suppose, to liven things up for her a bit. I'll see who I can drum up for the next weekend."

This decision gave him a feeling of relief, as it automatically solved the problem of his wife's discontent with rural life.

Arriving at Grand Central Station, Gilmore took a taxi to the office of his publishers and, less than half an hour later, was in conference with Atchinson regarding the unfinished novel. The latter was a dynamic sort of fellow, a voluble enthusiast, and their talk lengthened until it was past one o'clock. He had read the carbon copy of what had been written and felt that it promised to have a greater success than "Rogue's Paradise."

"We've decided to try illustrations with this book of yours," Atchinson was explaining. "I've selected Victor Sarbella to do the job. Sarbella draws splendid pictures—faces with life and character in them. He's one of those intense fellows. Half Italian, you know, although his mother was an American. You've met him, of course?"

Gilmore nodded. "Yes, I know Sarbella; interesting chap; and, say, that gives me an idea. I had been thinking of having some people down to Greenacres. Helen is finding it a bit lonesome. Wouldn't it be a good idea to have Sarbella come out?"

Atchinson beamed. "That's fine! He can pick out some of the dramatic situations with you and get the spirit of your characters. He's devilish slow in turning out work, and I don't want to run any chances of spoiling the drawings by rushing him. Suppose we call him up right now and get that part of it settled."

Word became action, as the publisher reached for the telephone and asked the firm's private switchboard operator in the outer office to get Victor Sarbella's apartment for him. A few minutes later the matter was arranged, and Atchinson glanced at his watch.

"Phew!" he whistled. "Half past one, old man; we'd better hurry out and have a bite of lunch. Speaking of Italians, what do you say to one of those Italian feeds? I'm always digging up new places to eat and I've run across a splendid little restaurant, where the food's uncommonly good even if the location is poor—in the upper Forties."

Kirklan Gilmore agreed indifferently. "Most anything will suit me," he said.

The two left the publishing-house building, and, Atchinson talking almost incessantly and not always to the point, they started out.

"Suppose we leg it," suggested Gilmore; "it may give me a little zest for lunch."

"I'm for that," Atchinson said heartily; "it's only a dozen blocks." How many things hinge on trifles! As they neared Eighth Avenue, passing along this cheap and squalid street, which one found it hard to believe was so near to pretentious Broadway. Atchinson's emphatic voice jarred to an abrupt stop, his hand caught at the novelist's arm.

"Hello!" he exclaimed. "Isn't that Mrs. Gilmore yonder?"

"You mean my wife? Oh, that's impossible. Where?"

But his eyes had looked too late. The woman Atchinson had seen was gone, disappeared swiftly into one of those grimy, ugly entrances before he could so much as glimpse her.

"I'd take my oath that was Mrs. Gilmore," muttered the publisher, giving a puzzled stare at the sign across the way which announced, "Furnished Rooms. Rates $3 Weekly and Up." Since Helen had worked in the publishing office for two months, he felt certain he had not been mistaken.

"That's ridiculous!" snorted the author. "She took the car and motored out to Tuxedo. Besides, what would Helen be doing in a neighborhood like this?"

Atchinson, feeling very uncomfortable, was wondering precisely the same thing. "Humph!" he grunted. "I must have been mistaken; yes, no doubt I was. Some one who looked like her."

But this was friendly diplomacy; he had got a square look, and he knew quite positively that he had not been mistaken. The woman who had hurried, almost furtively, into the cheap, unclean lodging house was Kirklan Gilmore's wife!

# CHAPTER 3

## HELEN ANSWERS HER LETTER

Entirely unaware that she had been observed, Helen Gilmore slipped furtively into the dark, musty vestibule of the ugly house. There were those unpleasant odors which accumulate in a decaying house, the smell that suggests neglect.

The opening of the second door automatically set a bell ringing, an unpleasant jangling that caused the woman to start and compress her lips, shutting back the nervous gasp which rose in her throat. When she closed the door the ringing stopped.

After a wait of a moment there came down the raggedly carpeted stairs a slovenly and haglike female, with straggling hair of dirty gray and the shoulders of a professional wrestler in their muscular broadness. The face of the slattern was, until she reached the bottom of the stairs, in the shadows. At the sight of it Helen instinctively retreated a step; she had never seen such a terrible face, she thought. A pair of narrow red eyes looked her up and down with appraising, impudent curiosity.

"Perhaps—perhaps I've made a mistake," Helen stammered. "I thought this was the right number; I—I wanted to see Don Haskins."

"You ain't made no mistake," came the response in a hoarse guttural. "He's upstairs. He told me he was lookin' fer comp'ny. Guess you're the swell sister he was tellin' me about."

"Y-yes," Helen answered faintly.

"Go right on up, deary; it's the thoid floor—the door at the end of the hall, the door with a busted panel, where the cops broke in. They thought, it bein' locked, Terry Mooney was there, but he wasn't." Her voice broke into a peal of cackling mirth. "No, he wasn't there; he was—somewheres else."

Starting toward the stairs, Helen turned, one hand resting upon the ancient rail.

"Then Don is wanted by—by the cops?"

"Ask him," grunted the woman with the gargoyle face; "ask him. I'll say he is, deary."

18

Helen went tremulously up the stairs, stumbled about the dark hallway until she found the second flight, which was narrow and, if possible, dirtier than the first. Here the boards were loose and clattered noisily beneath her step. Reaching the third floor, a bit of sun struggled feebly through the dust-filmed skylight and fell slantwise across the door with the broken panel, now patched with some unpainted strips torn from a chance packing box.

The occupant of the room had heard her approach—only a deaf man could have failed to be notified by the clatter of the loose stairway boards—for the door opened cautiously, and a haggard unshaven face looked out through a widening crack. A pair of thin lips twisted back into an unpleasant and gloating triumphant grin.

"So—so you've come, have you?" the man rasped and laughed harshly. "I thought you would. I give you credit for havin' that much sense. Real prompt, ain't you? Only mailed the letter yesterday." He moved back, making room for her to enter. His eyes, hard and glittering, followed her with a look of venomous hate that was at the same time one of admiration, as if her beauty stirred him.

The room was small, dark, and unventilated, and there was the vile odor of soured liquor that mingled nauseatingly with the stench of stale tobacco smoke. There was a narrow, tousled bed, with the white paint long since peeled from the metal framework, a broken-backed chair upon which rested a bottle of homemade whisky, that the old hag downstairs sold for ten dollars the quart.

"Why did you send for me, Don?" demanded Helen. She was plainly frightened. Looking at him she found it hard to believe that this haggard man was the same person she had first known as "Nifty Don." Don had been handsome—once.

Don Haskins placed the bottle on the floor and with a sarcastic courtesy waved her to the chair.

"Be seated, Mrs. Haskins," he sneered, and himself occupied the edge of the bed. Helen shivered, her fingers working nervously. For a moment he sat there staring.

"You still got the looks," he muttered thickly. "I—I guess I ain't ever goin' to get over bein' crazy about you, Helen—even—even when I'm hatin' you. His grimy hand reached out to her; his touch might have been tender, but at her shuddering recoil his eyes blazed again, and his fingers crushed about her white wrist until she gave a cry of pain.

"You always did think you was too good for your own kind," he snarled. "Now that I've got you where I can put on the screws, I ought to get you sent up; that's what I ought to do with you. After what you done to me—"

19

"I've done nothing to you, Don. Why did you send for me? You told that woman downstairs that I am—"

"Yeah, it was a good stall, tellin' 'Eighth Avenue Annie' that I gotta rich sister that would put up for me. See? Thirty bucks a week I gotta give the grafter for hidin' me away in this room, and ten dollars a bottle for this rat poison she calls whisky. I owe her a hundred now, and she won't let me skip until I pay up. If I don't pay—well, Annie fixes that by givin' the bulls a tip where I can be located. See? That's why I sent for you—to take me outta hock." He grinned sardonically. "When a guy's in trouble, ain't it the most natural thing in the world that he turns to—to his wife."

Helen shivered. "I'm not your wife!" she cried. "You know I'm not. I've never been your wife!"

"The law says different," retorted Don Haskins. "You married me, didn't you?"

"Yes," Helen admitted bitterly, "I married you. I liked you, and when you got into that trouble I—I thought I loved you. It was only pity. You rushed me into it so that I wouldn't have to testify against you—a wife can't be made to testify against her husband. I knew, before you got out of the Tombs, that I'd made a mistake."

This revival of old and bitter memories convulsed Don Haskins' face with anger.

"You lie!" he gritted. "When y' say I married you just to keep outta stir, you lie. I married you because I was crazy about you. You liked me, too, until—until you run into that other bird and fell for him. But when I got outta the Tombs I stopped that, all right."

"Yes, you stopped it," choked Helen. "I loved him—with every beat of my heart. You—you robbed me of my one chance to be happy. You—oh, why do you drag all these ghosts before me? Those are things I'm always trying to forget. I saved you from doing a twenty-year stretch, and you've been hounding me—hounding me ever since. That—that's your idea of gratitude!"

"Aw, cut out that stuff. I'm desperate. The cops is lookin' for me; I gotta make a get-away and I gotta have money."

"Oh, I see, you want money," nodded Helen, fumbling at her purse. "You said a hundred dollars—"

Don Haskins gave a contemptuous sneer.

"I said that's what I owe Annie, but I want more'n that—a lot more. Aw, I know you're well fixed. I know you married a guy that's got it. I got all the dope on you, see."

"How—"

"You thought you were pretty foxy, didn'tcha? It wasn't much trouble gettin' a line on you. When I went out West with Keegan and got nabbed pullin' the job we went out there to do in Chi, you thought I was in for a long stretch, and that you'd lose me. You changed your name, did the workin'-girl stunt, and hooked a live one—married a fellow that writes, Kirklan Gilmore.

"But the State's attorney out there made a little deal with me; I handed him some information he wanted, and he got me paroled. See? I come back, lookin' for you. Madge knew all about it, and I made her tell. Never trust a friend, girlie; that's my motto."

"So Madge told you?"

"She hadda tell; I'd have choked the life outta her if she hadn't."

"I—I suppose the past is one thing that never dies," Helen whispered. "I was a fool to think I could get away with it. I—I was a fool to take the chance."

"I ain't gonna stop you from gettin' away with it," grunted Don; "at least I ain't—providin'—"

"Don't beat around the bush, Don; get to the point. Providing—what?"

"I'll get to the point fast enough. I gotta be practical, I oughtta make you squirm, but I'm in a bad fix. What I need is a thousand bucks, and I need it quick."

Helen stared at him fixedly.

"I haven't got a thousand dollars, Don, but if two hundred will help any —" Her fingers were at the clasp of her hand bag.

"If you ain't got a thousand, then get it—from that rich husband you've swung onto."

"But he's not rich. You don't understand. He owns a house, an automobile, and lives well, but he's not rich. I doubt if he's got much money outside the royalties from his book. I—I don't see how I could ask him for a thousand dollars, without giving him some sort of an explanation, and I don't know what I could tell him."

"He ain't rich?" Don broke in skeptically. "Say, whatcha tryin' to hand me? If he ain't rich, whatcha marry him for—and risk doin' a trip for bigamy? Stuck on the guy, huh?"

Helen shook her head.

"N-no," she faltered. "I'm not 'stuck' on him. I wish to Heaven that I hadn't married him—now." Her lips twitched. "I—I suppose it looked like a chance to be respectable. I heard that you were in trouble out in Chicago, that you'd been put away for a long time. I took up typewriting after Tilliston's cabaret closed; I changed my name and got a job with a publishing house."

"Yeah, I got all that from Madge."

"Oh, what's the use going into the rest of it? I don't like to work; I never did. I met Gilmore. He was wild about me—still is. It seemed like such a wonderful chance, the wife of a famous novelist. I wonder what he'll do if he ever learns the truth? Perhaps—perhaps—he'll kill me!"

"Aw, can that stuff," growled Don Haskins. "Conversation don't help me any; what I want is that thousand bucks—quick. I'm due for a long trip up the river—or worse—if I don't jump town before the bulls nail me.

"I was in on a loft job. It was a water haul—not a ten-dollar bit between the three of us that was in on it. One of the birds got nabbed, and I know he's got a yellow streak in 'im as wide as Fifth Avenue. The cops won't have to more'n bounce a nightstick over his head when he'll come through with a squeal. I gotta get outta town, put distance behind me, because"— his voice sank to a low, hoarse whisper—"because the watchman got croaked, see! It—it's a chance of the chair, if 'Dago Mike' squeals on the other two of us.

"A guy ain't got no chance doin' a slide outta town these days unless he's well heeled. I'm flat broke. Do I get that thousand from you, or—"

"Say it, Don."

The man's eyes were narrowed.

"Or do I drop a note to Gilmore, tellin' him that his wife's got two husbands, that if he'll taxi over to Borough Hall in Brooklyn and look over the marriage-license records for October tenth, nineteen sixteen—"

"You—you wouldn't do that to me, Don?" Helen's face was deathly white. "You ungrateful rat—"

"If I'm a rat, then it was you made me a rat!" gritted the man. "When I got outta the Tombs that time and found you'd throwed me over, and was trailin' around with that swell with the Eyetalian name, it made a bum outta me. If I could have got my hands on you that first night—" His hands darted toward her, extended fingers twitching convulsively, as they neared her throat. With a stifled scream Helen protected herself with her arms.

"Don't! Don't! Don't look at me like that. I'll try to get the thousand dollars, but I don't know what—what I will tell him."

"It's up to you what kind of a song and dance you give 'im," he growled. "The big thing is—get it. It's that, or else— Now pass over that two hundred you was talkin' about; that'll help a little."

Helen's fingers trembled as she reached into her hand bag for the roll of bills. "Even if I give you the thousand dollars, I suppose I'll always be at your mercy—that you'll always be coming back for more, that you'll hound me, blackmail me—"

Haskins made no promises as to that; he grabbed the money avidly from her hand and counted it eagerly. Ten dollars lacking two hundred.

"When do I get the rest of it?" he demanded. "I can't wait long; it won't be safe—stayin' here with Eighth Avenue Annie."

22

Helen considered swiftly. "This—this is Monday," she said. "I may be able to get it by Wednesday. If I can get it at all I suppose I can get it by then. You—you'll give me until Wednesday?"

"Ain't got no jewelry that you can put in soak to raise the jack?" Don wanted to know.

"He—he would miss that, what little there is. I'd better try to get the money from him—if I can."

Haskins' lips twisted unpleasantly. "You better," he grunted threateningly. "Aw right, I'm givin' you until Wednesday, but if you ain't come across with it by then, I'll saunter out to that swell place I hear you're livin' in—and collect."

23

# CHAPTER 4

## "WHAT DOES IT MEAN?"

Returning from New York on the five o'clock train, Kirklan Gilmore stood for a minute or so on the station platform, looking along the assembled line of cars in which thoughtful wives were meeting their city-working husbands. He felt disappointed and hurt that Helen had not come for him, especially as this was his first absence.

Then it occurred to him that she might not have returned from her drive across the river; the country roads might have lured her farther than her announced destination of Tuxedo. A worried frown appeared over his eyes, as his imagination led him to take the unpleasant possibility that, since Helen was new at the steering wheel, there might have been an accident. A horrifying picture of a collision, his beautiful wife maimed, cut, bleeding, arose before him, but he brushed it aside with a shudder.

"I suppose all doting husbands do a lot of unnecessary worrying," he told himself. "I couldn't stand losing her."

Gilmore did not for a moment believe that it had been Helen whom Atchinson had seen on the street in New York; he considered it a bit of a joke on the publisher and intended having a good laugh by teasing his wife about her "double."

The village of Ardleigh is small, and, since it is surrounded with people owning their country homes and their own cars, there is small demand for taxicab service. There were just three of the ramshackle vehicles, but Gilmore delayed so long that the last one was occupied and started in motion, as he crossed the platform toward it.

Except that it might delay him getting to Helen, he felt no annoyance over this incident; it was only two miles from the village to Greenacres, and he often made the trip on foot by choice. It was a splendid, picturesque walk, which to him had never lost its charm.

Carrying his manuscript case of black leather, he swung off briskly, choosing the dirt road rather than the paved highway; this not only afforded the more scenic view, but also saved him nearly a quarter of a mile.

He was in a hurry for, try as he would, he could not help being rather anxious about Helen and her safe return.

The road ran along the backbone of a ridge, so that, while still some distance from the house, he was able to get a glimpse of the driveway through an opening in the trees, and he gave a breath of relief as he saw the car. His anxiety had been quite unfounded; his wife was home.

Approaching the house itself, he saw Joan on the lawn teaching tricks to the new collie pup, and she was so engrossed with the task that she failed to hear the crunch of his shoes on the gravel.

"Hello, Joan!" he called cheerily.

The girl, on her knees in the grass, dropped the puppy's paws and turned half toward him, the drooping brim of her hat shielding whatever expression may have been in her dark eyes.

"Hello, Kirk," she answered, getting to her feet.

"I see Helen's got home. I was just a little worried about her—she being new about driving the car."

"Yes, she's home," nodded Joan. "She drove in about five minutes ago; I think you'll find her dressing for dinner." She essayed a brief and fairly successful laugh. "I won't keep you, Kirk; I know you'll be anxious to see her after being away from her all these hours."

Gilmore hesitated for a moment. "See here, Joan," he protested, "I believe you're trying to get away from me. Somehow I've got the feeling that you've been trying to avoid me ever since you got back from your trip. You haven't told me a thing about it."

"I—I didn't think you'd want to be bothered; all your time belongs to Helen. I've thanked you for the glorious treat, haven't I? I know I intended to."

"There are no thanks due, Joan; you earned it—and more. Atchinson was speaking of some passages in 'Rogue's Paradise' only today, and, bless your life, most of them were yours!"

"It's nice of you to say that, Kirk," she murmured lifelessly; he would never know—must never know—what a labor of love it had been. There was an uncomfortable pause, during which Gilmore fumbled at his watch chain, and Joan bent over to pull gently at the puppy's ears.

"I guess there's something else I ought to say," he floundered. "I feel mighty guilty about Helen taking your room. I don't blame you for being hurt about it. I did my best to make her understand, but—"

"We'll not talk about that, Kirk. The house belongs to you; it was quite within your right. I'll get accustomed to my new quarters, and it will be all right, Kirk—quite all right."

It was strange that Gilmore, whose books were considered to contain keen analysis of the human emotions, should have missed the catch in her voice, the touch of pathos, as she tried to mask her true feelings with a careless, matter-of-fact tone. But miss them he did, and he felt relieved that she was being such a good sport about it.

"It's like you, Joan," he said warmly, "to take it like that, and I wish you'd try and make things as pleasant as you can for Helen. She still feels strange, and, I suppose, is overly sensitive. This is just between you and me, understand, but she has a notion that there is a feeling of antagonism, even among the servants, toward her. Of course that's ridiculous; no one could help loving Helen. She is wonderful, isn't she?"

Joan could not force the polite falsehood to her lips, but Gilmore rushed on, taking no cognizance of her silence.

"I've been honeymooning for the past three weeks, Joan, but I've got to get back into harness again—a very good simile, since my studio is a reno-vated stable—and rush the book to a finish. I've got to lock myself in and work.

"Well, I'm afraid Helen is going to get pretty lonesome unless some one looks after entertaining her a bit. Atchinson has arranged with Victor Sar-bella—you remember meeting Sarbella in town, of course—to draw the il-lustrations for my coming book, and he'll be out tomorrow for a stay of several days. He'll have time for loafing, while I'm working, and I wish you'd see to it that things are made as jolly as possible for Helen.

"It's partly selfishness that I don't want country life to pall on Helen; I've got to make her contented with Greenacres, or she'll be pulling me away from the old place and into town."

Joan's lips tightened. Kirk did not know, of course, how much he was asking of her. "You'd better be getting in to Helen," she said.

And when Gilmore had gone, striding swiftly to the house, Joan Sheri-dan dropped to her knees in the grass, hugging the collie pup close, the one living thing she would have permitted to see the tears now flooding her dark eyes.

"Oh, Laddie, boy," she whispered into one of the inquiringly cocked ears, "it's so hard to pretend—so hard! Oh, how I hate that woman—how I hate her! I didn't know there was so much hate in me."

Kirklan Gilmore entered the house and went directly upstairs. A mo-ment later he was rapping at the door of his wife's room and, after her muf-fled response from the other side of the panel, he went in.

Helen was not, as he expected, dressing for dinner. She sat by the win-dow in a listless, preoccupied attitude, and she had not so much as removed her hat. Her greeting was not that spontaneous explosion of welcoming joy that he would have liked after their first parting, even of the brief hours.

"Hello, Kirklan," she said listlessly. "How's everything in New York? Hot, wasn't it?"

Gilmore kissed her eagerly, but found her even more than usually unresponsive.

"Not so hot," he answered, "but the humidity was stifling. What's wrong, Helen? You look all out of sorts."

"Just tired, I suppose," she said. "Driving a car is a strain on the nerves."

"Yes, it is for a beginner; you shouldn't attempt such long trips until you're more accustomed to the wheel. Have any trouble?"

"I stalled the motor on a hill, but I just put on the emergency brake and worked the starter. That's what you told me to do in a case like that."

"Good headwork, Helen. The truth is, I'd worried about you a good deal. If anything had happened to you, my darling——" His voice choked, husky with emotion, and he put his fingers softly to a strand of bronze hair that had broken prison from under the edge of her hat.

When a man is in a soft mood, that is the best time for a wife to ask what she wants. Helen realized this and decided not to delay the matter of the needed thousand dollars. So she reached up and let her hand close about his.

"Kirklan," she said, "I—I am worried about something. I am ashamed to come to you with it, but——"

A look of alarm came into Gilmore's face, as he waited for her to continue.

"Oh, Kirklan, I—I am so—so ashamed. It's money."

He gave a quick, relieved laugh. "And it hurts your pride to ask your husband for a little shopping money. Since you feel that way about it, I suppose we'd better decide on a regular allowance. No doubt you'd like to have your own little bank account. I'll be as generous with you as I can, dear, but, as I told you before we were married, I'm no bloated capitalist. The royalties from the last book are coming in pretty regularly now, although we hope they'll be even larger. The sales seem to be growing. Did you have your mind set on any particular amount? Don't be timid about it, honey; if it's more than I can stand I'll have to tell you so."

"There—there are so many things I need, Kirklan; sometimes a man doesn't understand about a woman's wardrobe. I've been afraid you would think I am extravagant, and I don't want to be a burden on you." It had been in her mind to manufacture some past debt, but his suggestion of an allowance seemed to make it easier.

"How much do you want, Helen? You fix the amount, and, if I've got it, it's yours." Then, as she still seemed to hesitate, he suggested a figure that to his mind was generous. "Suppose I deposit five hundred in the village bank to start with? By the time you've checked against that, I'll have some more money coming in."

"I—I'd like to have a thousand dollars, Kirklan. Does that seem a great deal? Of course I won't have to ask you for any more for—oh, for quite a long time."

Gilmore was not displeased with her, but he was chagrined, for the reason that his own bank balance was three hundred dollars less than the thousand.

"Store accounts, of course!" he said. "I've charge accounts at several of the stores in New York, and you can buy what you want and charge it to me. The truth is, dear, that I haven't got a thousand in cash. We writer fellows aren't very good financiers and I've been living pretty close to the last dollar. But my credit is good."

Helen bit her lip. "I'd rather not charge things, Kirklan. If it would be just as convenient to let me have the cash—"

"I'll let you have it Friday," he agreed; "I'll drop a note to Atchinson and ask him to make me an advance. The publishing house makes out its checks on Thursday."

"Kirklan," she murmured, forced to try a new line, "I'll have to tell you the truth. I'll have to have some money by Wednesday. Oh, I know it's terrible, asking you to pay my old debts, but I'm so afraid of—of being sued that I—"

Gilmore patted her shoulder reassuringly. Had he stopped to think about it, he might have considered it strange that a girl in the humble position in which he had found her should have got into debt to the extent of a thousand dollars, but it was Helen, not he, who recognized this possible inconsistency, and she hastened to add with that glibness which even a poor liar may achieve in a moment of desperation: "It—it was money that I borrowed for my sister's illness. I had to sign some notes, and—"

"You shall have the money, Helen, but the truth is always the best in the first place, dear. I want us always to be frank with each other. I want you to feel that you can come to me with everything. After all, a falsehood is the most futile thing in the world. You should have told me the exact truth about the matter from the beginning. I'll get in touch with Atchinson on the phone tomorrow and arrange it. You shall have the money tomorrow night, but you must never lie to me, dear—under any conditions. A lie is one of the things I find it hard to forgive."

His tone was so gentle, his agreement to the request so prompt, and his faith in her so unquestioning that Helen was touched. It made her think that she might almost learn to love him; impulsively she brushed her lips to the back of his hand.

"That's good of you, Kirklan; you—you'll never know what a weight you've taken from my mind. You—you do love me a very great deal."

"Better than all else in the world, Helen!" he answered huskily.

28

There was a silence, to Gilmore an enraptured silence in which he felt closer to his wife than ever before. It seemed that suddenly there was a new bond between them.

"What does Atchinson think of the new book?" she asked him presently. "Does he think it will have the success of the last one?"

"Yes, even more. He's enthusiastic—even for Atchinson." His lips parted into a smile. "Speaking of Atchinson, that reminds me. He was trying to convince me that he saw you in New York this afternoon—going into some cheap dump just around the corner from Eighth Avenue."

With a startled gasp, Helen's hand jerked away from the fondling caress of his fingers and, clenched, went to her mouth. Her eyes became wide with something that was more than either surprise or bewilderment. Her gaze was fixed upon his face with a fascinated stare, and the smile that she attempted was only a sickly grimace.

"Why, Kirklan! In—in New York? How silly! You know very well that I drove the car to Tuxedo."

Kirklan Gilmore's blood was suddenly ice; his eyes were no longer smiling.

"Great Lord!" he whispered. "It's true. Atchinson was right. Helen, you've lied to me; you—"

"No!" she cried in a desperate frenzy of denial. "I swear to you—"

"I see guilt in your face. I know now; I know that you were the woman Atchinson saw in New York this afternoon. What does it mean, Helen? These lies, this deceit—what does it mean?"

Helen laughed hysterically.

"Don't—don't be so tragic—over nothing. I wasn't in New York; you just startled me, that's all. Please don't be so silly. Atchinson was mistaken; some one who looked like me, perhaps."

But, as much as he wanted to believe her, Kirklan Gilmore could not convince himself; her face had betrayed her. The blood was pounding in his brain, and he felt that the mystery of it, the doubts, the suspicions would certainly drive him mad.

29

# CHAPTER 5

## VICTOR SARBELLA

The next morning, after a sleepless night, found Gilmore haggard and hollow-eyed. There were moments when his wife's persistent denials almost convinced him that it was all a horrible mistake; for a beautiful woman in tears can be most plausible at dissimulation; and then, when trying hardest to believe her, there would come before him, with photographic clearness, the memory of her startled face, the sudden guilty terror in her eyes, and credulity would crumble.

He was up hours before the rest of the household, although the cook was stirring and brewed him a cup of coffee, which he gulped mechanically and then fled to the solitude of his studio, thinking that he might relieve the tension by forgetting himself in his work.

That, of course was ridiculous; there was no possibility of mental detachment with his brain in such a riotous tumult. Sheet after sheet of paper he drew before him to receive his thoughts, but, instead of smooth sentences flowing from his pen, he found himself tracing meaningless lines. He gave up any attempt at creation and tried correcting, ironing out rough spots in the manuscript, where he had left off three weeks previous, but in his present frame of mind all spots were rough, just jumbled words. He tossed down his pen with a violent force that crumpled the gold point and sent a spray of ink spattering across the desk top. Then he leaped to his feet and began to pace the floor like a caged beast.

"I've got to know the truth!" he groaned. "I think I could make myself forgive her anything, but the deceit of it is driving me mad! What could have taken her to that place—what is she hiding from me? Her reason for wanting the thousand dollars—perhaps, that too, was a lie."

It suddenly dawned upon him how little he knew of Helen's life; nothing more than she had been pleased to tell him, and that had not been much. She had seldom spoken of her family, and then only in a hazy, unenlightening sort of way. He had rather got the impression that her parents had died when she was a child, and that a shadowy, indefinite aunt had reared her.

Gilmore's love for his wife had been so blindly intense, so headlong that it had never occurred to him to weigh these things. He had loved her for herself, and that had been sufficient.

Until long past noon he remained locked within the studio, and no one came to disturb him. At last he could no longer endure the oppression of four walls; the day was hot, and he had neglected to open the windows; the air was stifling. So he flung himself out of the renovated stable and plunged, with hardly any sense of direction, across the open country—trying to think, trying to think!

Thus he missed the arrival of Victor Sarbella, his artist guest; in fact he had forgotten that Sarbella was coming. It was a quarter past four when one of the village taxis turned in at Greenacres, nosed along the driveway and, coming to a stop beneath the portico, deposited Victor Sarbella and his bags beside the long, cool porch.

One did not need to hear the name to be certain of Sarbella's Italian blood, for from his Florentine father he had got the intense black eyes and the tinting of skin which belong to that warm-blooded race. He was a handsome, powerfully built man, nearing forty. His hands, as he paid the driver, were revealed as long-fingered, tapering, such hands as properly belong to the artist.

With a honk of the horn the taxi moved off, and Victor Sarbella looked about him, his black eyes snapping with an appreciative light. The artist in him was delighted with the charm of Greenacres.

"My friend," he mused, "has a most beautiful home; a beautiful wife, too, I am told."

Attracted by the taxi's arrival, Bates, the butler, shambled out across the porch, followed by Joan Sheridan. Joan had met him at a literary affair in New York the previous winter, and of course she remembered him; Victor Sarbella was not the kind of man that one found it possible to forget. She met him with an outstretched hand.

"Welcome to Greenacres, Mr. Sarbella. Kirk told me last night that you were coming. I haven't seen Kirk all morning, but I suppose he's at the studio. Have you seen him, Bates?"

"Not all day, Miss Joan; as you say, perhaps the studio."

Joan nodded. "I'll find him, Bates, while you take in Mr. Sarbella's bags. He loses all track of time when he really gets to work, and he's got to make up for three lost weeks."

"Naturally my poor friend takes up hees pen like, as they say, a slave scourged to hees dungeon," he laughed. While he had spent a good many years in America with his mother who, following the death of his Italian father, had taken up residence in New York, there was a touch of foreign accent in the pronunciation of certain words. His education had been in Flo-

31

rence, and each winter he returned there for two or three months. "Tell me, Mees Sheridan, is hees new wife so beautiful as I have been told?"

Joan nodded. "Yes, she is beautiful, a very beautiful woman. Now I'll run and find Kirk. He'll feel much humiliated that he wasn't here to greet you. You're to make the illustrations for the new book. That's wonderful. I've always admired your drawings; there's such intensity in your pictures."

Sarbella, bowing, murmured an acknowledgment of the compliment and turned to follow the butler into the house and up the stairs to the second floor. A few minutes later he was unpacking his bags, as Bates drew a tub of water for him.

"What time is dinner, Bates?"

"A quarter past six, Mr. Sarbella."

"It is now nearly half past four," said the artist, glancing at his watch. "Every one dresses for dinner, I suppose."

"Oh, certainly, sir."

"Then I wish you would press my dinner coat, Bates; it's badly wrinkled. I was never good at packing. You may tell Meester Gilmore that I will not come down until six. There's no sense in dressing twice."

"Quite so," nodded Bates and, accepting the dinner coat, shuffled out of the room.

Sarbella took a brief plunge in the tub of tepid water, finished it off with an invigorating cold shower, and, slipping into a light bath robe, pulled a chair to the window and began to smoke. His thoughts evidently took an unpleasant turn, for his eyes glowed hotly, and his muscles tensed until his fingers crushed the burning cigarette, and the fiery end of it smoldered odorously in the nap of the rug at his feet.

"Today is the ninth," he smiled, half aloud; "day after tomorrow would have been hees twenty-third birthday—Andrea's twenty-third birthday! If I could but find her, that woman, I would kill her with my own hands! Heaven curse her! She—"

The tense soliloquy of hate was interrupted by a rap at the door; Sarbella turned with a start and called, "Yes, come."

Kirklan Gilmore, face still haggard, his eyes bloodshot, entered the room with tumbling words of apology.

"Can you forgive my discourtesy, Victor?" he exclaimed. "I should have been here to receive you. A fine host you must think me when—"

"Poof! That for your discourtesy, my good friend!" broke in Sarbella with a laugh and a snap of the fingers. "We are artists, you and I; you are an artist of the pen, and I an artist of the brush. So we understand each other. I think nothing of it. But, my friend, what has happened to you? Your face is that of a man who is ill."

32

Gilmore gave a jerky laugh. "It's nothing, Victor—nothing. Poor night's sleep, that's all." While their friendship was a warm one, it had never reached the point of intimacy; and to no friend on earth would Kirklan Gilmore have confided the truth. "We'll have a cocktail or so before dinner, and that will put new life back into me again."

Sarbella felt certain that this was an evasion and a very thin one; through Gilmore's eyes he saw a soul in torment. But he pretended to accept the explanation.

"The beautiful new wife, she must not see you so. It will make her unhappy."

Gilmore's lips tightened, and he hastily changed the subject. "Tomorrow, Victor, we'll dig in and talk over the illustrations you are to make. I have an idea or so, but I'll have to chase along now and dress for dinner. Did Bates tell you? A quarter past six? When you've dressed go on downstairs; we'll have the cocktails on the veranda. I'll be down ahead of you, perhaps; I'm a regular fireman for throwing on my clothes."

And he bolted abruptly from the room. Victor Sarbella stared after the closed door and shook his head slowly.

"Ah!" he murmured. "A poor night's sleep, he says. I fear it is nothing so simply remedied as that. It was tragedy I saw in his face—tragedy. We all have our tragedies; I, too, have had mine. Poor Andrea; he was so young to die. And our mother—" He blinked back the moisture which flooded his eyes and tossed off the bath robe of silk crape, starting to get into his clothes. Before he had finished, the butler returned with the freshly pressed dinner coat, uttered a few polite banalities, and departed.

Sarbella smoked another cigarette and then went downstairs to the veranda, where he found that Gilmore had preceded him, looking a little less pale than some minutes before. But the color in the author's cheeks was plainly artificial, induced no doubt by a nip or so from the bottle of liquor with which he was engaged in mixing the cocktails. The man was making a supreme effort to conceal the true state of his feelings, and being only moderately successful at it.

"The ladies will be down in a moment," said Gilmore, moving the cocktail shaker back and forth. "Joan tells me that she saw you when you arrived. Great admirer of your work, Joan; she's tickled to death that you're going to do the drawings for the book. She'll probably help you pick out some of the dramatic high spots; she knows the manuscript forward and backward. Here's my mother now; I hear her coming through the hall."

Victor Sarbella turned to greet Mrs. Gilmore, Kirklan's stepmother, whom he had not met before.

"Mother, this is Mr. Sarbella. Further introductions are unnecessary, Victor, because she's heard all about you."

As Sarbella bowed over her hand, Joan joined them.

"I think you can fill the glasses, Kirk," she said with a glance at the tray. "Helen was directly behind me, as I came down the stairs. You know, Mr. Sarbella, we're terribly punctual about dinner. The way the servants do discipline us these days!"

The screen door onto the porch opened again, and Helen Gilmore came out quietly, almost listlessly.

Kirklan was filling the last glass. "Victor, I want you to meet my wife; Helen, this is Mr. Sarbella—the artist, you know," he said. "Perhaps I neglected to tell you that he was expected."

There was a pause.

The polite, formal smile on the artist's lips was washed away by a tidal wave of emotion—surprise, incredulity, horror—which left his face white and rigid; into his eyes there blazed a scorching fire of hatred that, since his back was toward the others, was seen only by Helen.

At mention of his name Helen had stopped, her own features ghastly; but she quickly checked the startled gasp which rose in her white throat and, by the most tremendous effort, managed to control herself. However, her agitation escaped neither her husband nor Joan; both of them sensed what a dramatic shock the meeting had been to her.

Sarbella mastered his emotions wonderfully, and he came of a race that is essentially emotional. And while he could not hide the pallor of his face, he did mask that first flash of hatred which had blazed in his eyes. Yet he dared not trust his tongue. Silently he bowed.

Kirklan Gilmore's unsteady hand splashed the last cocktail all over the tray.

"Perhaps—perhaps you've—met before?" he suggested, alarmed by what was obviously an attempt to conceal a mutual recognition.

"No," answered Victor Sarbella, his voice husky despite himself, "Mrs. Gilmore and I have never met until this moment. It is a circumstance that I very much regret."

"Mr. Sarbella," said Helen, an almost hysterical catch in her voice, "is a total stranger. The name startled me. It is such an unusual name, and I once had a—a friend who—"

"Dinner is served!" announced Bates. He said it quietly enough, but it was like a thunderclap, this interruption.

"Here's how!" cried Joan, picking up her cocktail glass. "You'll go a long way before you find anything like this, Mr. Sarbella; it's some of the old stock that Kirk's father had in the cellar—oh, years and years ago." It served to break the tension. "Here's to the new book—may it be a tremendous success!"

"Great gods!" Sarbella said under his breath, as he mechanically lifted his glass. "It is she—the woman! I find her here, the wife of—of my friend. Merciful Heaven, his wife!"

Right: dish Sarbella and herd the touch as he made matter at Mina
Might Mina the rich woman and the face she looked at a Mina
Mona! I began his wife.

# CHAPTER 6

## IN THE STUDIO

There can be nothing so dismal as pretended gayety, nothing so mirthless as hollow, empty laughter. After that startling encounter between Victor Sarbella and Helen Gilmore, both of them fighting for self-control, all five on the porch drank the toast that Joan had offered in an attempt to save the situation. Joan, of course, could not know what it was all about, but she sensed the ominous trend of things. She had seen the look of frozen terror in Helen's face, had seen the muscles bulge and rise beneath the shoulders of Sarbella's perfectly fitting dinner coat, and, while she had not glimpsed his face, it was easy to know that he, too, had experienced a distinct shock.

"I have not tasted a better cocktail since my last trip abroad," exclaimed the artist, forcing a smile to his face. As a matter of fact, he had swallowed the drink mechanically, hardly tasting it.

"Now for dinner!" cried Joan, taking full command of things. Putting her fingers on Sarbella's arm, she led the way into the house and toward the big, old-fashioned dining room.

Kirklan Gilmore jerked himself together with visible effort; his impulse was to dash forward, face his wife and his friend squarely, demanding sternly, "What does this mean? Answer me! What does this mean?" But good breeding demanded restraint; his obligations as a host required a simulated appearance of naturalness. With a queer mental offshoot he wondered how he would have made one of the characters in his books behave under a similar circumstance.

A moment or so later the five were at the dinner table. Even Mrs. Gilmore, whom nature had endowed with no large store of astuteness, realized the strain, realized that something was tremendously amiss, and she, poor and well-meaning soul, made matters all the worse by the uneasy, inquiring glances that she cast about the table in nervous bewilderment.

Victor Sarbella managed to carry things off with fairly commendable grace, but not so with Helen Gilmore, who made clumsy mistakes with the table silver and not once lifted her eyes either to her husband or the others. The rouge on her cheeks made the paleness nothing short of ghastly.

36

Kirklan Gilmore's eyes, slightly narrowed and brighter than they should have been, shot quick, queer glances from his wife to his guest. Perhaps it was but natural that his mind swept to one conclusion—a previous affair between these two. His friend and his wife! The salad fork trembled in his hand. Time after time he suppressed the impulse to leap to his feet, voicing the demand that kept shrieking through his mind: "What is there between you two?"

Only Joan's persevering diplomacy kept them at fairly even keel; she rattled on with scarcely a halt. But the dinner was a thoroughly miserable affair, and by the time it came to an end the nerves of the five were raw.

Joan's heart ached for the suffering she saw in Kirklan's face, and there swept through her an intensified hate for the woman who had won the man she loved.

"She's going to wreck his life!" she said under her breath. "I know it—I know it! She's killing him—killing his soul! If she does that, I'll—" The thought that came into her mind frightened her, for she had not known that there was so much of primitive passion in herself.

The moment the unhappy dinner came to an end, Helen Gilmore murmured an almost incoherent something about a headache and fled upstairs to her room. The other Mrs. Gilmore, too, faded out of sight, still wondering what it might be all about. Joan was inclined to remain, but Kirklan showed very plainly that she wasn't wanted.

"Run along, Joan, if you don't mind," he said in a jerky, strained voice. "Sarbella and I"—it was to be noted that he had dropped the more cordial and customary name of Victor—"are going to—to talk things over. Come out to the studio with me, Sarbella; the manuscript of the book is out there."

Victor Sarbella was not deceived into any notion that Gilmore had in mind a discussion of the new novel, and, while he shrank from what he felt sure was going to be a cross-examination, he did not see how he could very well refuse.

"All right," he agreed with a nod, reaching for his cigarette case. Silently the two men left the house and cut across the lawn through the gathering dusk toward the studio. No word was spoken as they entered the building and mounted the stairs to the writer's workroom above. Kirklan Gilmore switched on the lights, and the two faced each other at the desk strewn with pages of the manuscript. Sarbella remained calm, but the other let himself go, and his whole body shook like a man in the grip of a chill.

"Well, let's have it—the truth!" he rasped, almost a sobbing catch in his voice.

Victor Sarbella finished off his cigarette with a long puff that slid the burning edge of the tobacco tube close to his lips; at the same time he reached for a fresh smoke, tapped it on the back of his hand, and then lighted it with the stub of the old. A thin trickle of smoke swam slowly through his parted lips.

"Just what do you mean?" he parried.

"Don't you fence with me, Sarbella!" Gilmore shouted hoarsely. "I've got to the breaking point. My nerves are stretched tight as piano wires; if something snaps—"

"That's the trouble, Kirklan," Sarbella broke in soothingly. "You're nervous and upset over something; that's the size of it. You were upset when I first saw you, and I—"

"That's got nothing to do with it, Sarbella. You know very well what I mean. I saw Helen—my wife—saw her face when I introduced you two on the porch. Introduced you!" His voice rose shrilly. "I guess you know her better than I do; I saw—"

"Kirklan," again interrupted Sarbella, "that is where you are absolutely wrong. I give you my solemn word of honor, my oath as a gentleman, that until this evening I never saw Mees Gilmore."

"Oath of a gentleman!" derided Gilmore. "You're the sort who would lie like a gentleman. Man, I tell you that I saw—her face! Helen, my wife, was afraid of you. Why was she afraid of you? Why did her face turn so pale? Why did she look as if she were fainting?"

"She said," Sarbella replied smoothly, "that it was the name—that she had once known some one named Sarbella. Why couldn't that be true!"

"It could be, but it isn't. Sarbella, you're hiding something from me, and I've got to have the truth." His hands were clenched, and his eyes blazed with jealousy. "Isn't it a fact that you were once in love with her?"

A harsh, humorless laugh, the sort of a laugh that it is not pleasant to hear, burst through Sarbella's lips.

"In love with her? Great Lord, no—a thousand times no! I—" He broke off, on the verge of saying too much, of betraying the truth in one exclamation of passionate, hot-blooded hatred. "I tell you again, Kirklan, that your wife and I never met until this very evening. That is quite all I have to say; you must take that or leave it."

Sarbella paused as if he would choke on one more word.

Chest heaving, lips twitching, Kirklan Gilmore leaned heavily across the table, staring into the eyes of this other man whom he had considered his friend. Suddenly he straightened and leaped toward the door, turning the key in the lock; swiftly he turned and faced Victor Sarbella.

"Take it or leave it, eh?" he panted. "Suppose I won't leave it; suppose I tell you that you're not to leave this room until you tell me what I want to know? What you are hiding from me?" His voice broke. "I—I can't stand these lies, these evasions, this deceit any longer. You have given me your word that you have told the truth, that you never saw Helen before today. I don't know whether to believe that or not. But, if it is the truth, you know something—something about her. In Heaven's name, man, tell me! Who is she? I ask you—what is she?"

Victor Sarbella shook his head slowly. "She is your wife," he answered, as if that might explain why he must keep sealed lips, but Gilmore would not have it rest that way.

"Yes," he groaned, "she is my wife, but who was she, what was she before—before she became my wife? I think you know." His shoulders shook with a dry sob. "Sarbella, can't you see what this is doing to me—that it is driving me mad?"

Again Sarbella's head described a sadly negative gesture. "I am sorry, Kirklan," he said; "believe me, Kirklan, I am your friend, and I am sorry, but there is nothing I can tell you. Set at rest any fears you may have had about"—his lips twitched into a bitter smile—"about any romantic attachment between us. Anything but that!"

Kirklan Gilmore took a step forward; the next instant he had flung himself on Sarbella, and, although he was the less powerful man, the latter was taken off his guard and staggered back into a chair.

"You tell me what you know, and tell me now, or I'm going to kill you!" he gritted. "Tell me before I have to choke the life out of you." His fingers squeezed about the artist's throat, and Sarbella had to fight him off to break the grip. With a tremendous heave of the muscles he flung Gilmore back, and the novelist, reeling, lost his balance and plunged heavily to the floor.

He lay absolutely still.

Victor Sarbella stood over him, staring down at him pityingly. "I am sorry for you, Kirklan," he said huskily: "yes, I am sorry—very sorry." He went to the door, unlocked it with the key, and turned, just as Gilmore was struggling up. "I cannot very well remain your guest now, Kirklan. Oh, I don't mean just this." His fingers touched his torn collar, the rumpled bosom of his dress shirt. "But I'll stay until tomorrow. We can't forget that we are under obligations to the publishers. Yes, I will wait until tomorrow; see if you can't pull yourself together long enough to talk things over."

Gilmore gave no sign that he had heard, and Victor Sarbella passed on out of the studio and down the old wooden steps of the stable. When the door closed, Kirklan Gilmore slowly dragged himself to his feet and moved toward the chair by the desk. Like a rheumatic old man with protesting bone joints, he lowered himself into the chair, his body sagging limply forward until he lay across the desk, his face pillowed in his arms. He lay like that, his senses numbed, almost as if he were dead, for a long time.

# CHAPTER 7

## THE GET-AWAY

Not for a moment did Don Haskins doubt that Helen Gilmore—legally Helen Haskins, by grace of an unsundered legal tie previously knotted—would "come through" with the thousand dollars that he had demanded as the price of his silence. She wouldn't dare refuse; bigamy is a sternly met crime in New York State.

With a thousand dollars to the good he felt that his get-away was safely assured, for a thousand dollars would enable him to put a long distance behind him. And so, sitting in the squalid, shabby little third-floor room in Eighth Avenue Annie's disreputable haven for those hunted men who can raise the price of her protection, he was laying his plans. Several points of the compass beckoned to him; California intrigued him, but he was also inclined toward Cuba, and, even at a lesser distance, Florida waved its picturesque palms beckoningly before his mental vision. He had thought, too, of South America, but was wise enough to know that this trip would have to contemplate the dangers of getting a passport. A passport is not readily secured by a man of Don Haskins' unsavory standing as a citizen; so he scratched South America off his list.

It had been Monday afternoon when Helen had called at Eighth Avenue Annie's, leaving a payment of one hundred and ninety dollars on account; it was now just gathering dark of Tuesday, and so certain was Don that the dawning of the following day would bring the remainder of the thousand that he was making his very definite plans for sliding out of town—quickly.

He had allowed his beard to grow; that would help some. Perhaps it wouldn't fool the eyes of a dick who knew him well—and many of them did—but it added materially to his chances. The cops, since he had no successful job to his credit, wouldn't expect him to be in funds. The thing to do, he reasoned, was the thing he wouldn't be expected to do; therefore with fifty of the one hundred and ninety dollars he had got from Helen—previously diminished by an even hundred that he owed his old hag protector—he had sent Annie out among the secondhand shops of Eighth Avenue to gather a wardrobe, a gentleman's wardrobe, at reasonable prices.

"Nuttin' flashy," he had warned; "respectable-lookin', but none of the race-track stuff, see."

And so Eighth Avenue Annie went forth among the clothing shops where stained, ancient garments are sponged, pressed, and advertised "Just Like New." True enough, Annie took her own reward for this service; to the suit of blue serge for which she paid twelve dollars and ninety-five cents, she affixed a price tag which read twenty-four dollars and ninety-five cents, and, as you might expect, put the difference into her own capacious and ever-hungry pocket.

There seems to be some persistent destiny that has the habit of sending policemen past a certain spot at a certain moment. It is always happening, as an almost daily glance at your morning newspaper will bear affirmative witness. As Eighth Avenue Annie was engaged in purchasing Don Haskins' get-away outfit, Detective Sergeant John Henry Tish passed the door of Abramson's dark, gloomy and somewhat odorous "Clothes Bought and Sold" establishment and chanced to glance within.

Detective Sergeant Tish was not perhaps nearly so good a detective as he thought himself to be, but he had a good record for arrests and convictions; when he made a "pinch" something usually came of it. He had been recently assigned to this district, on the fringe of the old Tenderloin, and he wasn't so well acquainted as he might have been. But he knew Eighth Avenue Annie; he had seen her in Jefferson Market Court not a great many months before, and Annie's gargoyle face, with the narrow, red eyes, her bulging, muscular shoulders, were not easily forgotten.

"Humph!" grunted Sergeant Tish. "The old hag is buyin' somebody some new rags—that is some rags that was new—one time. Looks as if there might be something in it."

So, instead of pursuing his way down Eighth Avenue, he loitered outside Mr. Abramson's cluttered establishment, to all intents and purposes interested in a suit of plaid which occupied the central space in the window. "Can't Tell it from New," read a card. "A Bargain at $22.69." Mr. Abramson, you see, was a great believer in the psychology of the odd cent.

Eighth Avenue Annie striding forth with that swaggering, Bowery walk of hers, a bundle under her arm, did not glance behind her. Had she done so, she would have seen Sergeant Tish, a short, well-fed-looking man, who didn't look much like the usual run of fly cops, lose interest in the plaid and follow her at a discreet and disarming distance.

However, when Annie turned in at her place of abode and harbored evil-doers just around the corner of the second block, Sergeant Tish quickened his pace and was directly behind her, as she stepped into the vestibule. It might have been the ringing of the automatic bell that dimmed her ears to the pad of the detective's shoes, for, as she turned, there was Tish, grinning at her wisely, his foot thrust forward to prevent the door being suddenly slammed in his face. He had no intention of finding himself on the outside looking in.

"Say!" growled Annie. "What's the game?" Sharp as were her red, narrow eyes, she failed to see the brand of headquarters in the plain-clothes man's round, fat face.

Sergeant Tish continued grinning, but it wasn't a grin to arouse any contagious mirth or even good humor.

"Who'd you buy the new rags for?" he demanded. "I wanna know a thing or two about that. Get me?"

Eighth Avenue Annie got him; there was the tone of authority in the man's voice.

"What's it to you?" she demanded with pretended indignation. "Ain't a lady gotta right—"

"Cheese it!" broke in Detective Tish. "I know you, an' I gotcher number. When a bird sends you out to buy 'im clothes, he's either a cripple or a crook—an' if he was that bad a cripple I guess he wouldn't need any clothes." He chuckled in appreciation of his own wit. "So don't try no bluff with me. Take your hand off that door."

Annie had often defied the law, but her defiance was never flaunted openly. When a cop said open the door, she opened it quickly.

"I ain't done nothin' wrong," she protested with a ludicrous pretense at innocence. "There ain't nothin' wrong, is there, in doin' a favor fer a gent roomer. Is there, now? He said fer me to go out an' buy 'em—"

"Where is this guy?" broke in Sergeant Tish. "I guess I'll give him the once-over. Chances are he's some bird that's wanted, tryin' to do a swift one outta town. Yeah?"

"I dunno," muttered Annie; "I dunno nothin' about 'im. I rents 'im a room; he pays his rent. I'm a poor lady tryin' to make an honest livin', I am."

"That's a double lie," snorted Sergeant Tish. "You ain't no lady, an' you never glommed an honest jitney in your life. Lead on, you; I'm gonna give this guy the once-over an' a free ride most likely."

The woman hesitated, for she was at a ticklish disadvantage. The surprise of the detective's visit was too complete to give her any opportunity to warn Don Haskins who waited in the vile little room on the third floor for his new wardrobe.

On the stairs leading to the top story there was concealed a very cunning little device that in six years of hiding hunted men for pay had not once been detected by the police. Two of the steps, by a simple mechanical oper-

42

ation, could be jerked upward into an opening large enough to admit a man's body. Below this was space large enough to accommodate several persons, the steps then dropped back into place, looking thoroughly innocent. But Haskins had not been given the secret of the third-floor stairs, and now there would be no opportunity to favor him with this belated knowledge.

"I'll run right up an' tell Mr. Smith to come down," said the old hag.

"Say," sneered Sergeant Tish, "do I look that easy? On the level, do you think I'd fall for that stuff?" It angered him that she should have so little regard for his intelligence. "What floor did you say?" He unbuttoned his coat which fitted somewhat tightly across his ample stomach, giving him freer access to his police automatic strapped beneath his arm.

Eighth Avenue Annie had not lived in the underworld for nothing; she knew the ways of the cops. She knew, for example, that the first overt move she made to protect her well-paying lodger would land her in jail on a charge of aiding and abetting a criminal. She wanted to help Haskins, not from any motive of sentiment, but because she expected to garner further money from Don's "swell sister," as she supposed Helen Gilmore to be.

"I didn't say what floor, off'cer," she muttered, "but I'm sayin' now. He's on the thoid. I ain't protectin' nobody that ain't right." She tried to affect a virtuous attitude. "I dunno nothin' except he spiels it to me his moniker is—um—Smith."

"Lead the way," ordered Sergeant Tish. "Not a word outta you either. Get me? No tip-off goes with me; try that, and it's the station for yours. If you think I won't, try it." Evidently Tish had not been deceived in the slightest by her attitude of innocence. "You go on up them stairs just like you was bringin' back his new duds. You say, 'Here's your clothes, mister.' I guess we won't use the Smith racket, either. His name ain't Smith, and you know it ain't."

"Yes, off'cer," agreed Eighth Avenue Annie.

"Not so loud with that officer talk," warned Tish. "Ease down on the lung power, you. Now, let's go."

He motioned to the bundle she had just brought in from Abramson's, and she obediently picked it up, starting up the dank, musty stairs. The detective followed, walking with surprising lightness of step for so corpulent a man. They reached the second-floor landing and passed around a bend in the hall to the next flight. There was no hope for Don Haskins now.

As they reached the top, lighted murkily by the dirty skylight, Sergeant Tish crouched low so that his head and shoulders would be shielded by the bulking form of Eighth Avenue Annie and her packages. The woman's shoes clattered noisily, and Haskins came to the door with the broken, patched panel, his unshaven face peering out.

"You got the stuff, huh?" he grunted. "I'll bet it's a tin suit."

Eighth Avenue Annie made no effort to warn him; that might mean shooting, and she wanted no shooting in her house.

"It's a good suit," she muttered in a hoarse guttural. "It cost—"

"Stick 'em up," roared Sergeant Tish, flipping out his gun, and rising to his full height, leveling the weapon at the now wide-open door. "Get 'em up, or I'll drill you."

Don Haskins' hands went up; he would have been a fool otherwise. His lips twisted, as they emitted a vicious snarl.

"Double crossed me," he said. "Took my good jack an' called in the cops. Curse you, I'll—"

"Shut your mouth!" Annie whispered hoarsely, her own face livid.

Sergeant Tish grinned delightedly; he was beginning to realize that it had been a fortunate circumstance looking so casually into the doorway of Abramson's secondhand clothing store. He had felt all along, of course, that the woman was lying, that she was keeping a man in hiding. And men do not hide unless they are wanted. It might be a big haul. He took another step forward and peered closely into the face of his quarry.

"I can't name him offhand, but I guess the Bertillon boys'll rap to 'im fast enough." He backed Haskins into the stuffy, dirty little room at the point of the gun and reached into the pocket of his coat for an ever-ready pair of nippers.

"Stick out them fins," he ordered. "I'll get these darbies on you, an' then we'll talk things over."

Knowing that the gun was beaded for his vitals, and that any fool can shoot straight with an automatic, Don Haskins stuck out his hands; the handcuffs snapped about his wrists.

"What's the pinch for?" he demanded with an effort at bluster. "You ain't got nothin' on me; I ain't done nothin'."

"Well, anyhow, I guess you've done time," Sergeant Tish said shrewdly. "What's your name down at central office?"

Don Haskins remained sullenly silent, his eyes glowing hotly, as they stared at Eighth Avenue Annie. The hag had let the bundle from Abramson's slide to the floor, and with both hands she pushed back the dirty gray hair that straggled down across her soiled face.

"Want to hold out on me, eh?" grunted Sergeant Tish, with a shrug of his flesh-padded shoulders, as he thrust the gun back into its holster. His chubby face wore a smile, for he was well pleased with himself; a single-handed capture is a thing that a cop delights in. And, if it turned out to be an important arrest—well, Tish had a hunch that it was just that, an important arrest. "Suit yourself, John Doe; you'll get the rap fast enough when I get you downtown."

Don Haskins knew how hopeless it was now. Ten minutes ago he had been daydreaming pleasantly of Florida, perhaps Cuba, and now—Sing Sing via the Tombs. It all depended on whether or not "Dago Mike," his confederate in the loft job, net profit ten dollars split three ways, had squealed. And he was sure Dago Mike had squealed. The warehouse watchman had been croaked, and that meant that not only the actual slayer, but Don Haskins, as a participant in the crime, was liable to the death sentence.

Haskins thought swiftly, desperately. The chair! The sickening vision of it swam before his eyes and drove his brain to cunning that was somewhat beyond his normal mental processes. He staggered back to the unkempt cot.

"Gimme a cigarette," he muttered thickly, his nerve apparently deserting him. "I'll talk—tell you who I am. I—I gotta have a fag first."

Sergeant Tish had seen that kind before. "Sure," he agreed readily enough and produced a package of his own. Don lifted his manacled arms and took a cigarette. It trembled between his fingers, wabbled between his twitching lips. The detective lighted a match and held the flaming stick toward him.

Haskins inhaled deeply and seemed to grow calmer; his eyes raised, taking his captor's measure. He noted with satisfaction that he was almost a head taller than Tish. Even then he found the time to wonder how he had managed to get on the force.

Tish did not rush his man. "Take your time," he encouraged. "No hurry; spill it when you're ready."

Eighth Avenue Annie edged to the door from the hall, peering inside with a horrible leer, as she considered that this man whom she had befriended—for pay, of course—was going to be a yellow skunk and "cough up." He would probably squeal on her, too; tangle her up in his own net of trouble. That was the way with some of these rats; they couldn't stand the gaff and wouldn't protect their friends. She muttered something that sounded like "scum."

Little did Annie know what was going on in Don Haskins' mind. Don had never been a swift thinker, and hard drinking of bootleg whisky hadn't added to his nimbleness of wit, but his brain was traveling in high now. He knew that it wouldn't do him any good to conceal his identity; lie as he would, there would be plenty of cops down at headquarters to remember him. More than that, his picture was in the rogues' gallery, his finger prints on file. But he didn't propose to make that trip down to headquarters. Desperation made him resourceful.

"My name is Haskins," he muttered. "They used to call me Nifty Don in the old days, but you ain't got nothin' on me. On the level, you ain't got nothin' on me."

Sergeant Tish frowned for a moment and then a look of delight spread over his round, fat face. "Guess again, Haskins. There's a general order out for you. You're wanted for a croak out in the Bronx; I forget the details, but you're wanted all right. Yeah, I'll say you are."

Don groaned. He had been right in his fears; Dago Mike had squealed. The handcuffed man got to his feet; his shoulders heaved, as he inhaled deeply on the now half-consumed cigarette. He filled his lungs to every cubic inch of their capacity. He took a step toward the detective and, opening his mouth, expelled a cloud of smoke directly into Tish's face.

Sergeant Tish, half blinded, was taken totally by surprise; he staggered back and made a motion toward his gun, but he was not quick enough. The prisoner's manacled arms flashed upward and downward, the metal wristlets catching the detective a stunning blow on the side of the head. The latter's knees sagged, but he continued to fumble for his gun, when Haskins struck again, and this time the plain-clothes man crumpled up on the floor, blood gushing from the edge of his scalp.

"My Gawd!" whispered Eighth Avenue Annie.

For the moment Haskins ignored her, as he knelt beside the form of his captor and took the police regulation automatic; then he began frisking the man for the handcuff keys.

"Here," he said harshly to the old hag, "get these cursed things off of me. Hurry!"

"You'se ain't croaked 'im?" gulped Annie, her eyes bulging.

"Naw," grunted Don. "Use that key, or I'll give you a dose of the same. I ought to, anyhow, you dirty double crosser. Tipped the cops off, didn'tcha?"

"He seen me buyin' the clothes; he follered me. See? I didn't have no chance to give you warnin'. Nice fix you got me into, brainin' a dick in my place. They'll send me away for this." She worked the key in the lock, and the handcuffs came free.

"I hope you get ten years," Haskins said viciously. "Gimme them clothes." A moment later he was changing in trembling haste, shedding the disreputable suit for the more respectable garments that Annie had purchased at Abramson's. His fingers were shaking, and he steadied his nerves with a drink from the bottle which rested beside the bed.

Eighth Avenue Annie was twisting her grimy old hands in an anguish of terror. She knew the aftermath of this, and the revenge of the outwitted detective was not a pleasant thing to consider. Had she dared she would have tried to square herself by preventing Haskins' escape, by sending out an alarm, but Haskins was armed and at her first move would perhaps kill her.

46

She flattened against the wall, sobbing hoarsely in self-pity, cursing the man who had sent Haskins to her for protection.

In his haste Haskins forgot something very important; he forgot that beneath the dirty mattress was the forty dollars that remained of the one hundred and ninety dollars Helen Gilmore had given him the previous afternoon. He didn't think of it until he had dashed down the two flights of stairs and had reached the street. As he realized this amazing oversight and turned back, he saw Annie sneaking out of the vestibule, running. He knew. She was calling the cops, trying to square herself. He didn't dare go back for the money. He wheeled in the opposite direction, walking swiftly.

Flight without a dollar in pocket is a problem, but desperation has cut many a Gordian knot. Eighth Avenue is not a well-lighted street, and darkness had settled down over the city. A taxi nosed through the gloom, and after but a moment of hesitation Haskins hailed it; the question of fare did not bother him—not with that automatic in his pocket. The taxi drew up alongside the curb; it was a nice new taxi, with a shining, spotless coat of blue paint.

"I wanna get to Yonkers in a hurry," said Don briskly. "Gotta important date out there. How quick can y'make it?" Yonkers was the river-bordered town which joined the New York city limits on the north.

"Hour and a quarter," answered the driver, giving Haskins a sizing-up look.

"O. K.," grunted Haskins. "Let's travel; go down Riverside Drive all the way." He climbed inside, and they were off.

Don had a particular reason for choosing the Riverside Drive route. Past One Hundred and Eightieth Street the Drive winds between the river and high-towering bluffs, with no houses on either side. He desired a quiet place for settling the matter of the fare. They had reached the spot which is called Inspiration Point, when the fleeing passenger rapped on the glass which separated him from the chauffeur's seat.

"Stop 'er!" he shouted.

The car ground to a halt, and Haskins leaped out, cursing volubly.

"Lost ring—diamond ring—slipped right off my finger. That rock cost me eight hundred bucks," was the excuse he gave.

The driver stared suspiciously, for his fare did not look like a man who would own an eight-hundred-dollar diamond ring.

"Aw, watcha handin' me?" he growled skeptically.

Haskins looked up and down the Drive. The nearest car was some distance away. His hand slipped to his pocket for the automatic he had taken from Sergeant Tish. At the same instant he sprang forward. He did not shoot, but brought the butt of the weapon down in a vicious swing on the fellow's head. With a grunting, choking groan the latter collapsed into black unconsciousness, still sitting at the wheel.

The approaching car swept past; another followed; and neither paused their swift progress. There was no reason why they should have noticed anything. Don Haskins lifted out the limp form and carried it well back to the side of the road, where he quickly rifled the senseless man's pockets, taking nineteen dollars and thirty-five cents in cash, a good watch, and the driving license. Then he donned the chauffeur's cap and climbed into the taxi; an instant later he was speeding on northward—alone. He was headed for the one place where he was sure that he would find money and protection—Greenacres.

# CHAPTER 8

## CAUGHT IN THE WEB

The wife of Kirklan Gilmore was not literary, had not even any tendencies in that direction; no literary qualifications had been required for her employment as a typist in Atchinson's publishing house. Her reading had been superficial, shallow, but she had an adaptable mind and was constantly picking up surface things, chance clever little quips and quotations, which, if she were not put to a severe test, might pass for an acquaintance with the classics.

When, overwhelmed by the appearance of Victor Sarbella as her husband's guest, she had fled to her room, it was with the realization that still another specter of the past had appeared to haunt and undo her. And there flashed through her mind a fragment of an old quotation:

*Oh, what a tangled web we weave,*
*When first we practice to deceive.*

Yes, what a tangled web she had woven—inextricably enmeshed in the snarled skeins of her ambitious folly. How circumstances had conspired against her.

"What a fool I was to think I could get by with it!" she whispered bitterly. "How will it end? It was bad enough without Sarbella. Him—him! It was like a ghost from the grave. He will tell my husband; of course he will tell him—he could want no better revenge than that. That look in his eyes —how he hates me!"

She began to think of flight, even made a half-hearted, indecisive move to gather up some of her things, but there was no train now until morning, and the thought of driving the car, novice at the wheel that she was, through the dark night terrified her. Besides which the car was probably in the garage, locked; and she did not have the key. There seemed nothing to do but wait.

Helen would have been a very blind person indeed had she not realized that Kirklan had sensed something amiss in the amazing meeting between her and Sarbella; and, as time dragged on—eight o'clock, nine, and then ten—she wondered why her husband had not come raging upstairs to fling

49

the past accusingly into her face, to order her out of the house, perhaps to kill her!

"Surely he would come if he knew," she told herself. "Hasn't Sarbella told him? Why, he—he must have told him!" It was past her understanding.

Wearily she went to her dressing table, removed the dress she had worn at dinner, slipped into a flowing-sleeved dressing gown that was charmingly open at the throat, and began to let down her glorious bronze hair which cascaded over her shoulders.

Detached as Greenacres was, the house was very still, so still that the many sounds which always fill a country night, floated through the window, magnified by her taut, tortured nerves to crescendo volume.

"Something has got to happen. Why can't it happen now and be over with!" she moaned. "The suspense, this awful suspense! I can't stand it—I can't!"

Nervously she went to the window, and, pushing aside the curtains, leaned out, staring into the night. The future, her future, was like that—black, impenetrable, void, and she felt that there could never be any dawn —not for her.

"My life's been nothing but tragedy," she told herself bitterly. "I thought I might be happy and respectable. There's a curse on me; that's what it is, a curse. I'd be better off dead, but—I don't want to die."

Helen, staring off into black space, did not see the skulking form that moved stealthily through the shrubbery, circling uneasily, furtively about the house. The slinking man stared upward at the lighted window, stopped, as she leaned out across the sill, framed in the open space by the light which burned within the room behind her.

"It's her!" he grunted, but, as he crept forward, intending to call softly, she disappeared.

Don Haskins had deserted the stolen taxicab two miles down the road; by cautious questioning he had learned the location of Greenacres and had walked the rest of the way, and here he was. It had been a troubling problem as to how he would get in touch with Helen. He had thought of going into the village and calling her on the telephone, but there were objections to this plan. In the first place he did not want to risk an appearance in the village; added to that, it might be bad business calling her to the phone so late at night. It had been his tentative idea to find a hiding place on the spacious estate until he could get in touch with her. Already he had considered the stable as a likely place for his purpose.

"That's her room," he told himself, still looking up at the lighted window. "Now, if she was alone—" He crept closer to the house the better to study the situation, and he found it very much to his liking. The window of

Helen's room opened out on the roof of the veranda which semicircled the house on two sides.

It might be risky business, but a desperate man, the prospect of the death chair looking him in the face, does not stop to weigh such minor risks as this. He reached an almost instant decision. He sat down in the grass and removed his shoes; tying the laces together, he swung them about his neck.

"I never done no porch climbin'," he muttered, "but it don't look so hard."

But it was hard, much harder than he had anticipated; the porch post was large of circumference, making it difficult to hug his arms about it with a freezing grip. Several times he slid pantingly down just as his straining fingers were within a few inches of the raised awning. The perspiration poured from his body and moistened the palms of his hands, so that he had to keep wiping them dry.

In one last desperate effort he got hold of the awning's edge and began to pull himself upward to the cornice. The triumph, however, was far from noiseless; awning hooks snapped loose from the wood, and the awning itself tore with a ripping sound under the strain.

Panting, breathless, exhausted, Haskins lay flat on the roof, waiting to see if the sounds would arouse the house. He marked the time by counting, one to sixty, one to sixty, until four minutes had dragged past. Not even Helen, within the room of the open window directly above, seemed to have heard.

Haskins began edging himself, a few inches at a time, across the shingles toward the patch of light that streamed out across the roof. Presently he had reached the sill and, drawing himself up, peered within.

Helen was again at the dressing table, mechanically applying bedtime cosmetics. Otherwise the room was empty; Don made sure of that before he pulled himself still further forward.

"Sh!" he hissed. "It's me—Don. Douse the glim!"

Helen Gilmore did not turn; there was no need. Through the dressing-table mirror she could see his unshaven face at the corner of the window sill. Her hand clapped to her mouth to stem the scream which rose in her throat. Her body rocked in the low-backed chair, but she did not faint.

"Douse the light!" Haskins commanded again in a piercing whisper. "Somebody might see me sneakin' in."

Helen stumbled unsteadily to her feet and snapped out the lights. In the darkness she heard him floundering through the window and into the room, heard the curtains rip, when he caught at them, evidently to keep his balance, as he lunged forward. She even heard his panting breath, as it wheezed through his mouth.

Don turned, lowered the sash, and drew down the blind. "Lock the door an' then flash on the lights again," he ordered tensely.

"The door is already locked," answered Helen, as she fumbled for the light switch. The next instant they were blinking at each other; she leaning limply against the wall, he standing in the center of the floor. "My God, Don, what made you come here—tonight of all nights? I can't stand any more; I can't. You gave me until tomorrow—"

"Blame the damn cops," he grunted. "It was them did it—them an' Eighth Avenue Annie. She sicked 'em onto me." He still believed that the old hag had double crossed him.

"You mean—"

"Yeah, they're after me. I'm in for it right. They had the darbies on me, but I beaned the dick that nabbed me, got 'em off, took his gat, swiped a taxi, an' here I am. My hunch was right. Dago Mike squealed on the loft-job croak."

"How did you—find me—this room?" gasped Helen.

Despite the desperation of the situation, Don Haskins grinned a little.

"Seen you when you poked your head outta the window; shinned up the porch, an' here I am."

"I—I haven't got the money, Don; I haven't got it—yet."

"But you're gonna get it tomorrow? I betcha y'are." His tone was menacing. "You gotta hide me somewheres until— Mebbe you can drive me somewheres in a car. Boston, huh?"

Helen lifted her hands in a weary gesture. "Everything seems to be happening at once," she whispered. "I—I don't know if I am going to be able to get the money or not—now."

The man glowered menacingly. "Don'tcha try to pull no stall on me; that stuff don't go. Understand?"

"Don, listen. My husband was on the same street yesterday when— when I went to that place to see you. His publisher saw me—the man I used to work for."

"Aw, say; you don't expect me to swallow no guff like that?"

"Sh! Not so loud, Don. It's true. Atchinson saw me. Kirklan didn't believe it at first, but now he feels sure it's true. At first he'd promised me the money. I told him that I wanted to pay an old bill, but I don't know what he is going to do now. Then"—a shudder went through her—"to make it all worse, a man came to the house tonight, a Mr. Sarbella. He—"

Haskins lifted his hand to his unshaven chin and stared at her dubiously. "Sarbella? I guess you're bats, ain'tcha? Why, that guy's dead!"

"Not—not Andrea," choked Helen. "Victor Sarbella. At first I thought— they look so much alike. He recognized me. Oh, the awful look of hatred that he gave me!"

52

"You mean that Sarbella spilled to Gilmore?"

"I—I don't know. I haven't seen any one since dinner. I—I suppose he did. He hates me, and he wants revenge. The newspapers said—"

"That he was gonna get you," finished Don. "Yeah, I remember readin' that. The papers made quite a piece about it—Eyetalian revenge an' that sort of spiel. I guess you're some scared that the Sarbella guy's gonna croak you, huh? Right here in the house, is he?"

Helen nodded. "Yes, right here in the house," she answered.

Don whistled softly. "Well, if that ain't the cat's eyebrows!" he murmured, as he stared at her suspiciously. If what she told him was true, he probably had lost the club he had been holding over her head to extort money from her. But he doubted if it were true; Helen, he told himself, was clever. Perhaps she hadn't found it easy to get the thousand dollars blackmail money from her husband, and she had made up this story as a pure bluff.

"Where's the Gilmore guy?" he demanded.

"I don't know. I told you that I hadn't seen any one since dinner. I can't understand why Kirklan hasn't come to me, if Sarbella has told him."

Haskins pursed his lips thoughtfully and wrinkled his shallow forehead; after a moment he nodded. "I gotcha; if Gilmore had the low-down on you he'd have come stormin' in here to have it out with you. Sure he would. No, I guess Sarbella ain't spilled to him. I guess that ain't his way of gettin' even with you. Stiletto! That's the way them Eyetalians do it."

Helen gasped; she hadn't thought of that possibility. She was inclined to treat the suggestion lightly, but there came back to her the memory of Victor Sarbella's black eyes flaming into her face, hot with a stored-up hatred, and she shivered.

"Oh, I—I don't think he would kill me!" she gasped.

"Then you don't know them Eyetalians," Don grunted sagely. "They sure is strong on the revenge stuff. If I was you I'd keep right here in this room, while he was on the premises. But that's your trouble, and I got troubles of my own. When do I get that thousand bucks you was gonna hand over?"

"But if Sarbella has told Kirklan who I am, what I was before—"

"Then you figger to pass me up, huh? Guess again. Even if Sarbella does, Gilmore won't squeal to the cops; a guy like him don't want no family scandal, see! Mebbe he'll show you the gate, but he ain't gonna send you up the river—not if he's crazy about you like you said yesterday. But me, that's different. You done me dirty; you throwed me over, made a bum outta me." His face contorted unpleasantly. "I owe you one, I do, an' I'm handin' you this on the level; if I get nabbed this trip I'm goin' to spill. I'm gonna send for the district attorney an' tell him—"

53

"I'll try to get the money for you, Don; I'll try my best," broke in Helen with a quick promise.

Don glared at her triumphantly, as he reached into his pocket for one of the cigarettes that he had taken from the unconscious taxi driver, lighted it, and, puffing slowly, began rocking to and fro on his feet. A silly smile spread over his face, as glancing down, he saw a bare toe protruding from one sock, where a hole had been rubbed by friction against the porch post in his climb of a few minutes before. He remembered that his shoes still swung from around his neck. With a chagrined exclamation he untied the laces and put the shoes on. Helen did not smile.

"Yes," she said again, "I'll try to get the money for you tomorrow." Her hands went out in a nervous gesture, and Don caught the sparkle of a diamond on her finger. She had not worn it on her visit to Eighth Avenue Annie's—for good reasons. Haskins stared at the ring and put a hasty appraisal of four or five hundred dollars on it.

"I'll take that for security," he said, pointing. She drew back against the wall in a move of refusal, and Don, eyes narrowed, darted toward her.

"Aw, I guess you will," he growled.

But, when his fingers touched the smooth, white skin of her arm and seized her in an effort to force the diamond from her, a change came over him. A fierce return of his old love for her swept through him. All his hate melted, like ice returned to its first form of water. His arm tightened about her, drawing closer; his unshaven, stubbly chin buried against her throat.

"The law says you're mine!" he panted. "You're my wife. I—I guess I ain't stopped bein' crazy about you even—even when I was wantin' to kill you—wantin' to choke the life outta you like—like this."

The fingers of one hand raised before her face, writhing, twisting, like tentacles; they neared her soft throat, toyed against the skin. Helen dared not scream, but she struggled in silent terror. Her arms flailed against his sides, and her hand struck against the bulky automatic in his coat. Her fingers slipped swiftly into his pocket and seized the butt of the gun.

"You ain't this guy's wife," he went on hoarsely. "You're my wife; the law says so, and you're goin' with me." He was so beside himself that he did not feel the tug of the pistol, as it came free from his pocket. And then there crashed through the stillness of the house the slam of a closing door. Don's arms dropped limp.

"What was that?" he whispered, returning to the realization that he was a hunted man, fleeing for his life.

"I think it's Kirklan," she whispered. "His room adjoins this one. Sh! He'll hear you."

Haskins took a flying leap across the room and switched off the lights; his hand went to his pocket.

"The gat—it's gone!" he muttered under his breath. "It musta dropped outta my pocket when I was climbin' up the porch." He groped through the darkness. "Helen!"

"Sh!"

"You gotta stash me away somewheres. If I get nabbed, what I said goes —I spill what I know."

Helen in the darkness concealed the automatic beneath the flowing sleeve of her robe. With the gun she was no longer afraid of Don, but she still did fear his threats, his power to send her to Auburn prison on a charge of bigamy. A moment before he had loved her madly; the next he might hate her again with just as much intensity. She had to aid him—protect him.

"I'll hide you," she told him, "on the third floor—an old storeroom. No one ever goes there. I'll bring you food. I'll try to get you the money; I'll get you money—somehow. I'll see that you get away. Follow me."

Cautiously she opened the door. The hallway was in friendly darkness. She groped along the wall, fearful that Don would betray their presence, but he followed her in stealthy silence.

The third-floor stairway was inclosed, and it was reached through a door which, since the third floor was seldom used, creaked dismally, as she swung it open.

"Up there!" she whispered. "The last door at the left; you'll know it. It's a storeroom. I'll see you—some time tomorrow."

The door closed again whiningly, inclosing Don Haskins within the stairway. He considered it safe to light a match and did so to illuminate the upward climb. He saw accumulated dust, evidence of disuse; Greenacres servants were not good housekeepers above the second floor, it seemed. Without any difficulty he found the storeroom and, striking another match, discovered that a kindly circumstance had left a discarded couch for him to rest upon. He sat down on the edge of it and felt in his pocket for his package of cigarettes, and then something dawned upon him. The gun had been in his pocket after he had got inside the house; he remembered the touch of it, as he had sought out a cigarette.

"Curse her!" he gritted. "She took that gat outta my pocket. What did she want with it, anyhow? I got a good notion to go back down there an'—" He lighted a fag and smoked nervously, indecisively. He wanted his gun. A desperate man feels safer with something to shoot with, but he could not quite make up his mind to risk a return to the second floor.

Helen had returned to her room without detection. She switched on the lights again, but in her agitation forgot to lock the door behind her. Stunned, nervously exhausted by this new-conspiring circumstance, the appearance of Don, she sank down into a chair, and, as her arms dropped listlessly down, the gun which a few brief hours before had been the property of Detective Sergeant John Henry Tish of the New York police department slid down to the rug with a faint thud and lay at her feet. She made no move to pick it up.

She faced the door, her eyes fixed vacantly upon nothing; hopelessness engulfed her. Don—her legal husband—here. Sarbella here, too. Both of them here with her under the same roof. No wonder that she was stunned, dazed; at times she felt that she must be in the midst of a terrible night-mare, that she would wake up with the grateful realization that it wasn't true.

For perhaps ten minutes she sat motionless, surrendering any attempt to think coherently. Suddenly her lax nerves snapped taut, a gasp escaped her lips, her eyes widened. There had been no sound of a footstep in the hall, there had been no rap at the door, but the knob was turning slowly, silently, and the door began to move.

# CHAPTER 9

## THE OPEN DOOR

The butler at Greenacres occupied a small room on the ground floor near the kitchen. He had been asleep for some time when the ringing of the doorbell sounded, a loud jangling in the night's stillness; he stirred, muttered grumblingly, and was about to tell himself that it must be a mistake, when the ring was insistently repeated.

"There ought to be a law against it," he declared, as he slid his thin old legs out from beneath the sheets, and, not more than partly awake, fumbled groggily for the light. The clock on the bureau told him that it was half an hour past midnight. "Fine time of night for people to go around ringing bells at respectable houses!" Again the bell started its clatter. "Maybe it's an automobile accident out on the road," he said, but he did not hurry. Bates was not the hurrying kind. He reached under the pillow for his false teeth, clicked them into his toothless gums, and then began to pull his trousers on over the old-fashioned nightshirt that flapped about his skinny legs.

Still grumbling under his breath, he shambled down the hall, switched on another light, and went to the front door, making sure that the safety chain was in place before he opened it. Bates did not have good eyesight even in the daytime, and at night he was little better than blind; squintingly he stared through the narrow crack at the form of the man out on the porch.

"What's wanted?" he snapped complainingly.

"It's me, Bates," came the answer.

"Heaven bless us, it's Mr. Kirklan!" gasped the butler, making haste to unfasten the chain and admit the master of Greenacres. "Was it you, sir, doing all that ringing?"

Kirklan Gilmore, still wearing his disheveled dinner coat, entered the house with a slow, dragging step. His face, as it had been all day, was haggard and drawn.

"Yes, I rang," he answered; "sorry to rout you out of bed, but I must have forgotten my keys when I dressed for dinner. It was the only way I could get in, and I didn't want to spend the night in the studio."

57

"Oh, certainly not, sir," Bates agreed hastily. "You mustn't think I am objecting to getting up to let you in. It's quite all right, sir—quite all right. But you gave me a surprise; I thought you were in bed hours ago. Have you been at your writing so late?" As an author, Kirklan Gilmore was one of those methodical fellows who worked just so many hours a day, usually eight, and at the most ten.

He laughed mirthlessly. "Writing? Man, I can't think, much less write."

"You are ill, sir," Bates murmured solicitously. "I noticed at dinner that you did not look well. I thought—" He broke off abruptly, realizing that thinking, especially as regards family affairs, was not one of his offices as butler.

"You thought—what?"

"Er—nothing, sir; I beg your pardon very humbly. Is there anything I can do for you before you turn in?"

Kirklan Gilmore's lips twitched.

"Thanks for offering, Bates; as a matter of fact, I was thinking of asking you to make me one of those old-fashioned toddies that you once were so good at in my father's day. With a dash of stomach bitters in it, you know. My nerves are all shot to pieces, Bates. You can see that; probably liquor won't do any good, but perhaps a good, long drink will help me get to sleep."

Bates' head wagged approvingly on its slender neck.

"Your father, Mr. Kirklan, always found them beneficial after a hard day at court. I remember one time when— But I mustn't be gabbing, when your nerves are jumping like that. I'll mix the toddy for you right off, sir."

"And I'll go with you," said Gilmore. "You know, as many of 'em as I've had, I don't think I ever saw you make one."

"There's a bit of a trick to it," Bates admitted modestly and shuffled toward the rear of the house, Gilmore at his slippered heels. A moment later the butler was performing a service for the author that, in the old days, he had performed many times for Kirklan's father. Kirklan wasn't so fond of liquor as his father had been.

"A full measure of orange juice—like this," Bates was saying. "Two squares of sugar and—" He droned on, illustrating his formula, as Gilmore watched him dully.

"Take one for yourself, Bates," he invited; but the butler shook his head.

"They say it's a poor doctor that won't take his own prescription, sir; but it would upset me at this time of night. Thank you just the same, sir. Ah, there you are." He handed Gilmore the glass, the square of ice clinking, and the latter accepted it, sipping slowly. He did not gulp it down hastily, as Bates had expected.

"Is Sarbella still here?"

58

The butler looked bewildered.

"Is he still here, sir? Why—why certainly, Mr. Kirklan. I took it for granted that he was down for a considerable stay. He retired to his room a little more than an hour after dinner."

Gilmore nodded.

"Oh, yes, of course," he murmured and took another sip of the toddy. "But I thought he might have gone. A little something happened—something that— My God, man, what's that?"

His body had tensed, and the glass slipped from his fingers, as a look of horror spread over his face. Loud, shrill, blood-chilling, there rang through the house a terrified scream—a woman's scream.

Bang! A sharp, staccato explosion reverberated through the night's stillness. Bates' thin legs were trembling beneath him, his mouth sagged open, and his eyes rolled wildly toward the ceiling as, struggling for utterance, he pointed a shaking hand upward.

"That was upstairs!" he cried hoarsely. "Something—something terrible has happened upstairs. It was a shot. And that scream—I swear that it was Miss Joan's."

Kirklan Gilmore stood, his muscles rigid, hands clenched at his sides, gulping hard.

"Joan's scream?" he muttered. "No, Bates, no! Something tells me, man, that it was my wife. I tell you it was my wife. Quick, the stairs! I've got to know what happened; I've got to know. Come!"

And, although it was Gilmore who urged haste, it was the butler who took the lead, heading for the stairs with a lame lope.

"I—I can't understand it, sir," the servant chattered as he went along. "There's no weapon in the house except your shotgun; and that report—it wasn't loud enough for a shotgun. It must have been a pistol; I am sure that it must have been a pistol."

When they were perhaps halfway up the staircase there came to their ears, unmistakably clear and permitting no possibility of a mistake, even in the tenseness of the moment, the sound of a hastily slammed door. Gilmore stopped dead in his tracks. An opening door, some member of the household aroused by the scream and the explosion, would have been perfectly understandable. But a closing door! There was the suggestion of hasty, headlong flight. Under the circumstances it was a sinister sound.

Nearing the top of the stairs, the two men, master and servant, saw a patch of light rays which came from an open doorway down the hall.

"That light!" panted Gilmore. "It comes from my wife's room. The door of her room is open—her light is burning!"

They had now reached that ominously opened door; it stood ajar for perhaps ten inches. Gilmore stopped again, the breath wheezing through his teeth, as if he might have had a presentiment of what he might find on the other side of that panel. The old butler went on forward, laid his withered hand upon the knob; but he was unprepared for the sight which met his eyes. With a gasp of horror he reeled back.

"You—you were right, sir," he whispered hoarsely. "It is your wife, and she— Be brave, sir—be brave!"

Helen Gilmore lay in a half-reclining posture on a wicker couch. Looking only at her face, one might have thought her sleeping, such was the repose of her features. But the bosom of her silk robe was stained crimson. On the floor, beneath the outflung fingers of one hand, there was an automatic pistol.

Gilmore took another brief step forward and over the butler's shoulder saw his wife, the light from one of the wall brackets flooding across her beautiful face—still beautiful even now. A shudder shook his shoulders, as if the hand of some invisible giant had seized him in a vicious grip.

"Your wife has killed herself!" cried Bates. "The poor woman has shot herself!"

"Is she dead?" Gilmore cried hoarsely. "I can't—I haven't the strength —the courage to go near her, Bates. Can you tell me if—if my wife is dead?"

The butler was trembling in his agitation, but he steeled himself to the ordeal and forced his unwilling feet forward. Even as he neared the couch, he thought one last, weak breath escaped the lips of his master's wife. But he might have been mistaken. His fingers reached out and touched her cheek.

"She is still warm," he gulped; "of course she would be—so soon after. But I think she must be dead. You see, sir, the bleeding has stopped. I understand that is a sign of death." He shook his head slowly. "Yes, Mr. Kirklan, I am sure that she is dead."

Gilmore collapsed into a chair; head lowered, his eyes closed, as if to blot out the terrible sight in front of him, he began to sob, brokenly, but without tears. A moment later he checked his grief.

"You'd better call Doctor Bushnell, Bates," he choked. "There—there might still be a chance of saving her."

The butler shook his head sadly. "I'm afraid not, but there is a way that I've heard the doctors use—" He shambled to Helen's dressing table where he picked up a silver-backed hand-mirror; then he returned to the limp form on the couch and held the glass close to her lips.

"Yes, I know," Gilmore muttered thickly, watching him with a fascinated stare. "If any breath of life remains, there will be moisture on the mirror." He leaned forward tensely. "What—what does it show, Bates?"

The butler inspected it briefly.

"There is no breathing," he answered; "I was right, sir; your wife is quite dead. But I will phone for the doctor; that is, I believe, the customary thing in cases like this."

As the servant moved toward the door, he paused suddenly, a startled look coming into his eyes.

"It is very strange," he muttered; "yes, very strange."

Gilmore looked at him dully. "What is strange?" he demanded heavily.

"That—that she should have shot herself with the door standing open, sir. If you will pardon me, I know that I wouldn't kill myself—with a door open. I would lock myself in. And"—his voice sank to a tense, vibrating whisper—"Mr. Kirklan, did you hear a door slamming shut, as we were coming up the stairs just a moment ago?"

"I heard a noise, Bates, yes. You are sure, Bates, that it was a closing door?"

"Quite sure of it!" cried Bates. "There is something else, too. If she shot herself, why did she scream? My word, sir, don't you understand? Your wife has been murdered!"

# CHAPTER 10

## COMMON SENSE

"Your wife has been murdered sir," repeated the butler, with growing conviction of his sudden theory. "I am not a detective, but I am sure, were it suicide, the door here would have been closed—locked. That is only common sense, Mr. Kirklan."

Kirklan Gilmore forced his eyes to that lifeless, crimson-stained form which so recently had been alive, that lovely creature whom he had married only three weeks before. His face was set in a rigid paralysis of horror, which did not change even when he turned his head away and closed his eyes.

"No, Bates, no!" he cried thickly. "It—it couldn't be. Look! There is the gun beside her, where it must have dropped from her fingers after—after she pressed the trigger. Your first impression was the right one; Helen has killed herself."

But the butler was not to be shaken.

"You heard the scream, sir," he argued; "the scream that sounded before we heard the shot—the scream that I thought was Miss Joan's."

"What nonsense!" muttered Gilmore, pressing his hands to his temple. "A scream is a scream, Bates; they all sound alike."

"Of course I was mistaken," the butler broke in hastily. "I had heard Miss Joan scream once, the time you were thrown by the horse, and we all thought you had been killed. It sounded so much like that, sir, I thought for a moment— But naturally it could not have been Miss Joan."

"Certainly not," said Gilmore. "Why do you stand there arguing about it? Go call the doctor, can't you? Tell Doctor Bushnell to come quickly."

Yet Bates delayed another moment to press his theory.

"Do you remember the scream, sir?" he whispered. "There was terror in it. Not at all the kind of a scream, Mr. Kirklan, that one would give unless faced with a terrible danger. And people do not scream when they are about to shoot themselves."

Gilmore groaned and tossed his hands wildly.

"Stop it!" he cried hoarsely. "Get out! Do what I tell you—call the doctor. You're a butler, not a policeman. In Heaven's name, Bates, get a move on you."

As the butler shambled into the hall, almost ludicrous in his haste, he narrowly escaped a collision with Victor Sarbella, who appeared from out of the darkness, a dressing gown thrown over his pajamas.

"What's happened?" demanded the guest of Greenacres. "I thought I heard a shot." His voice was strained, excited; there could be considered nothing strange in that, for there was certainly the promise of sinister, tragic things when the after-midnight stillness of a peaceable country house is shattered by the startling voice of exploding gunpowder.

"The younger Mrs. Gilmore is dead, shot—murdered!" panted Bates, and dashed on past so headlong that it seemed he would surely tumble down the steps.

A smothered exclamation broke through Sarbella's lips, and for a brief moment he did not move, as he stared toward the half-open door in front of him. His face was set into tense lines. From within he heard the sound of a groan, and, stepping forward, he saw Kirklan Gilmore, as his body sagged in a chair, twisting his hands with such intensity that it seemed he must snap the finger joints. And then the artist saw the dead woman on the chaise longue.

"Great Lord, Kirklan—"

The novelist turned, flinging out an accusing finger in a wild gesture. "You did this!" he screamed. "You—"

Sarbella's eyes narrowed, his face hardened. "Be careful what you say, Gilmore," he broke in. "It is no light thing to accuse a man of murder."

"I say you did it! Helen has killed herself, and you—you drove her to it —you drove her to her death."

Sarbella was naturally bewildered.

"Your butler says your wife has been murdered; then you accuse me of it, and now you switch everything around by telling me that she has killed herself. I don't know what it all means. What *has* happened?"

"Bates is an old fool," muttered Gilmore. "Of course she has killed herself. You see—there is the gun on the floor, where it dropped from her fingers. Any one can see that it was suicide."

One might have thought that a look of relief came into the face of the artist; he nodded his head slowly in agreement.

"Yes, that's the way it appears; but if that is the case, why is it that your butler says—"

"Oh, what's the use of discussing my butler's notions. He seems to think that he ought to be a detective, that's all. She killed herself, and"—his voice became edged with bitterness—"it was you who drove her to do it."

The artist tossed out his hands in an imploring gesture. "That is unfair," he protested. "Perhaps her conscience, but am I responsible for her conscience? Am I responsible for—for her sins?"

Kirklan Gilmore staggered to his feet. "What do you mean—her sins?" he cried hoarsely. "Am I never to know the truth about her?"

Sarbella shook his head. "Not from my lips," he answered; "she is dead. Let what past there be buried with her. It will be better that way, Kirklan—better for every one."

"Who is dead?" came a tremulous question from the hall. The novelist recognized the voice of Mrs. Gilmore, his stepmother, and leaped forward to prevent her entrance. He knew, high-strung, nervous woman that she was, the gruesome sight would be a tremendous, perhaps even dangerous, shock to her.

"You—you mustn't come in here, mother. Something—something has happened to Helen."

"You mean," gasped Mrs. Gilmore, clutching at the casing of the door for support, "that she is dead?"

"Yes, Helen is dead," finished Kirklan. "Go back to your room, please."

"I was awakened by something. I am not certain just what it was," whispered the little, gray-haired woman. "And then there was a shot. You mean, Kirklan, that your wife—"

The novelist inclined his head. "Helen has—has killed herself. Bates has gone to telephone Doctor Bushnell; there is nothing you can do—nothing. Now please return to your room."

Mrs. Gilmore began to sob wildly, perhaps not so much from grief as from the hysteria of horror.

"She has killed herself—suicide! Oh, the disgrace, the scandal of it; three weeks married and—a suicide. I—I knew that something awful would happen. It was in the air. I had a presentiment of it at dinner. All of you acted so strangely, so tragic. Kirklan, what made her do it?"

"I don't know," he answered thickly. "Perhaps the reason for it died with her. I—I don't want to talk any more about it, mother; it's all I can do to hold myself together. Won't you please go back to your room?"

Mrs. Gilmore, making a move to obey him, released her fingers from the support of the door casing and staggered; thus, unintentionally, she reeled just within the door. As she saw the crimson-stained form on the lounge, a scream tore up through her throat. She swayed dizzily, her knees crumpled beneath her, and she would have fallen to the floor in a limp heap, had not Kirklan reached out and caught her in his arms.

"Sarbella!" he called. "She—has fainted. I knew that would happen if—if she saw it. Won't you help me with her? I—I suppose we'd better take her to Joan's room; she can't be left alone in this condition."

Victor Sarbella rushed forward to lend his assistance, and between them they supported the limp, gray-haired figure down the hall to the wing of the house where Joan Sheridan's belongings had been banished by the coming of Kirklan's bride to Greenacres. This, the room of tragedy, had been Joan's until the coming of the house's new mistress.

"You'll find a light button there, near the corner of the turn," directed Gilmore, and Sarbella fumbled for the switch. "It's the last door to the right. She—she's heavier than I thought."

As the two men came to the door that Kirklan had indicated, there reached both of their ears the muffled sound of sobbing—convulsive, hysterical sobs. A tremor went through Gilmore.

Joan's room being somewhat removed from the other part of the house, it was reasonable that the sound of the shot might not have awakened her, but, being awake, how could she have failed to hear it? And she was not asleep! She was awake—weeping!

Apprehensive terror clutched at Gilmore's heart—the terror of a sinister something that he could not explain. Was it possible that, after all, it had been Joan who had screamed? Sarbella, too, looked startled and darted his host a quick, uneasy, questioning glance. His arms being occupied, Gilmore kicked his shoe against the foot of the door, as a substitute for rapping. On the other side of the panel the choking sobs suddenly ceased.

"Yes?"

"It's Kirklan, Joan. Something has happened, and your mother has fainted. We thought we ought to bring her here to you."

"Just—just a moment, Kirk," came the tremulous answer, "and I will let you in."

There was a brief wait and the sound of running water, as the girl within the room turned on a faucet. Then the door opened, and Joan stood before them. Although it was now almost one o'clock in the morning, she had not taken down her hair for the night; she had, late as it was, not yet retired. Evidently the sound of running water had marked her effort to undo the evidence of tears, but her eyes were red and her face was ghastly! After a first furtive glance her gaze avoided Gilmore's eyes.

"You can put her on my bed," she said in a shaking voice, but she did not ask why her mother had fainted.

"Something very terrible has happened, Joan," the novelist said hoarsely. "Didn't you hear it?" He had placed his stepmother on the bed and mechanically began to rub her wrists.

"Didn't I hear—what?" Joan asked so faintly that her voice was hardly audible.

"The pistol shot—just—just a few minutes ago," answered Gilmore.

The girl shuddered, her head averted. Her hands were clenched at her sides, and her lower lip was imprisoned between her teeth, obviously in an effort to keep it from trembling. She was making a tremendous effort to keep her self-control.

"I did not hear a pistol shot," she said, her voice still very low. "I did not hear any shot. Why do you ask?"

"Helen has killed herself, Joan; she shot herself with a pistol."

There was no startled cry of horror from Joan's lips, as she heard what might have been supposed to be her first news of tragedy. But was it news to her? There was not so much as an exclamation of surprise, not so much as a murmured word of sorrow or sympathy.

Standing a little to one side, Victor Sarbella stared at the girl in narrow-eyed, intent interest, evidently greatly puzzled by her peculiar attitude. Joan still said nothing; almost absently she began massaging her mother's ice-cold fingers.

"She faints very easily," she murmured. "It is never serious. She will be all right presently. Mr. Sarbella, will you please dampen a towel under the cold-water tap?"

"I had been out at the studio," Gilmore went on, the words tumbling out jerkily. "I think I must have fallen asleep out there. When I came to the house I found that I didn't have my keys, and had to ring for Bates to let me in. My nerves were in a bad way, so I asked Bates to mix me a toddy, a nightcap. I was drinking it, when both of us—Bates and I—heard a scream. Right after that there was a shot. Bates and I rushed upstairs to find Helen dead; that's all I know."

As his voice trailed off to a dull, lifeless stop, Joan gave a start and looked up to take the damp towel that Sarbella offered her. She placed it across her mother's forehead; Mrs. Gilmore stirred under this application and moaned faintly.

"I think mother will be all right now," said Joan. "I don't think it will be necessary for either of you to stay. If I need you I will call."

"Bates has telephoned to Doctor Bushnell. I will have him see mother when he comes, Joan."

Joan nodded.

"Perhaps it would be best," she agreed. "She is very high-strung, and may need an opiate. It was a tremendous shock to her—of course."

Kirklan began a retreat from the room, and Sarbella, after another queer glance at Joan, followed. No word was spoken until they had come to the room of the tragedy.

"I can't stand to go back in there!" Gilmore cried hoarsely. "It—it's all that I can do to hold myself together as it is. I think I'll go downstairs and have another drink."

Victor Sarbella, frowning so deeply that his eyes seemed to be closed, put out his hand impulsively.

"Don't do that, my friend," he murmured; "for your own sake—don't. Liquor will not help any at a time like this, and it will look bad, very bad, for you to be under the weather at a time like this."

The butler came hurrying up the stairs.

"I have had Doctor Bushnell on the wire, sir," he reported. "He had just got home from a call, and he says that he will be here as quickly as the car can bring him—a matter of minutes. It is only two miles from the village."

Kirklan Gilmore glanced shudderingly toward the door of his wife's room. "It doesn't seem right," he muttered, "leaving her in there alone, but I can't stand to look at her again. I—"

"There no use torturing yourself," advised Sarbella. "It is quite certain that she is beyond all human help. There is nothing that can be done until the doctor comes. Here, man, you're wabbly—all in; sit down here on the top step. Hold yourself together the best you can, my friend."

Kirklan laughed harshly, mirthlessly. "Stop calling me 'my friend,' Sarbella," he said unsteadily. "I won't have any more of that from you. If it hadn't been for your coming down here, Helen would—" He broke off abruptly, as he realized that Bates was within earshot, and that very little missed the butler.

Sarbella shrugged his shoulders, but made no verbal response. The house had become intensely still again. From the foot of the stairs there was the steady, measured ticking of the tall clock on the first floor, as the long pendulum moved to and fro. Gilmore sat down on the steps, shoulders slumping forward, as he laced and unlaced his fingers.

Why had Joan been sobbing in her room? What was the reason for her strange behavior? Why had her face been so ghastly pale, even before he had informed her of Helen's death?

He pondered this.

"Listen!" said Bates, breaking the uneasy silence. The other two men jerked into an attentive attitude. There came to their ears the hum of a powerful motor. An instant later an automobile horn blasted the stillness in brief announcement. Doctor Bushnell had arrived.

67

# CHAPTER 11

## BUSHNELL CALLS THE POLICE

The butler hurried stumblingly down the steps to admit Doctor Bushnell, who had been the Gilmore family physician for almost a dozen years; he swung open the door, as the doctor was stepping briskly across the porch.

"You got here in a hurry, doctor," said Bates. "It happened upstairs. Mr. Kirklan is up there now—at the top of the steps. She's dead; I held a mirror to her face and—"

"Yes, so you told me over the telephone," broke in Doctor Bushnell; he was a tall, crisp man, with a pair of gray eyes looking out from behind a pair of rimless spectacles.

"She—" began Bates again.

"This is no time for conversation, my good man," the doctor again interrupted firmly, but not impatiently. "You can talk later." He started swiftly for the stairs.

But Bates was not to be shaken off so easily.

"You didn't give me a chance to finish telling you over the phone," he said, blocking the way. "Mr. Kirklan says she killed herself, but I know better. She was murdered."

Doctor Bushnell abruptly halted. "Murdered?" he repeated.

"See if you don't bear me out, sir," whispered the butler. "I'm not a detective, but I've got common sense enough to know—"

The physician shook loose Bates' fingers. "There'll be time enough for that, Bates. Just now there's a chance—a bare chance—that you are mistaken, and that she is still alive. If there is any chance of saving her, there must be no wasted time."

Surgical kit swinging at his side, the doctor bounded up the stairs, two steps at a time. Kirklan Gilmore was waiting just outside the door of Helen's room. The doctor offered his hand, and they clasped silently for a brief moment, the grasp of the physician warm-hearted, sympathetic.

"Am I too late, Kirklan?"

The novelist bowed his head. "Yes, Doctor Bushnell, you are too late. She is dead—I am sure she is dead. She shot herself with a pistol. She is—

there." He pointed to the partly open door. "It—it won't be necessary for me to—to come in there with you?"

The doctor gave a pitying glance at the young husband, whose wife had been taken from him after three weeks of marriage; he saw the haggard, drawn face, the horror-filled eyes, the twitching lips.

"It will not be necessary," he answered quietly. "Perhaps you had better wait downstairs. If I need you I will call."

"Th-thanks," gulped Gilmore.

Doctor Bushnell, after a glance at Victor Sarbella, who, of course, was a stranger, passed on into the room and closed the door behind him. Being a doctor, he was steeled to death, but he was hardly prepared for the sight that shocked his eyes. Despite himself, his nerves reacted with a tingle of horror, and a gasp slipped through his lips.

Quickly he bent over the still form of the beautiful woman; it was the first time that he had seen Kirklan's wife, although gossip of the surprisingly sudden unannounced marriage had reached the near-by village. Little more than a cursory examination was necessary to verify the butler's earlier findings. Helen Gilmore was dead; she had succumbed to that bullet wound which the doctor found in the chest, just a little below the left armpit.

"She was murdered!" The butler's statement came back to Doctor Bushnell with a rush of conviction now. It would have been almost impossible for such a wound to have been self-inflicted. For the woman to have shot herself would have meant the holding of the weapon at a decidedly awkward and unnatural angle. Possible, perhaps, but highly improbable from a medical viewpoint.

Doctor Bushnell's face had become grim. Swiftly he unfastened the surgical kit and found a long, slender probe, with which he might approximate the direction that the bullet had taken. Ranging downward! Still further argument against the wound having been self-inflicted.

"Bates was right!" muttered the physician. "I wonder how he knew." He stepped back and glanced at the gun on the floor. He had, of course, noted that the moment he had entered the room, and he took it at the moment as proof of suicide. The pistol had every appearance of falling from the hand flung out over the edge of the lounge.

"Who could have killed her—this beautiful bride of three weeks?" he said under his breath. As a physician, as a surgeon, he knew the right thing to do at the right time, but now a feeling of helplessness came over him. Obviously something had to be done. What?

As he stood there in the center of the floor, staring down at the dead woman, debating, there came to his ears the sound of a muffled cough in the hall. He took a quick step toward the closed door, more than half suspecting that some one was eavesdropping.

"Oh, it's you, Bates," he grunted, as he saw the butler. "You might as well come in; there are some questions I wanted to ask you, anyhow."

"Yes, sir," murmured Bates, entering the tragedy chamber willingly enough. "Have you discovered anything, doctor?"

"Did you examine the body, Bates?"

The butler shivered.

"Examine it?" he whispered. "Heaven, no! I held a mirror close to her face; I touched her with my hand; that is all. Why did you ask me that, sir?"

"I wondered what made you so certain that it was murder, Bates, and whether you had observed the nature of the wound which caused her death."

"It wasn't that made me know it was murder; it wasn't anything more than just common sense. The door into the hall was open when we found her."

"The door was open? What significance was there in that?"

"Would you shoot yourself, sir, with a door standing half open?"

Doctor Bushnell stared and, after considering this question for a moment, shook his head. "No," he answered slowly; "since you mention it, I don't suppose I would."

"And you wouldn't scream, doctor, while you were getting ready to pull the trigger," added the deductively inclined butler.

"You mean—"

"I mean, sir, that she screamed horribly. Oh, it was a terrible scream, the kind of a scream that makes a man's blood turn to ice." Bates made no mention of his first impression that the scream might have been that of Miss Joan; he had, in his own mind, entirely rejected that possibility as too absurd for any consideration whatever. "As I take it, sir, she screamed when she knew that she was about to be murdered."

"Humph!" murmured Doctor Bushnell. "You've got quicker wits than I'd given you credit for. You figured that out like—well, like, I imagine, a trained detective might do it."

Despite the situation, Bates gave a faint smile of pleasure at this compliment.

"I have always read a great many detective stories, sir," he said. "I've not only read them, I've studied them. I might say that I am quite a student in a way. Had I not waited so late in life to develop my mental faculties, I hardly think that I should have remained a butler. In fact, I am quite sure that I would not."

70

"You're a queer fellow," mused the doctor. "What else have you deducted, Bates? Can you manage your tongue?"

"Why do you ask that, doctor? If you mean, can I keep from talking too much, I can be very discreet."

"All right, Bates; then I'll tell you that you were right. This woman has been murdered. The nature of the wound verifies your guess."

Bates looked grieved. "You don't call it guessing?" His tone was protesting.

"Well, no, not guessing," Doctor Bushnell answered slowly. "It had more foundation than a guess. Very logical, Bates, reasoning out that business about the door. What else can you tell about this business?"

"Very little, sir, very little, indeed. Mr. Kirklan and I rushed directly upstairs when the shot was fired and then—"

"Wait a minute. You rushed upstairs? What time was this?"

"A few minutes after half past twelve, very shortly before I had you on the telephone."

Doctor Bushnell gave the man a quick glance. "You had been in bed, hadn't you? I judge from your state of dress—"

"Quite so, doctor; I had retired early. I was sound asleep when I was awakened by the ringing of the doorbell. It was Mr. Gilmore; he had locked himself out and was trying to get in. He had been out at the studio—the old stable, you know, where he does his writing. The poor man was quite badly upset; he was in a terrible way, and asked me to make him a toddy."

The physician looked uneasy. "Good Lord, Bates," he muttered, "you don't think it possible that Kirklan—"

"Oh, certainly not, sir," the butler broke in quickly. "It was quite impossible. I was standing within four feet of him when we both heard the scream and the shot. The glass dropped out of his hand, and he stood there like a man of stone, his hands shaking, his face white as a sheet of paper. He said: 'My God, Bates, what's that?' And while we were both still listening, there came the shot; it must have followed the scream by half a minute, perhaps not so long as that. We both dashed up the stairs, I in front. While we were mounting the steps, sir, we both heard a sound that seemed to be the slamming of a door."

"Ah!" exclaimed the doctor. "The slamming of a door? Then you think that some one in the house—"

"That would be but guessing, doctor. The door of this room was open, the light was burning, and I was the first to see her. It seemed to me—I cannot be sure—that she took her last breath while I was watching her. The bleeding had stopped. Am I right, doctor, in supposing that the flow of blood stops when death takes place?"

Doctor Bushnell nodded. "Yes, when the heart action ceases," he answered. "What else, Bates?"

"The gun was just as you see it now, sir. It was only natural that Mr. Gilmore should be so firm in his belief that she had taken her own life. He was not even convinced when I mentioned the matter of the door and the scream. Poor man, he couldn't be expected to do any thinking at a time like that. He was very much in love with her; he seemed fairly to worship her. It was too bad that she wasn't the right wife for him. Miss Joan is the one he should have married; she's only his stepsister, you know, no blood kin. I guess it nearly broke her heart, poor girl, when—"

"What do you mean by saying she wasn't the right wife for him, Bates?" broke in the doctor, moving toward the bed, where he began removing a sheet with which to cover the body until an undertaker could be summoned.

"She had good looks, but she wasn't his kind," Bates replied. "She'd managed to climb up in the world—most likely from pretty near the bottom. A servant can usually tell, sir, from watching them at table, and a letter came—day before yesterday, I believe it was—a most disreputable-looking letter it was, sir, to be received at Greenacres, all smudgy and dirty. It gave her a shock, too, although she tried to pass it off casual."

"What the servants don't know!" murmured the doctor under his breath, and then added, aloud: "You think there may have been some connection between the letter and the murder?"

"As to that, I couldn't say, Doctor Bushnell, but she was much agitated, it seemed to me. I would say that it must have been written by some very low person, a most peculiar sort of a missive for Mr. Kirklan's wife to be getting."

"All these little scraps of information may prove valuable, Bates," the doctor said meditatively. "You were pretty sharp on naming it murder. Perhaps you have some theory as to who killed her."

Bates looked crestfallen; his slender stock of theory was completely exhausted, and then he brightened.

"Finger prints!" he exclaimed. "Perhaps the murderer's finger prints are on the gun." He made a move to pick up the weapon, but the doctor stopped him with a gesture.

"Better not," he warned. "I understand it's such a simple matter to destroy a delicate thing like a finger print. We'd better leave that for more practiced talents than ours; I'm afraid that all finger prints look alike to both of us."

"It wasn't robbery, sir," offered the butler. "She is still wearing some jewelry."

"Yes, I'd noticed that. There are no back stairs, Bates?"

"There are none."

"In that case, Bates, it hardly seems likely that the slayer could have fled from the second floor without you or Kirklan seeing him. That probably means that the murderer is still in the house. That would not give us a very large list, eh?"

The butler's eyes widened.

"You mean, sir," he whispered tensely, "that you think Mr. Sarbella could—"

"I mentioned no names, Bates. Sarbella—is that the man I saw in the hall when I arrived?"

"Yes, sir, that's him; he's a friend of Mr. Kirklan's, a guest who came out only this afternoon—yesterday afternoon it is now, speaking precise. He's some kind of an artist, I believe. I guess he's an Italian, sir. I don't want to go around accusing any one, Doctor Bushnell, but—"

"But what, Bates? This talk is strictly between ourselves."

"There was a most peculiar attitude at dinner, sir; Mr. Sarbella and her"—pointing toward the sheet-covered lounge—"did not so much as speak once, while I was serving. They were all on edge—even Mr. Kirklan. I didn't understand it; I don't understand it now. After dinner the younger Mrs. Gilmore went very quickly to her room; she was pale and nervous. I don't think I know anything more, doctor."

"Just one more question, Bates. You and Mr. Kirklan were downstairs. Sarbella was upstairs. Who else?"

"The elder Mrs. Gilmore, Miss Joan, and her." Again he pointed to the dead woman.

"What about the other servants?"

"Elizabeth, the maid, went to Yonkers yesterday, sir. She pleaded that her mother was ill, but I doubt it. She don't know what the truth is, that girl; she's always making excuses, and Mrs. Gilmore is that soft-hearted she never refuses her."

"Or doubts her stories," added Doctor Bushnell with a faint smile. "A most credulous woman, Mrs. Gilmore."

"Exactly, sir," agreed the butler. "Mrs. Bogart, the cook, does not sleep at Greenacres; she comes every morning from the village and goes home again at night. And the gardener isn't employed full time—only three days a week."

"To me it looks very much like Mr. Sarbella," murmured the doctor and glanced around the room. For all that the physician knew there might be clews within touching distance, but which he, untrained as he was in such business, would never be able to recognize as clews.

"I am going to lock this door, Bates," he said. "No one must enter it without my express permission. I am going downstairs now. I suppose you

73

might as well go to bed."

"What's the use?" muttered Bates. "Not a wink of sleep would I get after this."

The key was in the lock; Doctor Bushnell removed it and put it in the outside of the door. Then he turned off the lights, stepped into the hall, shot the bolt, put the key in his pocket, and went down the stairs. He found Kirklan Gilmore and Victor Sarbella in the library, the latter sitting in a chair, puffing nervously at a cigarette, while the novelist paced back and forth like a caged beast. At the doctor's step, Gilmore swung around.

"You found her dead, of course?" he muttered thickly.

"Yes, Kirklan, I found her beyond all help." Doctor Bushnell gave a quick glance at Sarbella, who returned it steadily for a moment with his intense black eyes. "I would like to talk with you, Kirklan, privately if I may. Suppose we go across the hall into the den."

Sarbella inhaled deeply at his cigarette and got to his feet.

"I am going to my room," he announced; "if you need me for anything, I shall be at your service." He moved perhaps three paces toward the stairs and then turned; his face was in the shadows, so that it was impossible to see any expression that may have been on his features, as he asked: "You discovered that it was self-destruction?"

"So it would appear," answered the doctor, deliberately indulging in a deceiving play on words. With suspicion pointing toward Sarbella, it was perhaps best that the man not know too much—just yet. If the artist were guilty, there might be something gained by keeping him in ignorance that the suicide sham had fooled no one. Sarbella moved on up the stairs; Doctor Bushnell would have given a pretty penny to have had a good look at his face, wondering if he might not see there a look of relieved suspense.

Kirklan Gilmore's hands fidgeted restlessly in his pockets. "You say that you want to talk with me privately?"

"Yes, suppose we go into the den."

"That isn't necessary now, is it? Sarbella has accommodatingly gone upstairs to his room."

"The den, if you don't mind," insisted Doctor Bushnell. "I'd prefer taking no chances of being overheard."

Gilmore's head jerked up. "I can't understand the reason for all this secrecy," he muttered; nevertheless he led the way across the hall to the room known as the den. It had in former days been his father's favorite room. The physician followed and gently closed the door.

"Sit down, Kirklan," he murmured. "I dislike to add to your strain, but there is something that I must tell you. Your wife did not kill herself."

The novelist winced.

"You mean—"

74

"Kirklan, it's murder."

Gilmore staggered and dropped limply into one of the big leather chairs, face buried in his hands. "But, Doctor Bushnell, it—it can't be that. There —there was the gun beside her. That is proof—"

"Only proof of an effort to make murder appear suicide," broke in the physician. "The nature of the wound is such as to preclude any reasonable thought of self-infliction."

"Murder?" Gilmore whispered dully. "Bates was right, after all, then? I can't understand it. Who would have killed her?"

"Ah, that is what remains in front of us. I am in a very peculiar position, Kirklan. I am your family physician, but at the same time I am a deputy coroner; I accepted the appointment only last month. It is my official duty to do everything in my power that the law may take its proper course. I don't suppose you know whom the gun belongs to?"

"I do not know."

"It is a heavy gun, Kirklan; not at all the sort of weapon that would belong to a woman, or that a woman would use if it were left to her own choice. I have not examined it; I have not so much as touched it. I was afraid that I might destroy possible finger prints; I thought it best to wait."

"Wound or no wound," muttered Gilmore, "I can't believe that it was murder. Why would any one have killed her?"

"Kirklan, I am going to put a frank question. How well do you know this guest of yours, the man Sarbella?"

"Great Lord, doctor, you don't think that he—"

"I'm afraid I don't think anything yet. I'm just stabbing around in the dark. Was Sarbella previously acquainted with your wife?"

"See here, I don't want any insinuations of that sort."

"I am not insinuating, only asking a question. Bates thought he noticed a peculiar, strained situation at the dinner table. Since you and Bates rushed directly upstairs, and since that is the only means of reaching the second floor, it seems quite certain that she was killed by some one who is still in the house. There is no evidence of robbery. There were but five persons in the house—Sarbella, your stepmother, Joan Sheridan, Bates, and yourself. Unless we want to suspect Mrs. Gilmore or Joan—"

"Oh, that's too absurd for words," broke in Gilmore, making no mention of having heard Joan's sobbing.

"And that leaves Sarbella."

The novelist beat his clenched hands against his knees. "Doctor, I tell you that you're wrong—wrong!" he cried. "Helen killed herself; there is no other explanation—none! I must tell you something; my wife asked me for a thousand dollars. She must have needed it desperately. Because I did not give it to her— What are you doing with that telephone?"

75

Doctor Bushnell had picked up the instrument from the desk and lifted the receiver from the hook.

"I am doing what I must do, Kirklan," he answered with quiet firmness. "I am calling the village police."

# CHAPTER 12

## "WIGGLY" PRICE

The local police authority in the village of Ardmore was vested in the person of Mr. Hamilton Griggs, who held the office of constable, and whose most important duty was the enforcement of the municipality's automobile laws. Since the roads were exceptionally good, and since Constable Griggs received a fee of two dollars and fifty cents for each arrest resulting in a collected fine, he found the office fairly lucrative during the touring months.

Constable Griggs—generally called "Ham" by way of brevity—was a widower and occupied with his daughter a neat, green-shuttered cottage on Hudson Street. His police equipment was a high-powered motor cycle, and his most profitable hours of patrol duty were between nightfall and a little past twelve, when automobilists were hurrying over the highways, probably feeling more secure in their breach of law under cover of darkness.

It had been a good night for speeders, and "Ham" Griggs was mightily pleased with himself; an even ten arrests he had made, the fines had all been paid, and the neat sum of twenty-five dollars in fees reposed in a trousers pocket of his khaki uniform. At a quarter of one his motor cycle putt-putted stormily into the yard beside the cottage. He shut off the engine, locked the ignition, and, going to the rear of the house, let himself in through the unlocked kitchen door.

Etta, his daughter, had set out a cold lunch for him, as was her custom, and the constable lost no time in "falling to." With a chuckle of satisfaction he took the little wad of crumpled bills from his pocket and tossed them to the top of the kitchen table, where he might enjoy the sight of them.

"Pretty good," he told himself with a grin. "Let 'em speed!"

There was even further reason for jubilation. During his patrol of the roads within the village's corporate limits, he had found the deserted blue taxi, where Don Haskins, fleeing the New York police, had left it to continue his journey to Greenacres on foot.

Taking the number, he had reported his find to the New York company which controlled an entire fleet of like cabs. There ought to be a ten-spot from the taxi company, the constable told himself. All in all, it had been a most satisfactory night.

Ham Griggs was a heavy-set, dull-faced man of forty-odd; he had, prior to his elevation into public office, been a caretaker for one of the summer homes which border the Hudson River. Having an appetite in proportion to his stalwart build, he ate with a gusty heartiness. When the last chicken bone had been picked clean, he leaned back in the chair, which creaked protestingly on its two rear, straining legs, loosened his belt, and took from inside his uniform cap, always the policeman's cigar cache, a rich-looking Havana which had been the ineffectual peace offering of a gentleman who had been doing forty miles per, when Mr. Griggs halted him.

"Ah!" murmured the constable, puffing deeply. "Betcha this is a twenty-center—mebbe twenty-five." He removed it from his mouth and examined the embossed band with utmost respect. "A smoke like this sure tops off a good feed."

His coat unbuttoned, his thumbs hooked beneath the straps of his wide-webbed suspenders, he continued smoking until the electric light seemed to be swimming in a sea of smoke. And then the telephone rang, a loud, insistent jangling from the front of the cottage. Ham Griggs' chair thudded down on all fours with such force that there was the sound of cracking wood.

"Now I wonder what that is?" he grunted. Ardmore being a quiet, law-abiding community, a night call for the constable was highly unusual. He lumbered hastily to his feet and plunged toward the sitting room, where the telephone was located. The bell was still ringing when he took down the receiver.

"Hello!" he shouted into the transmitter. "Hello there! Dang it, central, quit ringin' in my ear; you'll bust an eardrum!" Possibly in retaliation of this impolite tone, the switchboard operator buzzed again.

"Constable?"

"Yeah, this is Ham Griggs."

"Doctor Bushnell speaking, constable. There's been a tragedy at Greenacres—the Gilmore place, you know. Can you come at once?"

"Whatcha mean—tragedy, doc?"

"There'll be time enough for that when you get here," came the voice of the village physician.

"I gotta right to know," grunted Ham Griggs. "Let's have it." His voice was officially important now. "Y'mean robbery?"

"Worse than that, constable. Oh, I might as well tell you—Kirklan Gilmore's wife has been killed. It is—murder."

"Good Lord, murder!" cried Griggs, his voice rising thunderously loud. "Who killed her, doc? Who done it?"

"That's our job, constable, to find out. You'll come right away?"

"Sure I will. Whatcha think I'm constable for? How—how was she killed?"

"Shot, Griggs; let's not waste any more time talking now." And at the other end of the line the receiver clicked, breaking the connection.

It was not surprising that the persistent ringing of the phone and Ham Griggs' loud-pitched voice should have aroused the constable's daughter, Etta. She appeared in the sitting-room doorway, her hair done up in curlers, her rather plain face a glistening smudge of cold cream.

"What's happened, fawther?" she demanded, her none-too-plump arms hugged tight across her flat chest.

"Ain't I told you to cut out that 'fawther' stuff?" growled Ham Griggs.

"Yes, fawther, but did you say somebody had been murdered?"

"That's the size of it," nodded the constable, beginning to button his coat. "Out to Greenacres—Gilmore's new wife, so Doc Bushnell says."

"My Gawd!" gasped Etta Griggs, momentarily forgetting her little book, "Social English." Etta was ambitious for herself; she was engaged in writing a play, and wished to equip herself to move as one of the elect in literary circles, when the moment of her great success should arrive. "The—the author's wife? Why, they ain't—they haven't been married a month yet! Did he kill her, fawther?"

Ham Griggs was impatient of questions, eager to be off, but his daughter barred the sitting room's one door, and he knew that the only way to pass without absolute violence was to answer her.

"I don't know nothin' 'bout it," he grunted, "except what the doc told me, which was precious little. Seems like she's been shot. I dunno who done it. Now get outta the way, Etta, an' let me get goin'."

"Chances are he did," mused Etta; "we literati are so temperamental, so given to quick, strong passions."

"You just natcherally make me sick!" snorted her father, as he plunged past her. A moment later she heard his motor cycle bark into life and, with staccato explosions from the exhaust, race out of the yard and down the quiet village street.

Etta's rôle in the Greenacres tragedy was more important than one might imagine it could be, and for no greater reason than that she aspired to be a playwright. Her play had reached its fourth and final act; with a few minor corrections here and there, it was ready for its journey to New York. She had not the slightest doubt of its immediate acceptance and production.

She realized in a vague sort of way the power of the newspapers; and, little knowing into how many independent departments a great daily is divided, she was suddenly seized with an idea—a great idea. The murder of Mrs. Gilmore, she reasoned, was news, stupendous news; Kirklan Gilmore

79

was a famous novelist. The newspaper which she read regularly would, as she saw it, naturally feel grateful to her for giving them firsthand information regarding the tragedy. It would serve as a pleasant introduction to the editor of that great metropolitan publication, would tincture the review of her "play" with a personal kindliness.

What queer notions people do get into their heads! But the merit of her idea is neither here nor there; the important thing is that Etta Griggs did call the office of *The Morning Star*, and she was thus responsible for the appearance on the scene of a certain news hound named Jimmy Price, sometimes more intimately known as "Wiggly."

The news-gathering staff of *The Star* is a high-pressure, hectic organization; one would wonder how they could get out an intelligent paper in the midst of such a mad scramble. It was nearing press time for the final edition; Scoggins, the city editor, was bellowing at the top of his nasal voice; the copy desk was railroading a last batch of late news matter; the assistant make-up man, who is one of the important gentlemen who keep the type in the right columns, was screaming frantically about something of which no one except himself seemed to know anything, and, from the way the office boys were sliding back and forth across the floor, one might have thought the city room was the skating rink of an insane asylum.

And then, with a breathless suddenness—silence! In newspaper parlance, "the paper had been put to bed." From the street below there sounded the blump-blump of a flat-wheeled surface car journeying along Park Row. Scoggins, the city editor, gave a look at his news schedule, sighed, and jerked off the shade which protected his eyes.

"There's not a live piece of local news in the whole darn paper!" he muttered. "Here, Milne, take the desk; I'm going home, and—" He took a last survey around the long, paper-cluttered city room, and saw Jimmy Price, who was cognizant that he had incurred the displeasure of the gods, trying to do a quick sneak out.

"Hey, you, Price!" he bawled.

Jimmy Price turned, and it became apparent why he had been saddled with the nickname of Wiggly. In moments of inner excitement or of strong emotion, Jimmy's protuberant ears became animate objects. They were unruly ears, always wiggling when he least wanted them to; it seemed that Jimmy had absolutely no control over his ears. They were wiggling now, for their owner sensed what was coming. He turned slowly and retraced his steps toward the city editor's desk, which was set up on a platform. The boys called it "the throne," and certainly no monarch ever held more despotic sway than Caleb Scoggins, the city editor of *The Star*.

Scoggins was a good city editor, but he was a man of strong prejudices, and he was prejudiced against Wiggly's animated ears. It annoyed him to look down the room and have a perfectly good idea take sudden flight, as he was forced to stare in fascinated, almost hypnotized, interest at a pair of ears doing a sort of uncanny dance on the side of a man's head, while the owner of those remarkable appendages bent industriously over his type-writer entirely unaware of his innocent havoc. Bob Roddy, the star rewrite man, that high-salaried word slinger, whose supple brain and nimble fingers could paint a column word picture with no more material than a five-line news bulletin, was, likely as not, to be discovered staring, vacant-eyed, at "Wiggly" Price, while the desk was waiting for the rest of his story.

And Jimmy Price was a good reporter, a rattling good one, so good, in fact, that Scoggins had been at a loss for an excuse to fire him. But now he had the excuse.

"Price," he rasped, "you fell down on the Hammerslaw kidnaping case." His voice had the tone of doom, but Wiggly, except for the renewed twitching of his ears, moved neither of body nor tongue. He was too wise to point out that he had registered this one failure to fifty successes, or to remind Scoggins that no reporter can bat a thousand in the news-gathering league.

"Where you belong," went on the city editor with withering sarcasm, "is in a side-show tent, along with the rest of the freaks, not in a newspaper office. As a reporter—" He broke off, as the telephone rang; mechanically he spun half around in his chair and pulled the instrument toward him.

"Yeah?" he grunted.

Etta Griggs had chosen this opportune moment to call.

"Is this the editor of *The Star*?" came her sweetest, most cultured tones over the wire. Scoggins admitted it with a grunt.

"This is Miss Griggs, the playwright, and I am calling to give you a—a scoop, I believe you call it."

Had it been a busy hour, Scoggins would have switched the call over to his assistant; experience had hardened him to persons calling him up to give him a scoop. Usually they didn't pan out, these scoops.

"What is it, Miss Griggs?" he inquired with a deference that he never used toward his staff.

"It—it's very important news," went on Etta Griggs tremulously, almost overwhelmed by the realization that she was in conversation with the great editor of her morning paper. "There has been a murder—a very prominent family, and I thought you might be interested—"

"I should say I am!" exclaimed Scoggins, picking up a pencil and poising it over a sheet of paper. "What did you say the name was?"

"Miss Griggs. I am—"

"Not your name—the murdered person's name."

"Oh, of course! Why, Mrs. Gilmore—the wife of Kirklan Gilmore, the famous novelist, you know."

Now, as a matter of fact, Scoggins didn't know; he didn't read the book reviews, and Gilmore, while he had written a selling book, wasn't quite so famous as Etta imagined.

"You say she has been murdered, Miss Griggs?" he purred. "Where did this happen?" And, waiting for the reply, he put his hand over the transmitter as he said out of the corner of his mouth to Milne, his assistant: "Who the devil is Kirklan Gilmore, the novelist? Get the clippings on him outta the reference room. Picture of his wife, if there are any. Hurry! We gotta stop the presses and make a lift, if this pans out."

"Ardmore—Ardmore-on-the-Hudson," went on Etta. "The Gilmore estate is Greenacres. She was shot—killed. Poor thing, they'd only been married three weeks, too." Scoggins' eyebrows went up. In a flash he visualized the headline, "Bride of Three Weeks Slain."

There followed a few rapid-fire questions in which the city editor had all available information. The constable had been summoned—Etta neglected to state that this constable person was her father—and the village physician, a Doctor Bushnell, was at the house.

"Fine!" exclaimed Scoggins with that inhuman delight with which some city editors receive the news of a crime. "If you will give your name, I will have the business office send you a check, and then—"

"Oh, no!" cried Etta. "But I expect that my play will be coming out soon, and—"

"Certainly—certainly," Scoggins murmured mechanically and snapped the receiver to its hook. "She's a nut," he grunted. "Gotta verify this story before we can use it, but I guess it's safe enough at that. You, Kinsella, call up the Gilmore place, Ardmore, and ask for Doctor Bushnell. You, Roddy, bat out a coupla sticks for a lift on page one, and—" His eyes roved over the now empty city and then back to Wiggly Price, who had withdrawn a few feet from the desk. In the pressure of the moment he forgot that he had been about to fire the reporter with the animated ears; he only remembered that he needed a good reporter for a good story, and that Jimmy Price was a good reporter. He slid open a drawer of the desk and tossed over a roll of bills.

"Here's a hundred dollars for expense money, Price," he snapped crisply. "Gilmore place, Ardmore. Author's wife—bride three weeks—murdered. May have to take taxi. Get pictures—lots of pictures. Gotta hunch this is a good yarn." Wiggly's ears wiggled violently, probably registering his delight that the catastrophe of being fired had been so narrowly and unexpectedly averted, but Caleb Scoggins had turned his vigorous attention to other details of the new story—the only real piece of local news during the night—and he did not notice.

Price grabbed up the expense money and left the city room with discreet swiftness. Less than five minutes later he was in a taxicab, speeding out Broadway toward Greenacres.

# CHAPTER 13

## WHAT DID JOAN KNOW?

Awaiting the arrival of the constable, Doctor Bushnell was still in the den of the Greenacres house, while across from him Kirklan Gilmore sat, like a man dazed, in one of the great leather chairs, staring vacantly into space. He had not spoken for almost five minutes.

"So you had to call in the police," he muttered bitterly, breaking the silence. "They've got to come, snooping through the house, prying into things, asking questions, badgering, bullying—"

"You're taking the wrong attitude, Kirklan," the doctor broke in gently. "I know how you feel, of course; you abhor the legal procedure, but a crime has been committed, and the law must function. You would not want your wife's murderer to escape, would you, no matter what the price?"

"I can't believe yet, doctor, that it was what you claim—murder," protested the novelist with a shudder. "Your opinion is based on—just exactly what?"

"The nature of the wound, Kirklan. Look, here is my pipe." He produced from his pocket a straight-stemmed brier, holding it by the bowl. "Let us suppose that this is the pistol. Your wife is right-handed? Yes, I supposed as much; imagine any person holding a gun in the right hand and reaching halfway around their body and shooting themselves under the left armpit. You can see how absurd that is; even supposing she might have been left-handed, it is almost as ridiculous."

Gilmore debated this a moment.

"I suppose you consider that incontrovertible—medically," he argued, "but I've got a theory to suggest. I've had to study things a bit along such lines—the material for my books, you know. My last was a mystery story."

"Helen was lying on the lounge. The gun was heavy, hard for a woman to handle, as you have said. Suppose she used *both* hands in firing the pistol; one to support it in range, and the other to press the trigger?"

Doctor Bushnell toyed with his pipe for a moment; absently he filled it from a chamois pouch and struck a match.

"It's possible," he admitted, and then he shook his head, adding, "but improbable. I did work at Bellevue in New York, while I was at medical school. Naturally we had some suicide cases. It's a queer thing, but most of the men shot themselves through the head, while the women aimed for their heart—perhaps a natural horror of disfiguring their faces. But, looking back, none of them tried to reach the heart from so far around at the side. Always in front. Adding weight to the medical aspect of it, there are those very significant points that Bates raised. Quite an intelligent fellow, that butler of yours. He's been in the family a long time, hasn't he?"

"More than twenty years, I think; he was much attached to my father."

"It is significant, Kirklan, that you and Bates found the door standing open. And the scream—ah, there's the big point! Why did she scream? Not because she had reached a decision to end her life. As I consider the matter, this man Sarbella—"

"No!"

"Is your friendship for him so blind as that, Kirklan? Stop and think things over, man; on the second floor, when the shot was fired, were only your stepmother, your stepsister, and Sarbella. It must have been one of the three; there is no other explanation!"

As his voice came to a dramatic pause, there was a rap at the door.

"Doctor Bushnell," came the voice of the butler from the other side of the panel, "will you answer the telephone? There is a call for you."

The doctor looked puzzled. "There was no ring," he said.

"That is an extension," explained Gilmore. "There is no bell in this room."

"Oh, I see," murmured the physician, and, leaning across the table, he pulled the telephone toward him.

"Yes, Doctor Bushnell speaking," he said. "Who—what? Where did you get that information?" A pause. "Yes, that is true, but there will be no further information—positively none. You are quite wasting your time in pressing these questions." He cut the conversation short by clicking down the receiver.

Gilmore lifted his haggard face in a glance of curiosity. "Who was it?" he wanted to know.

"*The Star.* It is really quite amazing how quickly the newspapers get hold of a thing like this. Probably the telephone girl at the village gave them the tip."

"The newspapers!" groaned Gilmore. "The scandal they will make of it. Did—did you tell them that it was murder?"

The doctor nodded.

"They were already in possession of that report, and I verified it. There's no use kicking against the pricks, Kirklan; the best that could have been done was to keep it out of the papers for a few brief hours. There will have to be an inquest, you know; that is a public hearing. It's an ugly situation, but there's no escaping it."

"Yes, I suppose you're right," muttered the novelist, "but I want it expressly understood that no reporters are to be admitted to my house."

"They won't bother you until daylight, I suppose," said Doctor Bushnell, little thinking that already a madly speeding taxi was bearing Wiggly Price toward Greenacres. "They'll descend upon you in droves with morning, and they're a persistent lot, those chaps."

The two men in the den again lapsed into silence; Gilmore's muscles twitched spasmodically. It looked as if he were about to crack under the strain.

"I think I will give you an opiate of some sort and then get you in bed," the physician said gently. "You've about gone your limit, I'm afraid."

"That reminds me of something," Gilmore told him. "My stepmother fainted; I promised to send you to her when you came. And as for my going to bed—my room is next to Helen's. You couldn't expect me to spend the rest of the night there. But I will let you give me something, doctor; I feel as if my body were about to separate into atoms. Yes, give me something that will let me forget—for just a few hours."

Doctor Bushnell reached for a compact pocket medicine case and selected a vial containing some small white pellets.

"The constable ought to be here any moment now," he said. "Not that I expect Ham Griggs is going to be of very much help to us; catching speeders is about the limit of his abilities. But he had to be notified, and in the morning we'll notify the district attorney's office. We may get an intelligent investigation from that source. Ah, that must be Griggs now."

There had reached his ears the sound of the constable's approaching motor cycle.

"I'll have Bates let him in and keep him waiting downstairs until I have a look at Mrs. Gilmore. One of these pellets, Kirklan, and you'll be falling asleep in no time."

The doctor left the den and went upstairs, after pausing in the hall to instruct Bates that Ham Griggs should wait; passing the tragedy chamber, he tested the door and found it, as he had left it, locked. Then he made his way around the hall toward the room which, from previous professional calls, he knew to be the elder Mrs. Gilmore's. Kirklan had neglected to tell him that she had been taken to Joan's part of the house.

Ahead a gleam of light sliced out into the hall from a half-open door, the room occupied by Sarbella. The doctor's footsteps were audible, and the guest of Greenacres appeared at the opening.

"You were looking for me?" he inquired.

Doctor Bushnell paused, wondering if Sarbella had left the door open in an effort to keep in touch with what was going on; a guilty man, it was reasonable to presume, would be nervously anxious to know the progress of the investigation, to be forewarned of any suspicion turning in his direction.

"No, Mr. Sarbella, I am on my way to Mrs. Gilmore's room. Kirklan has just told me that she fainted some time since."

"Oh, but you're in the wrong part of the house, doctor; Gilmore and I took his stepmother to Miss Sheridan's room." He paused for a moment, and then added: "It has been a terrible night for all of us."

"It is a very puzzling business," murmured Doctor Bushnell.

"Very," nodded Sarbella.

"How long have you known the—ah—the dead woman?"

The artist hesitated briefly, and when he did reply gave the shrewd doctor the impression of carefully chosen words.

"I met her last evening for the first time," he said. "I had never met her before."

"During the dinner," pursued the physician, watching the man's face closely, "did you notice anything strange?"

Sarbella shot him a quick glance. "She may have been depressed," he answered evasively. "Other than that I can tell you nothing—absolutely nothing. Please do not let me keep you from attending Mrs. Gilmore."

The doctor had the baffled feeling that something was being hidden, that Sarbella knew a great deal more than he was willing to tell. Yet he felt that this was the wrong time to ply questions, that he would only muddle things until he was better fortified for a cross-examination. So he turned and retraced his steps around the hall to Joan's room.

Even before he rapped, he heard the sound of moans, punctuated by a hysterical rambling of speech. His knuckles descended upon the panel, and Joan promptly admitted him. Mrs. Gilmore tossed upon the bed like a woman in physical pain.

"I am glad you have come, Doctor Bushnell," murmured Joan. "Mother is almost beside herself with the horror of it."

"Kirklan was so upset that he didn't tell me until just a moment ago. Your mother fainted, I believe."

"Yes, she was awakened by the shot and went to investigate. She saw— her."

"I knew something was going to happen!" moaned Mrs. Gilmore. "It was in the air. I felt it—impending disaster. Every one acted so strange." There she broke off into wild weeping. The doctor reached for Mrs. Gilmore's wrist and took her pulse. He decided that it was safe enough to administer a soothing hypodermic. When this had been done, and the morphia had taken effect, Bushnell turned to Joan.

"What does she mean by saying that she felt something was going to happen?" he asked. "Did you notice anything peculiar in the behavior of Kirklan's wife last night?"

Joan hesitated, twisting her fingers and biting her lip. "I—I don't think she was quite herself," she answered, her voice very low. "She seemed greatly worried."

"And the guest, Mr. Sarbella?"

A gasp escaped the girl's lips, as she gave the physician a startled, wide-eyed stare. "Why—why do you ask about him?" she whispered.

"Joan, you are holding back something, and you have no right to do that. This atmosphere of secrecy, concealment—what does it mean? You are a sensible girl, and I feel that I can tell you something confidentially. Kirklan's wife did not end her own life."

Standing near the foot of the bed, one of the girl's hands clutched at the rail.

"Kirklan said that—that she had—killed herself. So you think that she was shot by some one else? What makes you think that?"

"Without going into the unpleasant details, it would have been practically impossible for her to have shot herself in such a manner. And there was her scream. You didn't hear it?"

Joan's face was white.

"N-no," she stammered. "I—I did not hear Helen scream."

"Scream she did—a terrible scream of terror, according to Bates. Added to that, the door of her room was found open, and—it was Bates who suggested it—people do not scream when they are about to kill themselves."

The girl's lips moved soundlessly as if she were trying to speak but could not find the words.

Her eyes refused to meet his, and the physician had a baffled, apprehensive feeling that she knew something she was very unwilling to tell. Her attitude was one of terrified concealment. Was she trying to protect some one? Or was she trying to protect herself? What did Joan know?

"But," she said, after this tense pause, "you—you don't think that Mr. Sarbella—"

Doctor Bushnell lifted his hands in a helpless gesture. "I don't know what to think," he replied. "From what I have gathered there is something under the surface and—"

Before he could complete the sentence Ham Griggs' voice bawled from down the hall:

"Hey, doc! Where are you?"

The constable was not disposed to bide his time downstairs; officially important, he had brushed the butler aside and mounted the stairs in search of the physician. Joan drew a breath of relief and Doctor Bushnell frowned.

"That's Constable Griggs," he said; "he's looking for me. Isn't there something you can tell me, Joan, that will throw some light on the tragedy?"

"Nothing," she answered faintly, "absolutely nothing. Only—I feel very positive that Mr. Sarbella did not do it."

"Doc! Where the thunder are you, anyhow?" Again Ham Griggs' raucous bellow, edged with impatience, boomed through the upper hall. The physician turned toward the door, having no choice but to respond. Joan's attitude troubled him. Why did she express such a positive conviction of Sarbella's innocence, the most obvious suspect?

He found Griggs around the turn in the hall, stern and grim.

"This is a fine howdy-do," Griggs rumbled, "keepin' an officer of the law coolin' his heels, when there's murder been done, an' there's a murderer to be put under arrest." His hand moved in his pocket, jingling a pair of handcuffs. "Who done it, doc?"

Doctor Bushnell sighed wearily, realizing that the constable was going to be a difficult person to deal with. There is nothing more trying than official bigotry.

"That's the job in front of us—to ferret that out," he answered.

"Reckon Gilmore—"

"No, Gilmore was downstairs talking to the butler when the shot was fired," broke in the doctor. Briefly he related the facts, as he had found them, but he confined himself strictly to facts, and indulged in no theories or suspicions; he was afraid to trust Ham Griggs with theories.

The constable listened, rocking his heavy body on his heels and frowning sternly.

"Hum!" he grunted when the other paused. "Where's the body?"

"I'll take you there," the latter answered. "I locked the room—didn't want anything disturbed, of course." He took the key from his pocket and led the way to the tragedy chamber.

For all of his outward bluster, Ham Griggs was inwardly nervous and uncertain, for this was his first murder case.

# CHAPTER 14

## THE GIRL IN THE SARBELLA CASE

As Doctor Bushnell unlocked the door and snapped on the lights, the constable was close upon his heels, staring at the lounge with its sheet-shrouded burden. From beneath the edge of the white linen covering, where it almost touched the floor, was the automatic pistol.

"Do you know anything about finger prints?" asked the physician. "I thought there might be finger prints on the grip of the gun; but I doubt it. The weapon was left behind to give the appearance of suicide; the murderer, being deliberate as that, would hardly have been fool enough to leave his signature behind him."

Ham Griggs neither admitted nor denied knowledge of the finger-print science; as a matter of fact, he knew precious little about it, but that did not deter him from stepping promptly forward, with great show of confidence, and picking the pistol up by the barrel. He did have gumption enough for that.

Stepping close to the electric light burning from one of the wall brackets, he turned the gun slowly, examining the butt plates at various angles.

"Gotta have a smooth surface, doc, to get finger prints," he grunted, tapping the corrugated rubber with his finger. "There ain't any—no, sir, there just natcherally ain't any."

Doctor Bushnell nodded. "You're right about that," he agreed.

"Guess I better keep this for evidence," said Griggs, handling it gingerly; ignorant of an automatic's mechanism, he did not know just how easily it might be discharged.

"Careful there!" warned the doctor. "It's ready for firing; the explosion, you know, ejects the shell and throws back the plunger for another shot. There's a safety catch on the side; I'll attend to it for you."

Griggs willingly surrendered the gun and glanced around the room.

"Don't look like there'd been no scuffle," he muttered. "None of the chairs is turned over, or nothin' like that. Don't seem like there is any clews."

Doctor Bushnell handed back the gun. "I understand that there are always clews, Griggs. No doubt there are plenty of them right here, but our eyes aren't trained for seeing them. We're just overlooking them, that's all, and I am afraid that we shall continue to overlook them. This is a job for a detective—a real detective."

Ham Griggs looked resentful.

"Just you hold your horses a little while, doc," he growled. "Gimme a chance, can't you? You don't expect me to clear this thing up in the battin' of an eye, do you? Mebbe if I'd been on the ground long as you have, an' talked to all the folks in the house, like you've done, I'd have got somewheres by this time."

"Yes—maybe," murmured Doctor Bushnell.

"Well, anyhow," retorted the constable, "I allow to ask a heap of questions. I ain't gonna stand here suckin' my thumb. Where's Gilmore?"

"I gave him an opiate, Griggs; the poor chap's a nervous wreck—naturally. Give him a chance to pull himself together. It would be rank cruelty to subject him to an inquisition until he's had an opportunity to come out from under the first shock. Remember, he had been married but a few weeks; a terrible blow, Griggs."

"Who else did you say was in the house?"

"Bates, the butler, the elder Mrs. Gilmore, Miss Joan Sheridan, Mrs. Gilmore's daughter by her first marriage, and a Mr. Sarbella, a guest from New York. Mrs. Gilmore is in a state bordering on nervous prostration, and, as her physician, I should certainly refuse to admit her to be questioned just now."

"Seems like to me," grunted the constable, suspicion in his voice, "they don't mebbe want to be questioned. The other three—they got prostrations, too?"

"No; there is nothing to prevent your cross-examining the others."

"The butler feller, you said he was downstairs with Gilmore when the gun was shot off?"

"Yes, that's right."

"An' that the two womenfolks an' this—whatcha say his name is?"

"Sarbella, Victor Sarbella."

"Sounds dago. So you say that Sarbella an' the two women was upstairs?" In his slow-witted, blundering way, Ham Griggs was arriving at the obvious. "That bein' the case, doc, I guess—hum—I reckon we better have a look at this Sarbella. I hope you ain't give him no chance to escape?"

"I'll call him," responded Doctor Bushnell, "but do you want to question him here?"

"Best place I can think of, doc; if he done it he'll kinda give himself away by bein' in the presence of the victim."

91

"Up to date," imparted the physician, "Sarbella thinks we believe she took her own life."

"That's good; we'll spring a surprise on 'im. Go get 'im, doc."

When Bushnell had responded to this command, Ham Griggs stepped to the lounge and drew back the edge of the sheet, staring at the beautiful face below him. He was surprised at the woman's beauty.

"Sure was a swell looker," he said to himself and drew the sheet back in place. With his stubby, thick fingers clasped behind his back, he took a turn across the room, so intent with his sluggish thoughts that he did not notice the trodding of his heavy shoes upon a bit of dark porcelain that lay upon the rug near the table which stood by the north wall—a bit of porcelain no larger than a silver dollar. It splintered beneath his weight, with a faintly crunching sound. In his preoccupation he did not hear it.

A moment later Doctor Bushnell had returned with Victor Sarbella. Ham Griggs turned and stared intently at the guest of Greenacres, who had himself well under control.

"The doctor tells me that you wish to see me," murmured Sarbella. "I am at your service."

"You betcha I want to see you," grunted the constable, motioning to a chair that faced the sheet-covered lounge. "What do you know about this case?"

Sarbella let himself into the indicated chair, facing the shrouded body without flinching. "Nothing," he answered steadily.

Griggs whipped the automatic from his pocket and thrust it before the man's eyes with what might have been considered an accusing gesture.

"Ever see this before?" he demanded, and, when Sarbella nodded, he went on with a triumphant exclamation: "Oh, you admit it, do you?"

"Yes," answered the artist, "I saw it on the floor, where it must have fallen from her hand, after she shot herself."

"She didn't do no such thing," the constable retorted belligerently. "It was murder."

Sarbella's head jerked up, and his hands suddenly froze rigidly about the arms of the chair. Into his intense black eyes there came a startled, narrow-lidded gleam that Doctor Bushnell, watching him closely, decided could have been guilt. But he recovered himself quickly.

"I don't believe it," he said flatly. "I begin to understand. You are hinting that I—"

"Matter of fact, now, ain't this your gun?" broke in Ham Griggs. "No use lyin'; we can trace it easy enough."

Sarbella did not become angry; he did not bluster.

"I do not know what has given you this ridiculous idea," he said quietly, "but I shall make a statement that, in so far as I am concerned, covers ev-

92

erything. The gun is not mine; I have never seen the gun until, aroused by the pistol shot, I saw Gilmore's wife dead. Never in my life had I ever seen the woman until I was introduced to her before dinner last evening. It did not for a moment enter my mind that it was other than suicide. If, as you claim, it is murder, I did not do it, and I do not know who did, or why. That is all I have to say." His tone had a firm finality that was discouraging to further questioning; over the room there fell a silence, a silence so tense and absorbed that none of the three men heard the automobile that sped into the Greenacres driveway and came to a halt beneath the portico.

Constable Griggs reached behind him and drew the sheet from the dead woman's face. Even the bosom of her crimson-stained silk robe was exposed to view. But no cry of guilty horror came from Sarbella; in fact, he seemed a little contemptuous of this dramatic play. His face was stonily hard.

Below, the taxicab bearing Wiggly, otherwise Jimmy Price, had arrived at Greenacres, and Wiggly, bidding the driver wait, leaped across the porch to the entrance. His finger pressed the bell button with one brief, curt ring. He waited grimly.

Now, Wiggly Price was wise in the ways of his craft; he knew that in a case like this, among such people, a reporter is emphatically unwelcome. From countless previous experiences he had learned that the big thing is to keep the door from being slammed in one's face. There was an old trick that he had used with success before; possibly it was chicanery, but the good reporter must get the story to hold his job. There are times when the exigency of the situation demands a blind eye toward strict ethics, and he knew that, unless he made good on the Gilmore murder yarn, Scoggins would complete the fatefully interrupted business of firing him.

There had been a day when New York newspaper men were given neat nickeled and numbered badges, issued by the police department to identify them in getting past the police lines at fires, parades, and the like. They looked official, these badges, and, although they had long since been withdrawn by the department, Wiggly Price had retained his; that word "Police" stamped upon the metal in much larger lettering than "Press" had more than once been the open sesame for him.

So when Bates, the Gilmore butler, opened the door in answer to the ring, Wiggly Price flipped back the lapel of his coat so that the servant might be misled by the brief flash and glisten of the metal.

"I'm here on the case," Wiggly announced briskly, knowing full well that if he revealed his true identity he would get about so far as "I am a reporter." Then the door would have closed in his face.

Bates readily admitted him. "Doctor Bushnell is expecting you?"

Wiggly, having no notion of committing himself, evaded the question.

"Hum!" he said. "Bad business, I understand. How long since it happened? I'll hear what you know about it before I see Doctor Bushnell."

Thus Bates, who would have let his tongue be cut out before he would have divulged so much as a grain of information to a reporter, was misled into telling all he knew. Thinking he was talking to a detective summoned by the doctor, he pridefully told of his own deductions of murder; he omitted nothing, and Jimmy Price's animated ears wiggled delightedly, as he realized how lucky he was.

"Fine!" he murmured. "You're a pretty good detective yourself. Now just between us—strictly confidential, y' understand—who do you think killed her?"

Bates looked around cautiously, and then lowered his voice to a mere thread of a whisper.

"Things began to be queer, sir, after Mr. Sarbella arrived. Mind you, I don't say that he did it, but—" His voice tailed off meaningly. Jimmy Price's ears moved rapidly—swift thinking.

"Sarbella?" he said under his breath. "Sarbella? I've heard that name somewhere before." And then aloud: "Where is the doctor now?"

"Upstairs with the constable; I think they are in the room where it happened. Who shall I tell him is here, sir?"

"Oh, don't bother about that," Wiggly Price said carelessly. "I'll go right on up. No, don't bother. Which room?"

"At the head of the stairs."

"Gee, but I'm one lucky bird!" chuckled Wiggly, as he hurried up the steps. "Now what's going to happen? Get pitched out on my ear, most likely."

Reaching the top of the stairway, there was no need for him to seek further directions. The door of the tragedy chamber was not fully closed, and there came to his ears the voice of Constable Griggs, badgeringly insistent, as he sought in vain to batter down Victor Sarbella's brief statement.

The guest of Greenacres remained calm. "I have told you all that I can about the case—the murder, as you insist," he was saying. "I have nothing more to say."

Wiggly edged closer to the crack of the door, peering within, and saw the face of the dead woman across which Griggs had not replaced the sheet. As he stared, his ears began to wiggle violently. Without any more hesitation he walked into the room. Ham Griggs looked up with a hostile and questioning frown.

"Who're you?" he barked. "Where'd you come from?"

"Price, Price of *The Star*," Wiggly murmured mechanically, as he continued staring at Helen Gilmore.

Doctor Bushnell took an angry step forward. "Mr. Gilmore issued specific instructions that no newspaper men were to be admitted," he said. "I don't know how you managed to get in, but I know how you're going to get out."

"Wait a minute!" muttered the reporter. "I've seen her somewhere. I never forget faces, and she— Wait a minute, I tell you, and I'll place her. Let a fellow think, can't you!" He moved a little closer, staring at the beautiful features. Victor Sarbella had strained forward in his chair, and there was something so tense in his attitude that Doctor Bushnell signaled to the constable that the intruding newspaper man was not to be interfered with for a moment. The constable did not notice that; he seemed little short of hypnotized by Price's animated ears.

"She must have figured in some story that I worked on," went on Jimmy Price, hardly conscious that he was thinking aloud. "And it must have been some time ago, or I wouldn't have so much trouble remembering."

The doctor made a suggestion that bore more fruit than he could have expected.

"Take a look at this gentleman," he said, pointing to the artist; "you don't happen to remember him, I suppose?"

Jimmy Price shook his head slowly and positively. "I am quite sure," he answered, "that I have never seen Mr.—Mr.—"

"Mr. Sarbella," supplied the doctor.

The effect of that name on Jimmy Price was startling. It seemed that his ears would surely work themselves loose from the side of his head.

"Sarbella?" he exclaimed, turning swiftly and looking again at the dead woman. "Sarbella? Yes, I know her now; she was the girl—the girl in the Sarbella case!"

A grunt of elation escaped Constable Griggs, as he stared triumphantly at the artist; this reporter had supplied the missing link between the dead woman and the suspect. Victor Sarbella's body stiffened and relaxed, as his shoulders moved with a sigh of weariness and defeat. The secret which he had guarded with his silence was out.

95

# CHAPTER 15

## SARBELLA SPEAKS

No longer was Wiggly Price an interloper, an unwelcome intruder facing eviction; for, instead of asking for facts, he was supplying facts, and extremely vital facts they seemed to be. Both the constable and Doctor Bushnell, since the Sarbella case stirred no memories, were both eager for further enlightenment.

"Yes," said Wiggly, "I am sure of it now; this woman was the girl in the Sarbella case. I think I must have written five or six columns about it; queer that I shouldn't have spotted her the minute I put eyes on her, but a fellow's memory does slip sometimes. The minute I heard the name just now it all came back to me with a rush."

"I knew you was hidin' something," grunted Constable Griggs, fixing Victor Sarbella with a stern eye. "I had a feelin' that you was lyin' about never havin' set eyes on 'er until last night. I guess you killed her, all right —that was the reason you wouldn't talk. Guess you thought you was pretty slick." He turned to the newspaper man. "I guess it wasn't nothin' short of Providence that let you get into the house just now. Queer, ain't it, how things is always turnin' out?"

"My statement," said Sarbella, his voice husky, "was entirely true. I had never seen the woman until last night—when my friend introduced her as —as hees wife. She—she the wife of my good friend!"

"I guess you think we're a lotta country boobs to swaller a thin yarn like that. Never seen her before, huh? That's likely—I guess not."

Doctor Bushnell looked eagerly at Wiggly Price, impatient to hear what was meant by "the Sarbella case."

"Let's hear what he's got to say, Griggs," he urged.

"Sure," nodded Ham Griggs; "talk right up, mister. I guess we're all wantin' to hear it —except Sarbella. You've put us on a hot trail, all right, young feller."

"For all I know," said the reporter, "he may be telling the truth about never having seen the woman before. It sounds reasonable enough, as you shall see.

"The Sarbella case got into the newspapers a little over two years ago. There was a young chap—handsome kid he was—a violinist. Born in Italy —forget what place—and came to New York in concert work. His first name"—he frowned meditatively—"I think it was Andrea."

"Yes, it was Andrea," muttered Victor Sarbella. "Poor Andrea! And that woman—death was too good for her!"

"He fell in with a girl, a beautiful girl, with bronze hair. The attraction of opposites, I suppose; he was dark—naturally, being Italian. But this girl's past wasn't as pretty as her face. A lot of it is coming back to me now —the details. She'd been raised on the fringe of the underworld. Maybe you know what I mean. Her father and her brother had served time. Oh, not her; she tried to pull away from that sort of thing.

"Anyhow, the young violinist fell in love with this girl, madly in love with her. I think they were planning to be married, and then he found out the truth about her. How? I can't tell you that, but he did. The note he left behind him told that—how she had lied to him, deceived him.

"He went into the bathroom of his hotel and shot himself through the heart. You see, this young Sarbella came of a very proud family—his father related to the nobility and all that sort of thing. He couldn't marry a girl like that, and he couldn't give her up. There was only one way he could forget her, and he took that way.

"In brief, gentlemen, that's the Sarbella case. The girl disappeared; the police didn't hold her, since it was so obviously a suicide. I saw her at the inquest; she seemed pretty badly cut up over it, but—well, you can't always tell about that."

"My word!" whispered Doctor Bushnell, aghast. "Kirklan Gilmore's wife was that woman, a woman of the underworld? It seems incredible, preposterous!"

"Sarbella," went on Wiggly Price, looking steadily at the guest of Greenacres, "had a brother who was in Italy at the time of the suicide. This brother caught the first boat to New York with the avowed intention—"

"I think that I am the best qualified person to finish your narrative," the voice of Victor Sarbella broke in.

"So you've decided to start your tongue workin'," crowed Constable Griggs; his chest bulged importantly. "It is my official duty to warn you that anything you may say will be used against you."

Sarbella waved his hand impatiently. "This is an explanation, not a confession," he retorted. "My first statement to you remains true, although I admit that I did not tell you all the truth—for two reasons.

"Yes, this dead woman," his voice dripped with bitterness, "was the girl in the Sarbella case. It is necessary for me to tell you that Andrea, my younger brother, and I were born and reared in Florence. Our mother was American, our father Italian.

"I came to America where I could find a better market for my drawings, and I brought with me Andrea, who was a violinist and expected to earn a great deal of money with his playing. He had wonderful talent, Andrea; even so young, his playing was attracting attention. Would to Heaven that I had left him in Italy. Then that woman would never have set his brain on fire, driven him mad with the madness of infatuation.

"It was the first winter that we were in New York, and I returned to Florence that I might accompany my mother back to America. She, too, was to make her home in New York, my father having died. It was while I was away that Andrea met this devil of a woman. How? I do not know, but he loved her madly; the letter he left behind for me told me the intensity of his passion for her.

"Andrea was young, idealistic; he thought her everything that was good, noble. And then there came to him a man; a low, common person, who was the woman's husband!

"You see how she had tricked him? She was not the innocent, lovely girl she had led my brother to believe. He had thought to marry her—soon. The shock of the truth dethroned reason; he could not have her, and he could not give her up. There seemed to him only one way that he could forget.

"If I could but show you his farewell letter to me, the letter that he wrote a few minutes before he fired the bullet through his heart!" Tears came into Victor Sarbella's eyes, and his voice trembled and broke. "Could you read that letter of Andrea's you would understand better.

"He was my brother, my only brother, and I loved him devotedly. News of his death was cabled to me, but it was not until the boat docked in New York that I knew how he had died—and why.

"My mother—Andrea was her very life. She—it killed her. This woman, this vampire, killed both of them—Andrea and our mother—as surely as though she had driven daggers into their hearts. And that—that would have been a kindlier way." He pointed a dramatically accusing finger to the couch. "There she is, a murderess, a moral murderess, and she has reaped as she had sown!"

Victor Sarbella's voice came to a pause.

"All right," said Constable Griggs, "let's have the rest of it. You killed her for revenge!"

"A life for a life!" murmured Wiggly Price, his ears twitching again, as he thought of a dramatic line for this amazing story that he was to write for *The Star*. "'The code of Latin vengeance!' Wow! What a whale of a yarn!"

Victor Sarbella shook his head slowly.

"Time passes, and the deepest of wounds heal—although there may be a scar," he said. "It is futile for me to deny that in my first grief and rage against this woman I made bitter threats, that I said I would hound her down and make her pay. I do not deny that I meant it—at the moment; I do not deny that I sought her in vain."

"But you did find her yesterday," exclaimed Constable Griggs. "I've heard tell of them Eyetalian vendettas. You hadda wait most three years, but you got 'er all right. Ain't no use holdin' out on me no longer, Mister Sarbella; we gotcha, an' we gotcha cold. Mebbe you can get by with that revenge business over in Italy, but you can't work it here."

Victor Sarbella looked tired, and his face was drawn, haggard.

"Yes, I found her here yesterday," he nodded. "I found her—this murderess—married to my good friend, who loved her madly—as poor Andrea loved her. While I had never seen her, I knew her from that picture of her that lay beside Andrea when he died. Every detail of that face was burned into my memory; I recognized her instantly. And she—the name and the family resemblance—she, too, knew me for who I am.

"Kirklan Gilmore saw that something was wrong, but I could not tell him. He was my friend; she was his wife; my lips were sealed. I swear to you that no thought of killing her entered my mind, although in the past I had thought many times of putting my fingers about her throat and—"

"Huh!" broke in Ham Griggs' grunt. "I guess you'd swear to most anything to keep yourself from goin' to the chair. What made you hold out on us about knowin' who she was, if you wasn't guilty?"

"As I told you a few minutes ago," answered Sarbella, "there were two reasons. One was that I wished to spare Gilmore, my friend, the torture of the truth."

"And the other reason," said Griggs, "was that you knowed blame well it would make things look purty black for you. You knowed that it would throw suspicion square on you."

Sarbella hesitated.

"At first," he replied slowly, "I had no other thought than that the woman had ended her life—driven to suicide by fear, fear that I would denounce her for what she was before her husband; but, when the butler kept insisting that she had been murdered, I knew that I had a vitally personal reason for keeping silent."

"But little good it did you—thanks to this feller," exulted the constable, jerking his thumb toward the newspaper man. "Victor Sarbella, you're under arrest for—"

"Be careful, sir—be careful," warned the guest of Greenacres, his face gray. "The gun is not mine, and you will never be able to prove that it was. If you subject me to false arrest—"

Ham Griggs hesitated, glancing at Doctor Bushnell for encouragement.

"I don't think you need worry about false arrest," advised the doctor. "An officer has a perfect right to hold a man on suspicion. There need not be positive proof, and there were but three persons on the second floor when the shot was fired—Mrs. Gilmore, Miss Joan, and Sarbella."

Victor Sarbella leaned forward in his chair, and he seemed on the verge of saying something further in his own defense, but did not speak. It may have been that he realized how useless it would be to say anything further in his own behalf.

The constable dragged from his pocket a pair of handcuffs. "Stick out your mitts," he ordered, holding open the steel jaws to receive Sarbella's wrists.

# CHAPTER 16

## THE FOUR CLUES

As Constable Griggs, proud as a pouter pigeon, departed with his prisoner, Doctor Bushnell replaced the sheet over the face of the dead woman, but not until he had looked again at the beautiful features, shaking his head, as if he could not understand the anomaly of countenance and character.

"A—a woman of the underworld! It's just a little hard to believe that a woman with that face—"

"On the fringe of the underworld, I think I said," corrected Wiggly Price. "Her associations were criminal, but I hardly imagine that she had led a vicious life, for that *would* show." He paused for a moment. "Sarbella told me something about her that I hadn't known before—that it was her husband who came to Andrea Sarbella and told him the truth about her. I was just wondering if—if she had gone to the trouble of divorcing him. It's a difficult thing, getting a divorce in New York State."

Doctor Bushnell looked grave. "Sarbella was right; she was a vampire. She tricked Gilmore, fooled him with her pretty face, as she fooled the other one—young Sarbella. I am apprehensive of the effect that this is going to have on Kirklan; already he is on the verge of a nervous breakdown, and when he learns the truth—well, I hope it can be withheld from him until he has had a chance to pull together." He made a move to depart, but Wiggly stopped him with a gesture.

"Just a moment, doctor. You're satisfied that Sarbella did the shooting?"

The physician seemed surprised by the question.

"Certainly," he answered promptly. "There were but five persons in the house; two of them downstairs, three upstairs, when the fatal shot was fired. You don't mean to tell me that you have any doubts—" He broke off, disturbed by the recollection of Joan's evasiveness and perturbation.

"I'm not saying Sarbella isn't the guilty man," answered Wiggly; "but I do say that it would be next to impossible to have a jury convict him on such evidence."

"But he was the only person in the house who could have any possible motive for the crime," argued Doctor Bushnell. "Revenge, young man—a trait that is strong with the Latins, particularly the Italian. You don't for a moment entertain a notion that Mrs. Gilmore, the gentlest soul I have ever known, or Miss Sheridan—"

"I admit the motive," interrupted Wiggly; "I admit the opportunity, and I admit that, on the face of things so far, he is the guilty man. But where is the proof—the proof that will convict him before a jury?

"The proof of guilt is somewhere—somewhere in this house; it may be right in this room. I have been a newspaper reporter for ten years, and a lot of my assignments have been crime stories. I did headquarters for nearly five years; experience tells me that there are clews, definite and convincing clews, that will convict. There are always clews."

"Yes, so I have gathered; but the room here—there is no evidence of a struggle—nothing visible—"

"The same things, doctor, are not visible to all eyes; seeing a clew is one thing, and observing it is quite another thing. A newspaper reporter gets to be a sort of detective, sometimes he's a darn good detective, and, if you have no objection, I'll look around a bit and see what I can find to clinch the case against Sarbella."

Doctor Bushnell hesitated. "Kirklan Gilmore gave orders that no newspaper men were to be admitted," he said; "still you have rendered valuable assistance, and—"

"And," added Wiggly with a faint smile, "I've already got my story. Even if you pitch me out, it won't stop my paper from printing the facts that I have gathered."

"Yes, that's true," nodded the physician, "and personally I've a profound respect for a good newspaper reporter. Gilmore naturally shrinks from the thought of having this thing blazoned across the front page; but, if he understood the situation, I feel sure that he would give you every chance to fix the guilt where it belongs. He seemed to resent the suggestion I made, that Sarbella was the most obvious suspect, but he did not know the past which linked the lives of his wife and his friend.

"The constable is little better than helpless in a case like this; his job is catching automobile speeders, and a murder is outside of his experience. It was nothing short of luck for Ham Griggs that you happened in and gave him the right tack. I intended urging Gilmore to employ a private detective, but if you can make any progress—well, I shan't stop you."

"That's mighty decent of you, Doctor Bushnell, and, before I start in Sherlocking, I'd like to ask you a question or two about the wound. The bullet pierced her heart?"

"No, it did not; I followed the course of the bullet with a probe, and it missed the heart by a fraction of an inch."

"Good Lord, you don't mean it! Then death was caused—"

"From the best I can determine, a punctured artery."

"In other words, she bled to death; isn't that what you mean, doctor?"

"Yes."

"Would she have bled to death so quickly?"

"That is hard to say—evidently very quickly. Both Gilmore and the butler are positive that she was dead when they reached the room here. They rushed upstairs immediately after hearing her scream and the shot."

"And that was a matter of less than minutes—seconds," mused Wiggly Price. "The bullet must have pierced the aorta, or one of its main branches."

"So it would seem, and I see that you know the anatomical terms."

"Some of them; a reporter has to know a little about everything. I was just wondering if perhaps she wasn't still alive when her husband and the butler reached the room."

"Bates thought he saw the last breath leave her body, but I wouldn't accept that with absolute finality. He is, of course, not a medical man, and he might have easily imagined it."

Wiggly Price's eyes searched the room with a slowly moving gaze, his animated ears twitching faintly. He seemed to be studying the rug, which was of a neutral shade; any discolorment, such as a bloodstain, would have stood out glaringly, and there was none.

"I've been thinking," he said, "that she might have been placed on the couch there—after she was shot. Yet, with all the profuse bleeding, if she had fallen to the floor there would be some signs of it. I wonder if you noticed whether she was shot while reclining on the lounge, or if the bullet was fired while she was standing?"

The doctor looked bewildered. "Great Heavens, man, how could you expect me to know that?" he exclaimed with a hint of asperity, suspecting that the reporter was trying to "show off." But he was mistaken about that.

"I feel that we may be able to determine that, if we take another look at the dead woman's clothing," Wiggly told him. "There's the law of gravity you know."

"Gravity? What's the law of gravity got to do with it?" Puzzled, the physician lifted the sheet to permit the reporter's examination. The latter leaned forward for a moment and took note, also, that the silk robe was powder burned—in fact, that the explosion had been so close as to scorch the undergarments as well.

Wiggly Price pointed to the meandering line of dried crimson which dyed the expensive dressing gown almost to the fur-edged hem of the garment. "Blood, like water," he said, "must obey the law of gravity and flow downward; she had to be standing on her feet for the crimson stream to seep down, almost level with her ankles. She was placed on the lounge by whoever shot her; that is evident. Gad, but she was a beautiful woman, wasn't she? It's no wonder that men lost their heads over her. You know, doctor, I've always felt sorry for a truly beautiful woman; so many of them end up in misery. But that's neither here nor there. The wound is in the side, isn't it?"

Doctor Bushnell nodded slowly. "I understand now what you're getting at. Yes, I can see that she must have been shot while standing on her feet, and either she staggered back to the couch herself, or was supported to the couch by the slayer. The wound—under the armpit?"

"The weapon must have been pressed close to her body judging from the evidence of burned powder. I see that the robe was set on fire, which burned quite a hole before it smoldered out. Doctor, wouldn't you say that it was a most unusual place for an intentionally mortal wound? Her arm would have to have been raised away from her body."

The doctor agreed with a tight-lipped "Yes."

"Of course," went on the newspaper man, "she might have turned suddenly, squirmed in the slayer's grip—I am taking it for granted that he was close enough to have seized her—but that's only speculation. What became of the gun?"

"Ham Griggs took it with him. It was an automatic, a large-caliber .44, I think."

"Finger prints?"

"The butt plates had a corrugated surface."

"I see; in that case there would have been no finger prints on the gun. Probably wouldn't have been, since the slayer deliberately left the gun behind. Only a very stupid person would have neglected to wipe away finger prints had there been any. Hello, what's this!"

Wiggly's foot had crunched against a bit of porcelain, and he leaned forward swiftly, picking it up; it was a rough-surfaced piece of pottery, black in color and, as much as he could judge from the fragment, had belonged to some convex object of which it was a shattered part.

"A broken piece of something—but what?" he murmured, holding it up for the doctor's inspection.

"I'm sure I couldn't say," answered Doctor Bushnell, who was not greatly interested. He considered it a waste of time to speculate over such an insignificant trifle, when there was murder evidence to be looked for.

"The Hitchcock murder last summer—remember that, doctor? It was solved by nothing more noticeable than a black pin, a mourning pin, and the widow of a man whom Hitchcock had ruined, confessed when she was faced with that pin. This is larger than a pin, doctor, but, to be frank, I doubt there's much value to it." He was near a small mahogany table by the room's north wall; the light was not very good, the chamber being lighted only by wall fixtures, and the incandescent rays were softened by parchment shades; but his eyes pierced the shadows and saw, on the floor beside the table, several other pieces like the one which he held in his hand.

"Ah!" he exclaimed. "Here's the answer to it, doctor. It's a vase, a black pottery vase; yes, here's the neck of it."

"That might be evidence of a struggle," suggested Doctor Bushnell. "The vase might have been knocked off the edge of the table, don't you think, when the woman tried to escape Sarbella's vengeance? She probably knew, the minute he got into the room, that his intention was to kill her."

Price's ears wiggled briefly, as he considered the matter of the broken vase, and with a dismissing gesture tossed down the broken bit which he held in his fingers.

"You may be right," he agreed, "it doesn't seem important enough to bother about, but—" His voice broke off sharply, as he stared toward the window directly in front of him; he had noticed the sagging curtain, where it had been ripped some two and a half hours earlier, when Don Haskins had made his surprise entrance into Helen's room. But, of course, Wiggly had no way of being aware of the fleeing crook's existence.

"Take a look at this, Doctor Bushnell," said the reporter; "this torn curtain. Funny we didn't notice that before; it's mighty near jerked off the rod."

"And what do you make of that?"

Wiggly's eyes were meditatively half closed, and his ears as well as his mind were active.

"I'd say one of three things," he answered slowly. "Either the murderer barred Mrs. Gilmore's flight through the door, and she was trying to get out the window—which somehow I don't take much stock in—or the murderer himself came in through the window, or, thirdly, that he got out through the window. In the last two cases it doesn't seem reasonable that he would have taken the time to shut the window behind him. It seems to me that the best thing to do is just store this away for future reference. It doesn't seem to mean much in itself."

"No, it doesn't," grunted the physician. "It might not have been torn tonight."

Wiggly glanced about the neat, precisely kept room. "She was particular about the orderliness of things," he said. "I don't believe she would have left a torn window curtain unrepaired for long. No, the curtain was torn tonight; but, as I said, we'll just store that away for future reference."

And then Doctor Bushnell made a discovery of his own, a half-burned cigarette that had been mashed down into the heavy nap of the rug, some eight feet from the chaise longue and even a farther distance from the door. He gave a brief exclamation, as he pointed to his find.

"Sarbella is a cigarette smoker; if this is his brand—"

Wiggly Price picked up the cigarette, which evidently had been flattened out beneath the pressure of a shoe.

"It's a little hard to believe, doctor, that a man with premeditated murder in his mind, would walk into his victim's room smoking a cigarette," he said quickly. "For that matter, it might be the murdered woman's cigarette —so many women do smoke 'em these modern days." He examined the flattened thing which, as it happened, bore the name of the brand. "Cheap —ten cents a pack. Hardly a woman's cigarette, I'd say. Perhaps Gilmore himself dropped it."

"Not Gilmore; I happen to know that he doesn't smoke anything except an occasional after-dinner cigar; but I do recall very clearly that Sarbella was smoking a cigarette downstairs. If he smokes that kind, it's clinching proof that he is the guilty man!" The doctor was becoming quite excited over this clew. "Since Gilmore doesn't smoke them, who else could have dropped it on the rug? Answer me that!"

Wiggly took a piece of copy paper from his pocket, carefully wrapped the cigarette butt in it, and tucked this important, or unimportant, bit of evidence in his vest pocket.

"As you say, doctor, if it's Sarbella's brand of cigarette it means something—but it's rather difficult to imagine a chap like Sarbella smoking this cheap fag; just about as hard as it is to imagine him walking into this room, a gun in one hand and a cigarette in another, ready to avenge his dead brother. However, when I get to the jail, I'll see the constable and check up on this. I'll have a look at Sarbella's cigarette case."

Although, as he had just said, it hardly looked like the sort of cigarette a woman might be expected to smoke, he was thorough enough to look about the room, and he even went to the dressing table in search of any proof that Helen Gilmore herself had been addicted to a little puffing now and then. But there was no telltale flickings of ashes, not so much as an ash receiver.

Wiggly compressed his lips.

"You know, doctor," he said slowly, "this cigarette thing bothers me a little—quite a little, too. She isn't a smoker unless she does it on the sly and— Oh, confound it, it just isn't reasonable that this is Sarbella's cigarette butt. I've got a hunch that this business runs deeper than we think."

Doctor Bushnell gave an impatient gesture. "Stuff! You're trying to manufacture a mystery; the papers like mysteries so that they can spread the story out over days and days. You're afraid that the solution is going to be too easy, too tame."

"Tame?" exploded Wiggly Price. "I can imagine nothing more dramatic than Sarbella being the guilty man—beautiful vamp, handsome, talented young foreigner, related to nobility, a suicide, a brother's vendetta, an unexpected meeting, arranged by Fate, at the home of a friend who is a popular novelist, and then—revenge!

"Good Lord, I hope you don't call a yarn like that tame! Scoggins, my city editor, will weep with joy if it pans out that way—and probably give me a raise in salary, although it's his burning desire to fire me. But I'm making the guess that the cigarette butt that we've picked up out of the rug didn't belong to Victor Sarbella." He paused, looking about the room again. "Electric lights are so tricky to the eyes; it's so easy to overlook something, some little thing that might be tremendously important. It still lacks some time of being daylight, and I'm anxious to scoot over to the jail and check up on this cigarette clew—make sure whether or not it's Sarbella's. Are you going to remain here for a little while, doctor?"

Doctor Bushnell glanced at his watch.

"Yes," he answered; "at least until the undertaker arrives—probably later. It's my official duty to remain, I suppose."

"Your official duty?"

"As it happens, I am a deputy coroner."

Wiggly showed his surprise. "You hadn't mentioned that; I hardly think that even the constable realized it. Of course you understand, doctor, that, in a case like this, your authority exceeds that of any other official. You are the commanding officer, so to speak."

Doctor Bushnell nodded. "In a way my position is somewhat embarrassing. I have been the Gilmore family physician for a good many years."

"I was wondering if I should be able to get inside the house again," said the reporter; "but, if you are the—"

"Deputy coroner," corrected the physician. "Doctor Whitestone, the coroner, is vacationing at Saranac Lake."

"Anyhow, doctor, you are in charge, and all I need is your permission."

"Probably it can be arranged," Doctor Bushnell said after a moment of hesitation. "Of course it will be rather difficult to admit one reporter and bar the others, and there will be a regiment of them swooping down on us; but you have rendered valuable assistance that makes it very hard for me to refuse you. You will let me know, just as soon as you have clinched the matter, whether the cigarette butt was dropped by Sarbella." He was taking the door key from his pocket and was starting to leave the room.

"Certainly," answered Wiggly, moving to follow. "I came out from the office in a taxi, and it's waiting downstairs. I shall come back immediately after I have—" His voice trailed off, as he squinted at the floor, where the chaise longue with its tragic burden cast a shadow over the rug. Swiftly he bent forward and picked up something.

Doctor Bushnell stared; it was nothing more startling than a hairpin, and he was rather impatient that the newspaper man should subject it to such an apparently interesting scrutiny.

"As I said," murmured Wiggly, "artificial light is tricky. Either one of us should have noticed this before."

"It's nothing but a common, ordinary hairpin," grunted the physician; "there's nothing in that—probably fell out of her hair."

Price's forehead was wrinkled into a frown, and his ears were wiggling again.

"It dropped from some one's hair," he muttered. "Her hair? I wonder if it did?"

"Don't be ridiculous," snapped Doctor Bushnell.

"Look at it!" the other commanded tersely. "What color is that hairpin?"

"Black, of course," the doctor said impatiently.

"Exactly—black! The dead woman's hair is blond. Step over to her dressing table, and perhaps you'll be puzzled, too. See, she uses bronze hairpins, doctor. Any woman with hair the color of hers, would. A black hairpin! I wonder if this is a clew, a real clew?"

"Rot!" retorted the physician. "Any one might have dropped it; the maid —"

"Where is the maid?"

"Bates said that she went to Yonkers."

"And has the maid black hair?"

Doctor Bushnell considered for a moment, trying to remember. "Dark hair," he nodded; "perhaps not black. I couldn't say as to the identical shade."

"The other Mrs. Gilmore?"

"Quite gray."

"And the other—what is her name?"

The doctor frowned indignantly. "Such a suspicion is too ridiculous, too absurd!" he protested. Yet with a vaguely uneasy feeling he remembered Joan Sheridan's strange behavior, her anguished protest of Victor Sarbella's innocence—and Joan's hair was black, jet black!

# CHAPTER 17

## KIRKLAN PROTESTS

Hint of the physician's disturbed thoughts must have shown in his face, for Wiggly Price gave him a keen, curious look, which seemed to increase the former's discomfiture; he dallied nervously with the fraternal charm attached to his watch chain.

"What color did you say, doctor?" pressed the newspaper man.

"It's ridiculous, absurd!" Bushnell repeated explosively. "What if Joan's hair is dark? Confound it, you make me downright angry, casting an insinuation like that, just because of an inconsequential thing like a hairpin."

Wiggly gave a faint smile which was grim rather than humorous.

"I haven't insinuated anything, doctor; just asked a question, that's all. Oh, I admit there's nothing conclusive about a hairpin, and yet—well, there was the Hitchcock case that I mentioned, solved by a black mourning pin."

"For murder there's got to be a motive," argued Doctor Bushnell; "no one besides Sarbella had a motive. I don't care what you find, I'd never believe that any one except Sarbella—"

The door was flung open with a startling violence, and Kirklan Gilmore lunged into the room, hair disheveled, eyes wide and staring.

"What—what does this mean?" he cried hoarsely. "Bates tells me that the constable has arrested Sarbella. Is that true? Come, answer me, what does it mean?"

Under his breath the doctor cursed the butler for adding this to the man's nervous strain.

"I thought I gave you a sleeping tablet, Kirklan. Bates should not have excited you by—"

"Certainly he should have," Gilmore broke in. "I've a right to know what's going on in my own house. Bates was perfectly right; but what does it mean? Bates says that Sarbella was taken away—handcuffed. It's true, isn't it?"

Doctor Bushnell nodded. "Yes, Kirklan, it's true; Sarbella is being—ah —detained, pending—well, at least pending further investigation of your

109

wife's murder. Certain things developed which made it advisable and necessary."

"Great Lord!" whispered Gilmore, his shaking fingers raking back a tangled shock of hair that fell across his forehead. "You mean—you mean that Sarbella has been arrested for—for that?" His other hand went out, pointing to the couch.

"Try and calm yourself, Kirklan," soothed the physician. "I hadn't intended that you should know this until you had pulled yourself together somewhat. I knew that it would be a tremendous shock for you to know that your friend, a guest in your home—"

"Why," broke in the novelist, "was Sarbella arrested?"

Doctor Bushnell hesitated over the answer, and Wiggly Price drew back to one side, making himself as inconspicuous as possible.

"I demand to know," insisted Gilmore, and the doctor saw that there could be no further evasion.

"As I told you downstairs, Kirklan," said Bushnell, "we have established beyond all question that it was murder. Since she was killed, some one had to kill her."

"But why Sarbella?" the author pressed impatiently.

"Obviously," went on the doctor, "an effort has been made to make it appear suicide, but the effort failed; such efforts usually do. It's hard to destroy evidence, next to the impossible. There were but five persons in the house; you and Bates downstairs, your stepmother, Joan and Sarbella upstairs. Taking the list into consideration it was only natural that suspicion should turn to Sarbella. And then—"

"But that's not proof, doctor—that's only suspicion," broke in Gilmore. "If you had no evidence, I don't see how you dared—"

"We had a little more than that," said Doctor Bushnell with obvious reluctance, realizing that circumstances had made it unavoidable that Kirklan should know the terrible truth about Helen's past life. "You see, Kirklan, we discovered that Sarbella had a motive."

"A motive?" Gilmore muttered dully. "What do you mean by that? What reason could he have had? Out with it! Why do you torture me with this suspense?"

Doctor Bushnell stepped forward and put a hand on the other's shoulder.

"Heaven knows that I wish I could spare you this, Kirklan, but it's bound to come out at the trial and in the newspapers. You were not aware, I suppose, that there was a previous relationship between—" He had phrased it clumsily and Gilmore started back with a shudder, a look of anguished horror on his face.

"You mean that Sarbella and my wife were— He lied to me—he lied to me—gave me his word of honor that he had never seen her before. I knew

110

there was something wrong; I saw her face when she met him; I knew—"

"No you misunderstand me, Kirklan. There was nothing like that. Perhaps you did not know that Sarbella had a brother, a younger brother named Andrea, who—"

"Who shot himself," finished Gilmore. "Yes, I'd heard of it; that happened before I knew Victor. But what has that got to do with this?"

"Young Sarbella shot himself because of a woman," went on Doctor Bushnell. "Because a woman, a very beautiful woman whom he loved madly, had misled him about herself. She lied to him, tricked him, and then —the woman's husband came to him and told him the truth."

Kirklan Gilmore stared dully; he seemed not to grasp the inference of it all. The room was tensely quiet.

"I—I don't understand," he muttered thickly, "what that has to do with Sarbella and my wife."

"Andrea Sarbella," the doctor went on gently, "was the idol of his mother and his brother. Shock of the tragedy cost the mother's life, and Victor, it seems, took an oath that he would avenge himself on the woman responsible for his double bereavement."

The dawning light of comprehension showed in Gilmore's horror-stricken eyes; a cry arose in his throat, as he staggered back into a chair and buried his head within his hands.

"You mean," he choked, "that the woman was—was—my wife!"

"Yes, Kirklan, your wife was that woman. Now you can understand why Sarbella has been placed under arrest."

Again the room was silent, silent except for the choking sob which came from the man huddled low in the chair. After a moment he staggered to his feet and flung his arms wildly.

"It's a lie!" he shouted. "It's a lie! I don't believe it; I'll never believe it. Why, if what you say is true, she—"

"Calm yourself, Kirklan. Sarbella has admitted what I have told you. We might have never known the truth except that this young man recognized her and put us on the right track."

Gilmore, for the first time, seemed aware of Wiggly Price's presence.

"Who are you?" he demanded hoarsely. "What do you mean by coming here with these lies—about my wife? Answer me—who are you?"

"My name is Price, and I am a newspaper man."

Gilmore wheeled accusingly upon the doctor. "Who let him in?" he shouted. "Didn't I tell you—"

"Easy, Kirklan, easy now. I can't answer as to how Price got into the house, but I'll say it's a lucky thing for us that he did. Except for him we might still be beating our heads against a stone wall. When you've calmed down you'll thank him instead of berating him. It may be that he is the agent who will bring your wife's murderer to justice. No matter what the woman did, a murder has been done; Sarbella had no right to take vengeance into his own hands."

The novelist dropped limply back into the chair, his muscles twitching, as he stared at the sheet-covered body.

"Sarbella?" he muttered thickly. "What—what does Sarbella say?"

"Naturally he denies it," answered the doctor. "We hope to find proof. We must find proof; I doubt if he could be convicted on the purely circumstantial evidence that we have so far. Unless we can establish his ownership of the automatic pistol, we will have to find something else. If he thought the gun could be traced he surely would not have left it behind."

Gilmore lifted his head slowly.

"Then there is no proof—only—only suspicion?" He paused for a moment and then added: "I can't believe it! I can't believe that Sarbella killed her. And she—she was—that kind of a woman!"

Doctor Bushnell touched his shoulder. "Try not to grieve, Kirklan," he urged quietly. "You were in love with the woman you thought her to be, and she did not exist. She wasn't worth a good man's grief. We do not even know—in fact, I doubt—if her marriage was legal."

"I can't believe that Sarbella did it," repeated Gilmore dully. "She—she must have killed herself to escape the truth."

"Did you happen to notice the brand of cigarettes that Sarbella smokes?" asked Wiggly Price.

Gilmore's resentment against the newspaper man seemed to have vanished; he displayed no curiosity over this apparently idle question, only shook his head absently, like a man in a daze.

"And your wife," pressed Wiggly, "I don't suppose that she used a cigarette now and then?"

Again Gilmore shook his head, almost stupidly and without verbal response, his hands dangling inertly across the arms of the chair.

"Sarbella didn't do it," he muttered again, as if talking to himself; "she did it to escape the truth. Nothing will ever convince me—nothing!"

Around the edges of the drawn curtain was creeping the light of a graying dawn. Price moved toward the door.

"I'm going down to the village," he said in an undertone to the doctor; "I'll come back when I've talked with Sarbella about his brand of cigarettes. Remember my hunch and the black hairpin."

With that he hurried down the stairs and to the still waiting taxicab, with its driver napping behind the wheel.

# CHAPTER 18

## TWO BRANDS OF CIGARETTES

The Ardmore jail was located in the basement of Borough Hall, and, since it was but a place of temporary detention until prisoners could be removed to the county seat, it consisted of a single cell, a narrow steel cage tucked away in one corner adjoining the furnace room. It was here that Victor Sarbella, who had ceased his protests and had lapsed into a stony silence, that took no cognizance of Constable Griggs' persistent and exasperating questioning, had been lodged.

Wiggly Price found Borough Hall locked, and the place was in darkness. Griggs had decided to let the prisoner "cool his heels" for a while, and he had gone home to freshen himself with a nap before continuing the cross-examination. The village was still soundly asleep, and Wiggly, thinking that the constable must return shortly, made himself as comfortable as possible in the cab.

Time dragged past, and the reporter considered the Greenacres tragedy and its various angles. A great little rider of hunches was Wiggly, and, in the face of the obvious, he was riding the hunch that Sarbella hadn't shot Helen Gilmore. And the black hairpin, small a thing as it was, occupied a conspicuous corner of his thoughts. The broken vase he thought of only casually. The half-burned cigarette butt he admitted might have some importance, but he much doubted that it had belonged to Sarbella. As he had told Doctor Bushnell, he couldn't conceive a murderer, smoking a cigarette, would walk in on his victim. It just wasn't reasonable.

The east was bright with the dawn of a brilliant day; the sun mounted higher, and still Ham Griggs had not returned. Wiggly glanced at his watch with a growl of impatience; he knew that it wouldn't be long until other news hounds would be keen on the scent of the big story.

"Confound that fellow!" he muttered. "Where's he gone to? More than likely he considers the case solved and has gone home to tell his folks what a great detective he is!"

From far up the deserted street just one sound broke the stillness, a particularly cheerful, but tuneless, whistle which, as it came nearer, brought into view an elephantine youth who approached with a flat-footed shuffle, his shoes flapping noisily, as if they might be trying to mark time to their owner's musical efforts. The village fat boy, drawing closer, left off whistling and turned to song, singing in a shrill treble, "Yes, we have no bananas. We have no bananas today."

Wiggly stepped from the cab to intercept him, and for no reason at all, unless it were taken for granted that it was outward evidence of an otherwise unexpressed mirth, Wiggly's ears twitched.

"Say, son," Wiggly said briskly, "do you know where Constable Griggs lives?"

For the moment Master Frederick Throgmorton, as the local juvenile heavyweight was named, was totally bereft of speech, completely hypnotized by the amazing gymnastics of Jimmy Price's ears.

"Huh?" he finally gulped. "Whatcha—whatcha say?"

"I said: Do you know where Constable Griggs lives?"

"Sure—sure thing," gasped Fatty Frederick. "Right—right down this street—third block, second house from the corner. Say, mister, tell a feller somethin'—how did you learn to do it?"

Wiggly flushed, as he always did when reminded of his refractory appendages, and he dived swiftly back into the cab, as he gave the chauffeur further directions. The taxi shot forward with a jerk. Less than a minute later they had negotiated the three blocks, and the New York newspaper man was on the sidewalk and at the picket gate of the Griggs cottage.

Etta, the constable's daughter, was ambitious, but her ambition was centered upon becoming a playwright and did not, as a rule, extend to early rising. But this morning she was up, fully dressed, and, at the moment of Wiggly Price's ring, pressing her father for further details of the Greenacres murder. For once in her life she was actually taking some pride in the fact that her parent was a constable. And Ham Griggs willingly sacrificed his intended "forty winks" that he might elaborate, none too modestly, on the part he had played; after all, it was something to be a hero to the critical and exacting Etta.

"I wouldn't be a lot surprised," he was saying, "that the reporter feller will be wantin' my pitcher to put in the paper. There ain't no use for me to deny, Etty, that I done a purty slick piece of work. I knowed the minute I clapped eyes on the Eyetalian that he was the one that done it. Wouldn't be surprised but what I'd better scoot down to Jess Burnside's pitcher gallery an' have some new pitchers struck; I ain't set for a pitcher since—" He was interrupted by the ringing of the doorbell. Father and daughter had been so absorbed that they had not heard the arrival of the taxi.

"I'll answer it, fawther," said Etta, and for once Ham Griggs did not correct the affectation which ordinarily so annoyed him. They had been sit-

114

ting in the kitchen, and Etta had put on a pot of coffee which, entirely un-
noticed, had boiled over. Ham tilted back in a chair, uniform coat thrown
open, snapping his suspenders smartly against his chest.

Etta frisked through the brief hallway to the front of the cottage. As she
opened the door, the upper portion of which was glass, with a frosted design alleged to be artistic, she faced Wiggly Price, who neglected the polite
formality of removing his hat.

"Constable Griggs live here?"

"He does," admitted Etta, one hand resting upon her practically hipless
waist, chin slightly tilted. "Who shall I tell fawther is calling, please?"

"Price, of *The Morning Star*."

"O—oh," gasped Etta, flustered. "Come—come right in; I'll tell him."

But there was no need to tell him. Ham Griggs, the intervening doors
being open, had heard him and came striding out from the kitchen, morally
certain that his prediction was well founded, and that the reporter had come
for a photograph.

"Come right on in, son," he boomed hospitably. "Etty's just fixin' me up
a cup of Java, an' I guess she can scare up a flock of eggs. Guess you ain't
had no breakfast, huh? Come right on into the kitchen an' make yourself to
home."

"Fawther!" cried Etta in embarrassed indignation. "Ain't you—haven't
you forgotten your manners? In the kitchen? Why the very idea! I'll set the
table in the dining room, and—"

"The kitchen for mine! Don't bother, Miss Griggs. I'm in pretty much of
a hurry, but I can't turn down a cup of coffee after being up all night."

"Sure," the constable nodded complacently and then added: "Guess
nothin' new turned up out at Greenacres, huh? I nailed the right man, all
right; not a bad piece of work for a hick constable, if I do say so myself."
With a laugh he led the way into the kitchen, while the mortified Etta bit
her lip in chagrin; but there was no choice in accepting the situation. She
recalled a line from her "Social Etiquette" which told her, "When embarrassed by an unexpected caller, the hostess should at once accept the situation in good grace and make her guest feel welcome." But a guest in the
kitchen! Her little reference book was mute as to that.

"I want to see Sarbella just as quickly as I can," said Wiggly, sitting
down and hitching his chair close to the table. He sniffed avidly. "Ah, that
coffee does smell good!"

"Sure," agreed Ham Griggs. "But whatcha want to see him about?
What's happened?"

"Nothing's happened—exactly," Wiggly answered cautiously, knowing
that the constable would in all probability resent any intimation of Sarbella's possible innocence. Even a seasoned detective, once he has made up

his mind, does not relish the idea of being shown that he had been wrong. In Griggs' case, it would be a hard blow to his exuberant vanity. "But, as you may realize, our evidence against the man is so far purely circumstantial."

"Oh, don't you worry about that," the constable said complacently; "he'll come through with a confession, after he's had a good taste of jail. Stubborn as a mule he is so far, but he'll break down; they all do."

"Isn't it thrilling!" broke in Etta, pouring coffee. "It's what you call a big story, isn't it?"

Wiggly gave a smiling nod. "It's about the best murder story I've ever worked on."

Etta beamed. "It was I who called up your editor and told him about it," she announced.

"The thunder you did!" grunted Ham Griggs.

"If it's a scoop," promised Wiggly; "I'll tell the city editor to have the business office mail you a fat little check for the tip."

"Oh, no! I didn't do it for any mercenary reasons. But, if the editor wants to say something nice about my play—"

"Eh—your play?"

"I expect it to be produced this fall. It's nearly finished; I have promised to let a New York producer stage it."

"Yes, I see," murmured Wiggly gravely. He had the good sense not to indulge in a smile, but his ears moved faintly. "And I'll certainly speak to the dramatic critic about it—I certainly will." Under his breath he added: "Lord, what the play bug does to people!"

Etta was so excited by what she considered the total success of her plan to establish a cordial personal relationship with the press that she tipped a cup, spilling hot coffee over the back of her father's hand.

"The murder at Greenacres has given me the inspiration for another play," she said. "It shall be a mystery play; they're so popular in New York."

"A good mystery is about the most interesting thing in the world," declared Wiggly, dropping a spoonful of sugar and stirring vigorously.

"And the Gilmore tragedy—fawther has just finished telling me all about it—isn't it dramatic?"

"It certainly is, Miss Griggs," agreed the reporter, wishing the girl were in Halifax.

"And to think," she rushed on, "that Kirklan Gilmore's new wife was such an awful woman. So pretty, too; I saw her only the other day. You know it was such a surprise when he married her. Mrs. Huggins—she's a seamstress and used to sew for the Gilmores—thought it was certain that he would marry Joan; such a sweet girl, Joan."

Wiggly's wandering thoughts suddenly became centered upon what the gushing Etta was saying.

"Joan?" he murmured.

"Young Mr. Gilmore's stepsister, you know. Didn't you see her? Such a sweet girl! Oh, I suppose some people would consider it unusual for a man to marry his stepsister, but Mrs. Huggins thought it would turn out that way. She's got sharp eyes, Mrs. Huggins has, and she said that Joan was simply in love with Mr. Gilmore; she used to help him so much with his work, I understand. And then, while she was away in Europe, he married the other one. It was such a terrible surprise to everybody. And Mrs. Huggins said—" Her gossip broke off into a gasp, as she stared at the reporter's ears which were now wiggling almost violently.

So Joan was in love with her stepbrother; she had dark hair; and he had found a black hairpin on the floor beside the slain woman's body! This certainly was food for thought—not only food, but a feast! The Greenacres story gave promise of being a live mystery.

And there was the cigarette butt; the husband did not smoke cigarettes; therefore it could not be explained by his dropping it there, and, if it wasn't Sarbella's— There was another angle.

During Etta's moment of speechlessness, Wiggly debated these matters swiftly, as he gulped down his coffee, and Constable Griggs embraced the opportunity to get back into the conversation.

"Whatcha say you wanted to see Sarbella about?" he demanded.

"As I said," answered Wiggly; "there's no proof against him except that he might be considered to have a motive, and that he also had an opportunity to commit the crime. Juries don't send men to the death chair on that sort of evidence. Of course, if he makes a confession or we can trace the murder gun to him, that automatically solves our difficulty; but Sarbella is probably shrewd enough to realize what a weak case you've got against him; if he does realize that, and if he is guilty, he'll have sense enough to keep his mouth shut."

"Whatcha hittin' at?" growled Ham Griggs.

"After you left Greenacres, Doctor Bushnell and I looked around a little, and we found a half-burned cigarette mashed down into the rug of the room where the woman was killed. Since Gilmore doesn't smoke—"

"Sarbella smokes 'em," broke in the constable. "Sure he does; purty near one right after the other. Regular cigarette fiend, the feller is. That clinches the case on him, huh? Is that what you're drivin' at?"

"If he smokes the same sort of cigarette as the one Doctor Bushnell found on the rug, I'd say it was pretty much a clincher. It would be evidence that he had been in the room."

"Of course it's his cigarette!" exclaimed Ham Griggs, lumbering swiftly to his feet. "I'd bet a hundred dollars on it. Come on, son, we'll get right down to the jail and prove it."

"Why, fawther!" came Etta's protest. "Won't you let Mr. Price wait until I have cooked the eggs? I was going to put them on the fire this minute."

"Speaking for Mr. Price," said Wiggly, "the coffee is sufficient. Thanks just the same." He pushed back his chair and moved to follow the constable.

"Like as not when we face 'im with this," suggested Griggs, "he'll break down an' make a clean breast of it."

"Oh, Mr. Price," called Etta, "you won't forget to—to speak to the dramatic critic about my play?"

Wiggly promised, without committing himself as to just how he would speak of it; there are some things, from a diplomatic standpoint, best left unsaid.

The constable clumped briskly out of the house with the reporter following. As they got into the taxi, Ham Griggs wondered if he were not to be asked for a photograph with which to adorn the first page of *The Star*; already he had visualized the caption: "Figures in Gilmore Murder Case— Local Officer Who Solved Baffling Mystery."

"If you want my pitcher for the paper," he suggested, "I'd better see about havin' one struck. Of course I ain't lookin' for no puff, but—"

"No use going to that expense," Wiggly broke in; "we'll probably have a staff photographer down during the day, and he can snap you on the scene—examining the murder gun, you know, or something like that. Action pictures always more interesting, Mr. Constable," he ended emphatically.

The brief trip was completed, and, as the machine again drew to a halt in front of Borough Hall, the chauffeur entered a protest.

"Say, boss," he exclaimed, "you don't expect a guy to sit at the wheel forever, do you? A man's gotta sleep some time. Guess you'd better pay what the meter reads an' let me skim back to the big town."

Wiggly paid the charge, which was twenty-seven dollars, gave a three-dollar tip, and let him go. Griggs entered the village's public building and led the way down into the basement, where Sarbella was lodged. At the sound of their footsteps, ringing on the concrete floor, the prisoner left off his nervous pacing of the cell's narrow confines and came to the steel door of the cage. His attitude was weary, dejected.

"Mebbe you're ready to speak up, huh?" grunted Ham Griggs, facing him from the other side of the bars.

"I have nothing to add," Victor Sarbella answered; "you already have the only statement I care to make," he paused briefly and then added, "for the present."

"Silence ain't goin' to do you no good, for I aim to keep you right where you are until you get ready to start talkin'," blustered the constable. "We know you killed her; we've dug up some more evidence on you—little matter of a cigarette that you dropped on the floor of that room out to Greenacres."

"Cigarette?" muttered Sarbella.

"May I have your cigarette case for a moment, Mr. Sarbella?" requested Wiggly.

The prisoner hesitated, gave the newspaper man a wary glance, and, evidently realizing that they would take it away from him by force, if he refused, slid his hand into his pocket, producing a silver case inlaid with gold stripes. He shrugged his shoulders.

"I don't know what it's all about, but you're welcome; please do not destroy the smokes. I've only two left."

Wiggly Price took the elaborate case, which Sarbella passed through the bars, and snapped it open. One glance was sufficient to verify his logical doubts that the butt of the cheap cigarette which Doctor Bushnell had discovered on the floor of the tragedy chamber had not been the artist's. The two cigarettes before him were of an expensive imported brand, straw-tipped and monogrammed with the man's initials.

The constable was looking over his shoulder, as Wiggly extracted from his vest pocket the flattened bit of evidence upon which both Doctor Bushnell and Ham Griggs had expressed so much faith. He unfolded the strip of paper that enwrapped it.

"They are not the same," he announced. "I didn't expect them to be. The question now is—to whom did this belong? It looks very much like another man—a man with cheap tastes in tobacco—was in that room last night!"

Victor Sarbella pressed his body tensely against the bars, but not so much as a syllable passed his lips. Perhaps there was a look of relief in his face.

# CHAPTER 19

## ENTER SERGEANT TISH

The constable and Wiggly had left the basement, and Griggs was almost apoplectic with anger. He glared at the reporter with indignant disgust and, as they entered the room used for the sessions of the borough council, flopped down in a chair.

"Now if you ain't made a fine mess of things! An' I give you credit for havin' some sense! I might have got a confession outta him except for your meddlin'. Dog-gone you, anyhow! He'll think now that he's got a chance to get out of it after you tellin' him that there must have been another man in the room where the woman was killed."

"You've got to admit that it isn't Sarbella's cigarette butt," defended Wiggly.

"If I'd have known you was goin' to pull a stunt like that, I'd never have let you in to see him," raged Ham Griggs. "Next time I'll have better gumption than to let some fool reporter gum the cards for me—you just bet I will."

"Let's talk it over," Wiggly urged placatingly. "Let's use a little simple logic. You admit, don't you, that this isn't Sarbella's brand?"

"I don't admit nothin' of the sort," raged the constable. "Chances are that he dropped that cheap cigarette on the floor as a blind, tryin' to leave a false scent to fool us."

Wiggly shook his head. "That won't hold water, constable; you forget that the murderer tried to make it appear suicide. And, as I tried to impress on Doctor Bushnell, can you imagine a man set on murder slipping in on his victim—smoking a cigarette?"

But Ham Griggs was in no mood for logic; he considered that he had solved the case in arresting Sarbella, and he wanted it to stay solved. A re-opening of the facts led him into water over his head, and he foresaw himself floundering helplessly beyond his depth.

"Sarbella done it!" he shouted. "He killed the Gilmore woman; he shot her to get even. He shot her—with this gun." Dramatically he dragged forth the automatic pistol and waved it almost wildly. "And you've gone

120

and messed things up by lettin' him think he had a chance to get off—darn your hide!"

The outburst was checked by the opening of the door which led into the council room from the outside entrance, and there entered a short, rotund man who wore his hat perched upon a bandaged head.

"Where's the chief of police?" was the stranger's greeting.

"I'm the constable; it amounts to the same thing in Ardmore," Griggs answered shortly, "but I ain't got no time to be bothered."

The corpulent little visitor moved back the edge of his coat, revealing a badge of the New York police department.

"I'm Detective Sergeant Tish—New York headquarters," he announced. "Your name Griggs? You telephoned last night to the Consolidated Taxicab Company that you'd picked up an abandoned taxi on one of the roads near Ardmore?"

"Yes, I did," grunted Constable Griggs, "but I ain't got no time to bother about taxicabs now. I've got a murder on my hands."

"And I want to get my hands on a murderer," shot back Sergeant John Henry Tish. "That taxicab was stolen by—"

"Don't give a hoot if it was!" shouted the constable. "The taxi's at Presley's garage. Go get it, if you want it." He even forgot that he had expected to receive a ten-dollar gift from the taxicab company.

Sergeant Tish, however, was not to be put off so easily. He projected his short, portly form closer and occupied a chair beside the council table, with the air of having something to say and being determined to say it. He wasted no time.

"Listen!" he commanded, wagging a pudgy forefinger with a forceful gesture. "This is just as important to me as your case is to you. See this?" He tapped his bandaged head. "The man I'm after did this to me, and I'm going to get him. He knocked me cold—after I had the nippers on him, see? I've got to get him.

"There may be some time when you'll want a favor from the New York department. I want a little information—and a little courtesy. I'm no windbag, and I won't keep you long."

"All right," grunted Constable Griggs. "What is it you want?"

"Thanks," said Sergeant Tish. "First, where was it that you picked up the machine?"

"Out on the Hudson Road, 'bout half a mile from the village proper. I called Presley's garage an' had 'em drive the bus into their shop—and that's all I can tell you about it, every blessed thing. I notified the taxicab company."

"Sure, I know that, and they flashed it right to headquarters. There was a general alarm out for that taxi. So it was run into the garage—under its own power, huh? That means Haskins didn't ditch the car because something went wrong with the engine. That may help some. Pretty swell folks live out on the Hudson Road, eh?"

Griggs nodded. "Most of 'em is rich," he agreed; "either rich or pretty well fixed."

"Sounds like it might be a warm trail," said Sergeant Tish, puffing out his plump cheeks. "Y'see—well, I'll have to give you the inside for you to understand just what the situation is."

Despite his first impatience, Constable Griggs became interested and offered no protest.

"This bird I'm after," pursued Tish, "is named Don Haskins. He's got a record as long as an income-tax report. Done a couple of short stretches at Sing Sing, one out West—Illinois—and has been in the line-up down at headquarters and in the Tombs. It would take an expert accountant to keep the count. He used to be a slick crook, nifty dresser and free spender, but he'd started slippin'. They all do. Clever—and hard-boiled."

Here Tish told the constable of his encounter with Haskins.

"Humph!" grunted Constable Griggs. "I see. And you're looking for your man in these parts. Sorry I ain't got the time to help, but—"

"Just a minute," broke in Sergeant Tish. "I ain't quite through yet. I'm right at the nub of it. Eighth Avenue Annie, I guess, wanted to cover up; anyhow, she runs out on the street yellin' bloody murder, and a couple of uniform men rushes in to find me laid out, dead to the world. But they brings me around, and then—oh, the grillin' we did give old Annie! We still got her locked up on a technical charge.

"Before we got through with her, she comes through with a lot of dope she didn't want to cough up. She hadda admit that Haskins had paid her big for his hide-out, and that he was gettin' ready to make the big jump out of town; that he had a rich sister, a real swell, who made him a visit and give him some dough. She was goin' to come back with more.

"Now, that's the funny part of it; one of the boys down at headquarters knows Don Haskins from the first time he went to Elmira Reformatory, and he says that Haskins did have a sister, but that she died eight or nine years ago, and that she didn't fit the description which Annie give us. No matter about that, it's a cinch that some swell jane did bring him the money. Annie says she was the class.

"Now, I was just wondering, gents—Haskins leaves the swiped taxi out on Hudson Road. The engine was O. K. That's proof that he left it there because he wanted to, and not because the car stopped on him. Where was he headin' for? Mebbe this swell who calls herself his sister lives around here. Now, you've got the whole works. I want somebody to help me check up. See?"

122

Ham Griggs' cap was on the desk which belonged officially to the borough council's president, his honor, Mayor Ripley. The cap accidentally—not from any design—covered the automatic pistol which had killed Helen Gilmore.

"As I told you," reiterated the constable, "I'm too busy this mornin' to do anything for you. Mebbe this afternoon, when I've got a confession outta the prisoner I got downstairs, I'll have more time." He reached for his uniform cap with a gesture of unshakable finality.

Sergeant Tish suddenly strained forward, his eyes bulging from out of his plump round face, staring in open-mouthed and bewildered amazement at the .44 on the desk.

"Where did you get that gun?" he gasped, lunging out of the chair and making a dive for it, getting his hands on it before Griggs could stop him. "Where did you get my gun?"

Ham Griggs snorted derisively. "Your gun? This here ain't your gun. It belongs to that prisoner I got downstairs, and he shot a woman with it last night. That's the murder case I'm workin' on."

Tish's face was a strange study of emotion. "It's my gun!" he shouted. "Here's a little place chipped off one of the butt plates. Sure it's my gun. Police department issue—you can tell that by the serial number. Sure, it's my gun—the one Don Haskins took off of me yesterday when he knocked me out. And you say that a woman was shot with it—murdered? You say that you took it off a prisoner, and that you've got him here? You mean that you've got Haskins locked up?"

The questions all jerked out with no pause, leaving him breathless, his fat cheeks quivering. Constable Griggs was speechless, and Wiggly Price's ears seemed determined to work themselves loose from his head.

"You're dead sure, sergeant, that it is your gun?" Wiggly demanded tensely. "It—it's very important that there should be no mistake about this."

"Don't you suppose I know my own gun?" snapped Sergeant Tish. "That's a funny question, askin' a cop if he knows his own gun. I want Haskins, and I want him now."

Constable Griggs found things happening just a little too fast for his slow wits. "I think you must be plumb crazy," he sputtered. "The prisoner we got is named Sarbella, an Eyetalian feller; he's the one that shot the woman with the gun. Gimme it back."

"Like thunder I'll give it back!" retorted Sergeant Tish.

"Wait!" said Wiggly. "I—I think I'm beginning to see some daylight. Haskins was a crook; some good-looking, swell-dressed woman brought him money—posed as his rich sister. And the minute Haskins got nabbed he made tracks for Ardmore. The cheap, ten-cents-a-pack cigarettes! Just the kind that Haskins might be expected to smoke. Haskins had Sergeant Tish's gun—and that's the gun that killed her. Don't you understand, constable? We've made a bad mistake because we didn't know anything about Haskins. The murderer was Haskins—the crook!"

And for the moment Wiggly forgot all about the black hairpin.

# CHAPTER 20

## A QUEER JUMBLE

"Haskins killed her!" Wiggly Price repeated excitedly. "We're on the right trail; there doesn't seem to be any other explanation now. Haskins, the crook, shot her—with that gun."

While Sergeant Tish's identification of the murder gun, as the same automatic pistol that Don Haskins had taken from his unconscious person the previous afternoon, plus the certainty that Haskins had deserted the stolen taxicab at no great distance from Greenacres, made it an obvious theory that it might have been the crook who had murdered Helen Gilmore, Constable Griggs sputtered protestingly. No man likes to admit a mistake. For a moment he was too eternally flabbergasted for words; this sudden development, the appearance of a new and unknown suspect, floundered him helplessly in a sea of bewilderment.

Possibility of Victor Sarbella's innocence endangered his triumph and put the brakes on his ego, for, by that mental process which makes men heroes in their own eyes, Ham Griggs had given himself a good deal more credit than he was really entitled to. He forgot that it had been the newspaper reporter's well-functioning memory, identifying the slain woman as "the girl in the Sarbella case," which had supplied the vital link, the possible motive, and that, except for Wiggly, there would have been nothing upon which to have detained the artist.

Not that Wiggly Price begrudged the constable feeding his vanity fat; for Wiggly was interested only in the story and concerned not at all with whatever transitory fame might attach to the solver of the mystery. Give Wiggly the story, and he was willing that Constable Griggs should monopolize the credit.

Sergeant John Henry Tish, realizing the importance that attached to a positive identification of the automatic, examined it still more carefully, reaffirming an already firm conviction that it was his. His own excitement, too, matched that of the newspaper reporter.

"There's no doubt about it, gents," he declared. "It's my gun."

125

"Huh!" grunted Constable Griggs, at last finding his tongue. "There must be hundreds of guns like that, as much the same as peas in a pod." His skepticism was, of course, backed by the wish that it be a mistake. "Mebbe it looks like your gun, mebbe it *has* got a busted place on the butt plates, but that don't prove—"

"A cop gets pretty well acquainted with a gun when he's packed it as long as I've packed this one. There's a lot of little marks on it that I recognize. I know it's my gat, and the serial number will prove it; the department keeps a record of the numbers."

"It's a police regulation, all right," grunted Wiggly Price. "I ought to have noticed that the first thing, but I didn't. I don't think there's much chance of Sergeant Tish being mistaken, constable, especially since the deserted taxi gives us proof that Haskins did come to Ardmore last night."

"Well, I ain't sayin' that it ain't, but at the same time I ain't sayin' that it is," growled Ham Griggs. "Nor am I goin' to admit that Sarbella didn't do the killin'; if he's so all-fired innocent, what makes him keep his mouth shut so tight? If you think I'm goin' to turn him loose just because somebody else *might* have done it—"

"Oh, I'm not trying to have you turn Sarbella out of jail, constable," said Wiggly. "I've no interest in him, personal or otherwise, beyond seeing you put hands on the guilty man. Detain him long as you like, so far as I'm concerned."

"You betcha life I'll detain him long as I like!" blustered the constable with a glare.

The rotund Sergeant Tish stood impatiently to his feet, shoving the automatic into the empty holster, where it belonged.

"It sure looks like Haskins is wanted now for two croaks instead of one," he said gruffly. "Suppose we make tracks for the place where the woman was killed. Just wasting time here."

"Huh!" sneered Constable Griggs. "You don't think the feller you're after will still be out to Greenacres?"

"Hardly," answered Tish, "but we've got to start from there, anyhow. Haskins won't get far, I guess; there's already a general alarm out for him. When they do nab him, I aim to have the goods on him—right."

"Yes, we've got to go back to the Gilmore place," agreed Wiggly. "We've got an entirely new angle to work on now."

Ham Griggs, still voicing a half-hearted protest, perhaps further embittered that this New York detective was now upon the scene and would probably try to take all the glory for himself, got grudgingly to his feet. The three men left Borough Hall and went out to the street.

"Confound it!" complained Wiggly. "It must be a two-mile walk out there to Greenacres. Why didn't I keep that taxi? And there's a real hurry, too. Where can we get a machine, constable?"

"Presley's garage—if Presley has opened up," Ham Griggs answered sourly. "It's right around the corner."

"Ain't necessary," said Sergeant Tish. "I came out in one of the department's flivvers. Got it parked just around the corner. It's only a two-seater, but I guess we can manage it. The main thing is to get out to that place quick as we can."

He led the way around the corner, where stood the roadster with "Police Dept." painted upon the sides. The New York plain-clothes man got in first, wedging his portly form in behind the steering wheel. Constable Griggs, too, was a man of considerable bulk so that, even without Wiggly, all available seat room was occupied.

"The running board for mine," Price said cheerfully and climbed up. "Let 'er go, sergeant."

Tish started the engine, manipulated the foot pedals somewhat awkwardly, and the little car started forward with a violence that almost jerked the newspaper man to the ground; to save himself what might have been a bad spill, one arm encircled Ham Griggs' neck, adding to the latter's ill humor.

"I've always heard that you newspaper fellers was a pesky nuisance," he muttered.

If Wiggly was tempted to a retort, he gave no signs of it, merely murmured an apology. There was a moment of silence, the constable frowning deeply.

"We do know why Sarbella would have killed her," he argued; "because she vamped his brother and drove him to suicide, but why would this Haskins feller have done it? Answer me that!"

"Haskins is a hard guy," growled Sergeant Tish. "He wouldn't have needed much motive, that bird. Look at the way he clouted me over the head with his handcuffs. Like as not he had some sort of hold on her. The murdered woman must of been the swell dame that Haskins told Eighth Avenue Annie was his sister. See?"

"That ain't nothin' but guessin'," said Constable Griggs. "How are you goin' to know if she was?"

"It may be guessing, but it's a darn' good guess," replied Tish. "And, far as that's concerned, we can have Annie down to look at the body and tell us whether or not it was the skirt who come to her place and handed Haskins some dough."

"But *why* would Haskins have killed her?" persisted Ham Griggs.

"Well, I can't say positive as to that," answered Tish, "but it would be a pretty safe bet to figure it out. When I dropped in on him at old Annie's yesterday afternoon, he had to beat it in such a hurry that he left his money under the mattress; perhaps he made tracks for this Greenacres place to get money. Y'see, constable, she was going to bring him some more jack Wednesday—which is today—but I spoiled that. Since she couldn't come to him with the dough, he come to her. Like as not she was a little slow in coming across with the money, and he croaked her."

"Robbery, huh?" demanded Ham Griggs. "Ain't that what you're drivin' at?"

Sergeant Tish admitted that this was his tentative theory regarding the murder at Greenacres. The constable's grim face broke into a triumphant smile, for he had led the New York detective into a deliberate trap.

"That ain't no good," he said with a grunt of satisfaction. "There wasn't no robbery, Mr. Tish, for the Gilmore woman was still wearin' her jewelry when we found her dead. There must have been diamonds and the like worth a good many hundred dollars. Wouldn't he have taken the jewelry? I ask you, wouldn't he?"

"Well, I didn't know about that," answered Sergeant Tish, looking not so crestfallen as Griggs would have liked. "That seemed the most plausible, and it's still not impossible, for Haskins may have taken money and have been too pressed for time—you haven't told me anything about the facts, you know—to strip off the jewelry.

"Anyhow what we *do* know is that Haskins did go to Greenacres, and that murder was done with the gun which was in his possession. If Haskins didn't kill her, then—how did the murderer get this automatic pistol?"

Constable Griggs could not, of course, answer this question. Wiggly Price, his feet planted firmly upon the running board of the little car, and his fingers wrapped tightly about the rods supporting the top, thought of something which added, to his mind, a fresh puzzler to the whole mysterious business.

"There's something else, Sergeant Tish," he said, raising his voice so that he might be heard above the sound of the motor and the rush of the wind, as they hurried along. "If Haskins killed her, why did he leave the gun behind? He is a desperate man, already in open flight to escape one charge of murder, and a man in a position such as his would want to be armed. Chances are that he would shoot it out before submitting to capture. You say that Haskins is a clever crook, and—"

"Used to be," broke in Tish. "Been going down grade for some time. Booze—dope, too, likely as not."

"If he had any head on him at all," continued Wiggly, "he would have known that there was every chance in the world of that gun being traced. There's something else. The gun was planted beside the dead woman's body, an effort to give it every appearance of suicide. Why should Haskins have done that?"

128

"I wish you'd give me the low-down on the case," urged Sergeant Tish. "How do you expect me to get anywhere when you gimme the facts in jerks and starts like that?"

Constable Griggs' face wore an elated expression as he listened to Wiggly. The reporter had declared his positive conviction of Haskins' guilt, and yet here he was shooting his own theory full of holes.

"So you've come back to my way of thinkin', eh?" he crowed. "Come on now and admit that I put the handcuffs on the right man. The Eyetalian done it. Sure he did. I was right all the time."

The reporter's ears twitched meditatively.

"I'm not saying positively that Haskins didn't kill the woman," he answered. "But I do say that I can't understand why *he* should have been so anxious for it to appear suicide. It's very easy to understand a possible link between this crook and Gilmore's wife; she began life, I think I told you, on the fringe of the underworld. Oh, I admit that I'm stumped—bad, but there must be a hidden something, somewhere, that will put us right."

The detective sergeant's car was now at that point of the road where it ran in front of the Gilmore place.

"Turn in here, Sergeant Tish," grunted the constable, as they neared the driveway, and Tish turned the wheel sharply. Before they had quite reached the house, Tish stopped the machine.

"Listen, gents," he said crisply, "let's get down to cases. It looks to me as if Haskins did the job here at this place, although, as our reporter friend says, it *is* queer that he left the gat behind. I want to put my mitts on Don Haskins, whether he did the croak or not. And you wanna get hold of the same bird, for, if he didn't do it, you want him to tell you how this gun of mine got away from him.

"I want Haskins, and you want Haskins. Circumstances puts us in the same boat, and we ought to work together on this business." He suppressed a wise grin, as he saw the look of displeasure on Griggs' face. "Aw, don't worry, constable, I'm not going to butt in on your territory. I'm not tryin' to steal your thunder."

Sergeant Tish paused for a reply.

"Humph!" grunted Ham Griggs, not finding any valid excuse for refusing this offer of coöperation.

"About all I know to date," pursued Sergeant Tish, "is that a woman was bumped off with my gun, the one that Haskins lifted from me, when he handed me a knock-out at Eighth Avenue Annie's, that the pistol was left beside the body to make it look like suicide, and that you've gathered in a guy named Sarbella. If I'm goin' to help you any, I've got to have the low-down. See?"

129

"Yes, constable, we'd better tell him," said Wiggly Price, as Griggs remained silent. "If you've no objection, I'll give him a brief outline of the facts."

"All right," agreed Griggs, and Price related to Tish the facts in the case.

Sergeant Tish listened thoughtfully to Wiggly Price's digest of the tragedy, and, puffing out his plump cheeks to a balloonlike roundness, nodded his head.

"It's sure a queer jumble, ain't it?" he grunted. "I don't blame you, Griggs, for thinkin' this Sarbella fellow pulled the job, but how would Sarbella have got hold of the gun? No, it still looks like Don Haskins to me. Nobody else to be suspected, I suppose?"

Wiggly thought of the black hairpin and that germ of suspicion which Etta Griggs had planted in his mind by telling him of the suspected one-sided romance between Joan Sheridan and her stepbrother. He hesitated a moment and decided to keep this to himself, at least for the present. Let Sarbella and Don Haskins, walking so unexpectedly into the mystery, be eliminated before other complications were added. He sidestepped this question by ignoring it entirely.

"Surely," he said, "if Bates had let Haskins into the house, he would have mentioned it."

"Why don't we ask him whether he did or not?" grunted Constable Griggs, for at this moment the butler had stepped out of the house into the warming sunlight of the wide porch.

130

# CHAPTER 21

## A CRY OF TERROR

The three men left the little police car where it stood and walked the remaining few yards to the house. Bates saw their coming; as a matter of fact, he had from within noticed their approach, and he had come out to meet them. Despite his evident weariness, he was patently eager for any news. Constable Griggs, quickly forestalling any move that might tend to crowd himself out of the major role, planted himself directly in front of the butler, frowning sternly.

"When was the last time you saw the dead woman alive?" he demanded.

"Immediately after dinner," answered Bates; "she went directly upstairs, and I did not see her again until—until she was dead."

"How long had you been in bed when it happened?"

"It was some time, sir; at least two hours, I am sure."

"What I'm hittin' at is this," explained Griggs; "we've got some new dope that may mean something, and then again it may not. Did you let a strange man into the house last night, or did you see any strange man prowlin' about the place?"

"I—I don't believe I understand," murmured Bates. "A strange man, sir —prowling about the house?"

"That's what I said," grunted the constable, "and it's evident that you didn't. Was the doors locked?"

"Absolutely," Bates answered firmly. "I always lock up before turning in for the night. I have been very careful about that, especially since the burglar scare that we had last year."

"Then the man couldn't have got into the house unless you had let him in?" pressed Griggs.

"The woman herself might have let him in, constable," interposed Sergeant Tish. "If the butler had gone to bed she might have done it without any one hearing her."

"Huh!" retorted Ham Griggs, with a quicker flash of reasoning than might have been expected. "How would she have known Haskins was about, unless he rung the doorbell, or called her on the phone, or something

131

like that? Until you, Sergeant Tish, trapped 'im in that place in New York, he didn't know his own self that he was comin' to Greenacres."

"I am positive that there was no ring of any sort, either doorbell or telephone, until Mr. Gilmore got me up to let him in—just before the shot," offered Bates. "Any sort of ringing would have awakened me. But this strange man—I do not understand. Who—"

"Might as well tell you, I suppose," grunted the constable. "We've found out that the murder gun most likely belongs to this man"—he jerked his head toward Tish—"who is a detective from New York. The gun was taken away from him by a feller named Haskins, who swiped a taxi in New York to make his get-away, and that same taxi was found by myself out on the road, 'bout one and a half or two miles from here. So—"

"Then it isn't Mr. Sarbella's gun?" broke in Bates with a gasp of surprise.

"That don't mean I've turned Sarbella out of jail, not by a whole lot, it don't," growled Ham Griggs. "He might have got hold of the gun somehow; he might—" But, being unable to supply any further theory of Sarbella's guilt, his voice stopped abruptly. There was a moment of silence, broken by Bates.

"Did I tell you about the letter?" he asked in his thin voice. "No, I think not. It was Doctor Bushnell that I told about the letter."

"What letter?" demanded Griggs.

"The letter that came for Mrs. Gilmore on Monday," supplied the butler. "I considered it most peculiar at the time, a very dirty envelope, addressed with a lead pencil. She seemed much upset over it, although she tried to pass it off."

"It might have been from Haskins at that," spoke up Wiggly Price, and he turned to Sergeant Tish. "It was yesterday—Tuesday—that you cornered Haskins in the place you call Eighth Avenue Annie's. What day was it that the swell-dressed woman called on the man at that place?"

"Monday," answered Tish.

"Ah!" exclaimed the newspaper man triumphantly, and his ears wiggled a bit. "It was Monday that the murdered woman got this letter that Bates tells about. Bates, did she go to New York on Monday?"

"I don't think to New York, but she did drive somewhere in the motor— out into the country, I believe she said."

"Yes, so she said," nodded Wiggly with meaning emphasis. "That doesn't make it true that she didn't go to New York. Any one accompany her on this motor trip?"

"She went alone; she returned late in the afternoon."

"Say!" exploded Ham Griggs with a glare. "One would think *you* was the officer in charge the way you're bustin' in with all these questions."

"Just one question more, Constable Griggs," urged Wiggly. "I'm not trying to be officious. Bates, let us suppose for a moment that this man, Don Haskins, did get into the house in some way or another, would he have had time to get down the stairs before you and Mr. Gilmore rushed up—and then let himself out of the house, while you and Mr. Gilmore were upstairs?"

Bates debated this question for a moment and then shook his head positively.

"He would not," he replied; "but he might have easily found a place to conceal himself in one of the rooms upstairs. There is one bit of detail that I may have forgotten to mention. When Mr. Gilmore and I were about halfway up the stairway, I am positive that I heard a door slam very loudly—very loudly, indeed."

"Huh!" grunted the constable. "That don't mean anything much. It might just as well have been Sarbella rushin' back to his room after havin' shot her." And then he indulged in another bit of reasoning which did him credit. "If it was the Gilmore woman who went to see Haskins in New York, we know she wasn't too afraid of him to go see him in that cheap joint Sergeant Tish told us about. And yet she was afraid of the one who come in on her last night—because she screamed. Why did she scream? I'll tell you why she screamed; it was because she knowed that Sarbella had come to kill her! Just put that in your pipe and smoke it a while."

"Not a bad deduction," nodded Sergeant Tish, "but the thing that puzzles all of us is—how did Sarbella get the gun away from Haskins? We're just wastin' good time arguing back and forth. Let's go upstairs and see if we can't pick up something new."

"The—the body has been removed," the butler informed them. "The undertaker left an hour since. Doctor Bushnell was very careful that nothing else should be disturbed, and the room is locked. Doctor Bushnell—"

"And took the key off with him, I suppose," growled Constable Griggs.

"Doctor Bushnell, as I started to say," went on Bates, "is still here. Mr. Gilmore seems to be in quite a bad way, and the doctor is looking after him."

"We'll go on upstairs," declared Griggs. "Tell the doc that we want him to come right on up and let us into that room."

Wiggly Price did not follow them immediately; he loitered downstairs until Bates had delivered the message to the doctor and had returned. The butler, luckily for Wiggly, had not been told the reporter's true interest in the case, else he would have doubtless guarded his tongue most carefully.

"It's a bad business, Bates," said the newspaper man to begin the conversation.

133

"A terrible business," agreed the butler. "You don't think that Mr. Sarbella killed her?"

"You do?"

"What else could I believe, with all the queer happenings? But I hope not—as much for Mr. Gilmore's sake as anything, sir; he seems to take Mr. Sarbella's arrest almost as hard as the murder."

"She was a bad lot, your master's slain wife, Bates."

"I am not surprised at that," murmured the servant. "I sensed that she wasn't the right sort. I think we all realized that—except Mr. Kirklan."

"Of course he wouldn't; she was a remarkably beautiful woman, and he was in love with her. Quite a sudden marriage, I understand."

"Very sudden; a surprise and a shock to all of us."

"It's much too bad, Bates, that Mr. Gilmore did not marry a woman of the right kind—Miss Joan, say." Wiggly's tone was disarmingly careless, and Bates did not understand that information was being sought.

"Yes, it certainly is," agreed the butler earnestly, falling straightway into the little trap. "We were all hoping that it would turn out that way. All of us, except Mr. Kirklan, could see with half an eye that Miss Joan was in love with him, even if she is his stepsister; it cut her up terribly when she came home from Europe and found her here. Not only here, sir, but in Miss Joan's own room."

"The room where the murder was committed?"

"Exactly, sir; that was Miss Joan's old room—the one that she had occupied since she was quite a small girl. When she came back I didn't have the heart to tell her about the room. 'Bates,' she says to me, 'take the bags up to my room.' And I didn't have the heart to tell her—knowing how much store she put by it."

This information, verification of what Etta Griggs had told him, might mean something or nothing, Wiggly knew; probably nothing. It was just that he had that avidity of the trained newspaper reporter for all the facts, because experience had taught him it is often the smallest detail which, in the light of other things, achieves prime importance. And there was the black hairpin; he was thinking of that again.

That could not be overlooked.

At this moment Doctor Bushnell appeared from the room on the first floor, where he had placed Kirklan Gilmore, and whose bedside he was just leaving.

"Gilmore is in a bad, nervous state," he imparted after a nod to the reporter. "You saw him upstairs before you left for the village; he was bad enough then, but I'm afraid of a complete collapse—one of those highstrung, emotional chaps, you know. If his thoughts are allowed to torture him, they might even drive him to insanity; he must be kept quiet. Poor devil! It's much too bad that a love like that should have to be wasted on a woman like her. Then, to make matters worse, to make the shock double, the man whom he considered his friend—"

He paused, remembering the cigarette butt that Wiggly had taken down to the village.

"What did you discover?"

"That it was not Victor Sarbella's cigarette that had been dropped upon the rug. More than that, doctor, we've got another suspect now."

"Another suspect? What other suspect could there be?"

Briefly Wiggly Price told the physician of Sergeant Tish's appearance at Borough Hall, his identification of the murder gun, and the other matters which turned the finger of suspicion so strongly toward Don Haskins, the crook who had already been in flight from one murder charge. This information left Doctor Bushnell almost speechless.

"It's astounding!" he gasped. "Positively astounding! It—it does have a plausible sound, for a fact."

"The thing that bothers us," Wiggly told him, "is why Haskins should have been so careful to have it appear suicide. Surely no one besides Helen Gilmore knew that he was inside the house. Obviously he came for money —he had a hold of some kind on her; probably knew about her past and was levying blackmail; but there's no evidence that he got any money, and he didn't touch her jewelry."

"You can't spend jewelry without first pawning or selling it," the doctor said shrewdly; "possibly he realized that it would be too dangerous for him to risk appearing in a pawnshop. Perhaps he did get money."

"He wouldn't have had to kill her for that," countered Wiggly. "If he did know of her past, this knowledge alone was sufficient to extort money. He wouldn't have had to kill her. But let's be getting upstairs. Griggs and Sergeant Tish are waiting for you to let them into the murder room. Now that we're working from a new angle, it's best to go over the ground again, and we've daylight now."

The physician nodded and started for the stairs.

"The crook's guilt would be the most satisfactory solution," he said, "but it did look bad for Sarbella. Is he still being detained?"

"Yes. You can't blame Griggs for holding him; the murder isn't solved yet, and it won't be, to my notion, until a number of points are cleared up," answered Wiggly.

As they reached the second floor, Ham Griggs and Sergeant Tish were waiting, the former with considerable impatience. Doctor Bushnell unlocked the door of the murder chamber and threw it wide. The body of Helen Gilmore, as the butler had informed them, had been removed, but the

135

chaise longue, its creton upholstering stained with dark splotches, bore its mute testimony of the tragedy.

"Here we are," grunted the constable, "but I dunno what you expect to find more'n has already been found."

Sergeant Tish projected his rotund form to the center of the room, glanced about briefly, and then went to the windows, raising the shades to their full height so that all possible light would be admitted. At the second window the ripped curtain dangled before him and drew his attention.

"It would be my guess," he said, pointing to the curtain, "that this means one of two things: Either it was done in a struggle with the murdered woman, or when the murderer beat it through the window." He paused a moment and added: "Still, it doesn't look as if he'd have taken the time to shut the window behind him."

He peered through the glass to the roof of the porch, puffed out his round cheeks, and quickly threw up the sash. There had been no rain in weeks, and the porch shingles were covered with a coating of dust. This film was broken where Don Haskins' body had wiggled upward from the cornice in his careful approach to the window, and, in more places than one, the imprint of the man's stockinged feet showed. At Tish's grunt of elation, Constable Griggs dashed forward, with Doctor Bushnell and Wiggly behind him.

"Somebody either entered or left this room through the window!" exclaimed Tish. "There's his trail in the dust on the shingles."

"Entered!" said the newspaper reporter, his ears twitching. "You can see that those footprints—and the man was in his stockings—are all turned this way. Yes, he came in by the window, but he didn't leave by the window. Another check in Sarbella's favor.

"The man must have torn the curtain here, as he came into the room."

Constable Griggs gulped, but said nothing. Sergeant Tish bent forward and examined the pane of the raised sash. Clear and distinct there were the prints of a man's fingers—on the inside of the glass. These prints were punctuated with downward streaks, as if the fingers had slipped, but the whorls had not been obliterated; in fact they were clear and distinct.

Tish reached his pudgy fingers to the breast pocket of his coat and drew forth a Bertillon card which he had borrowed from headquarters, and which bore, in addition to rogues' gallery photographs, full-face and profile, of Don Haskins, the crook's finger prints.

He bobbled his head back and forth, getting the light at the best possible angle, and then he compared the finger prints on the window glass with those upon the card. He gave a grunt of satisfaction and nodded his head in affirmation.

"Yep, this clinches it, gents. These are Haskins' finger prints on the window. Good thing I brought this card along, huh?" It is hard for a man with a chubby face like Tish's to look grim, but his voice certainly was grim, as he added, "Haskins is wanted now for two murders. The job now is—find Haskins."

Wiggly Price leaned closer, and he, too, observed that the finger prints were on the inside of the pane.

"That means," he said, "that Haskins came in the window and closed it behind him. Those smudges at the top of the prints show that his fingers slipped a little on the glass, and that his pressure was downward. And, had he been raising the window, the finger prints would have been at the top of the sash rather than at the bottom."

"That's true," Tish agreed absently, returning the Bertillon card to his pocket and turning away from the window. "Haskins must have climbed to the roof from the porch below. Guess we'll find evidence of that, too, on the porch pillars, although it's not particularly important how he got up; the thing that counts is that he did, that the man was in the house, in this very room."

Ham Griggs realized that this new evidence, the incontrovertible proof of the finger prints, completely knocked the legs out from under his persistent theory of Sarbella's guilt, and for the moment he surrendered to a stunned and bewildered helplessness.

Doctor Bushnell's eyes remained upon the windowpane, with an intent and fascinated interest.

"Most remarkable!" he murmured. "How much can be proven by such a small thing as the touch of a man's finger! The one witness, I understand, that cannot lie. But what is the next move?"

"Find Don Haskins," Tish answered promptly.

"And that's a big order," sighed Wiggly Price. "The man's probably miles away from Greenacres by now. However there's nothing like being thorough, and, if Constable Griggs can get a posse together—"

"Huh!" snorted the constable. "You don't think he'd still be hangin' anywhere around Ardmore?"

"That depends on whether he got hold of any money," replied Sergeant Tish. "He was broke when he left New York, y'know." He took a step across the room and bent forward, as his foot crunched down upon a piece of the broken vase on the floor beside the table. He picked it up and held it in his fingers.

"Haskins probably lurched against the table and knocked it off," said Wiggly, explaining what it was. Tish glanced with slight interest at the shattered bit of porcelain and tossed it down. It did, of course, seem too trivial a thing for any serious consideration.

"We've put in a pretty good quarter of an hour here," grunted Tish, "and I guess we've done about all— Good Lord! What was that?"

From out in the hallway there had come to the ears of the four men the sound of a choking, terrified cry, a jarring, dull thud, a rending crash of broken glass. And then—silence.

138

# CHAPTER 22

## WHAT THE COOK SAW

There is no drama greater than the drama of life. The actors are more than often thrust into rôles that are not of their choosing, and they respond to cues that they do not recognize as cues, blindly obeying the director as he plunges them into unsought situations.

Mrs. Bogart, the Gilmore cook, who came to Greenacres each morning and returned to her home on the outskirts of Ardmore each evening, was in the kitchen; and, although it was baking day, not so much as a cup of flour had been sifted. She had arrived shortly after daybreak, to be greeted with news of the murder, and immediately she gave herself over to intermittent outbursts of weeping. Not that Mrs. Bogart, wide of hips, ample of bosom and stolid of countenance, with straight, black hair brushed severely back from her low and usually damp forehead, had any great feeling of bereavement; but, for all of her phlegmatic aspect, the cook was given to strong emotions. At the funeral of a comparative stranger, for instance, it was the sound of her sobs which arose above the muffled grief of the immediate family.

So Mrs. Bogart, except for brewing a bit of breakfast tea and toasting some slices of bread—badly burned, at that—neglected her kitchen work and gave way to her emotional nature. From Bates she had learned that the undertaker had arrived, and that "the new Mrs. Gilmore" had been, as she phrased it, "laid out" in one of the spare bedrooms on the second floor.

Now, Mrs. Bogart, her attendance at funerals amounting to an obsession, had gazed into the face of death innumerable times, but she had never known the thrill of looking into the features of one who had been murdered. People about Ardmore were in the habit of dying prosaically in their beds. This was an opportunity that might never come to her again; and well-to-do folks, she had observed, frequently had their funerals conducted privately, turning back the pryingly curious.

For some time Mrs. Bogart, whose place was strictly the kitchen, and who had no other household duties, had been trying to think up an excuse to visit the second floor, considering that this might offer her an opportunity of viewing the dead woman. Not possessing a particularly agile mind, it took her some little time to arrive at this bit of pretense, and she wouldn't have thought of it then except for some empty fruit jars. And, while the jars might have better gone to the basement, Mrs. Bogart craftily decided to carry them upstairs to the third floor and into the seldom-used storeroom.

"Goodness knows," she murmured, "I've been threatenin' for days upon days to get 'em out of the kitchen."

Straightway she mounted to a chair, took the fruit jars from the shelf where they had been temporarily placed, used a dish cloth in improvising a sling which would carry the full ten of them, and started for the third floor. At some time or another there had been a back stairs to the Gilmore house, but this had been closed off in making some modernizing alterations, so that Mrs. Bogart perforce had to wend her way to the reception hall and up the wide front stairway—hoping that Bates would not see her and order her back to her own domain.

Bates, however, did not appear to interrupt her little pilgrimage of morbid curiosity. She reached the second floor and, having to pass the room wherein Helen Gilmore had been shot to death, paused for a moment outside the narrowly open door, as she sought in vain to get anything like a good look inside. And, while she could not see much, her ears certainly got her a thrill, for it was at this moment that Sergeant Tish had said: "Yep, this clinches it, gents. These are Haskins' finger prints on the window. Good thing I brought this card along, huh? Haskins is wanted now for two murders. The job now is—find Haskins."

Mrs. Bogart's eyes bulged, and the empty fruit jars came perilously near crashing to the floor. Two murders! What did they mean? Who else had been murdered, and who was Haskins? Up to the moment of her last talk with Bates about the tragedy all suspicion had been leveled at Sarbella.

She tarried a moment, but there was nothing of the conversation on the other side of the door to enlighten her; not wishing to run the risk of being caught at eavesdropping, she moved on down the hall toward the stairs, the top of the house, and the seldom-used storeroom.

The entrance to the third floor stairway was inclosed, and it was reached by means of a door. Mrs. Bogart's hand went out to the knob; her strong fingers closed about it with a muscular grip, and then a startled gasp sounded on her lips, and a chill swept over her body. The door had yielded a bare inch when she felt a retarding pressure, holding it shut against her. Some one was on the other side!

"Mebbe—mebbe it's just stuck a little," she muttered in a gulping whisper. "Mebbe I imagined it." She braced her body, took a fresh and determined grip on the knob, and tried it again. Under exertion of this strong pull the door, still in the grasp of that opposing, unseen force, came toward her a bare inch or so, revealing to her staring eyes, indistinct in the shadows of the inclosed stairs, a bleary, unshaven face—a face hideously haggard, terrifying.

Mrs. Bogart staggered back with a choking, frightened cry upon her lips; the fruit jars crashed to the floor, with a thud and the sound of splintering glass, and the woman herself toppled over in a dead faint. From the side of her face there gushed a stream of blood, where the ragged edge of a broken jar had slashed the flesh. After the woman's cry, the four men in the room up the hall stood staring at each other for a brief moment.

"What's happened now?" gasped Wiggly Price, and Constable Griggs was too utterly stupefied to make a sound.

"It sounds like a woman's scream," said Doctor Bushnell, looking no less dazed than the rest.

Sergeant Tish was the first to leap into motion, projecting his pudgy body out into the hall with the other three at his heels. At the sight of the prostrate Mrs. Bogart, surrounded by broken and unbroken fruit jars, with the blood still streaming from her face, the New York detective stopped dead in his tracks.

"What's this?" he shouted. "Who is this woman, and what's happened to her?"

Constable Griggs edged forward and made a number of queer sounds before he finally found voice.

"It—it's Mrs. Bogart—she that does the cookin' for the Gilmores!" he gulped. "She's all bloody. Do—do you reckon that she's been murdered, too?"

Doctor Bushnell brushed past and knelt quickly to the floor at the side of the unconscious woman.

"She's not dead!" exclaimed Wiggly Price, noting the rapid rise and fall of Mrs. Bogart's bosom.

"Nor badly hurt, I think," said the physician, as he made a rapid examination. "The blood here is from a superficial wound; she's been cut by this broken glass. I wonder what *has* happened to her?" He jerked his head toward the newspaper man. "Get my medicine kit, Price," he commanded. "You'll find it downstairs; I left it on the table in the library."

Wiggly dashed down the stairs in instant response. Yes, what had happened to this woman whom Griggs identified as the Gilmore cook? Was this another angle to complicate the Greenacres tangle?

Passing through the hall into the library he heard a familiar voice; it was "Tip" Gregory, a star reporter for a rival New York newspaper, *The Transcript*, pleading with the butler for admittance and information, and Bates was sternly refusing him either. Wouldn't Gregory have gnashed his teeth in baffled rage if he had known that Wiggly Price had things so sweetly to himself!

But the situation was too tense for wasting any time or thoughts upon what was, after all, only an accidental triumph. He had the silly Etta Griggs to thank for being here, on the inside of a big story, instead of spending the morning canvassing the other papers for a job. In the library was Doctor Bushnell's medicine kit; he grabbed the handle of the little bag, wheeled and raced up the stairway again.

Mrs. Bogart was stirring, a moan passed her lips, but she had not returned to consciousness.

"Is she badly hurt, doctor?" Wiggly asked, as he placed the kit upon the floor.

"No, this cut would not cause unconsciousness. She must either have fainted and fallen, or fainted because she fell. Sometimes sudden and profuse bleeding causes—"

The physician's words broke off at the sound of a stifled cry coming from the turn of the hall, where the corridor led off to the wing of the house. Joan Sheridan, alarmed by Mrs. Bogart's scream of fright, had hurriedly left her room to investigate. Her face told of a sleepless, harrowed night, and now her eyes were wide and startled with this threat of fresh terror.

"Oh," she whispered, "it's Mrs. Bogart. In Heaven's name what—what has happened now?"

"That's what we are not exactly certain of, Miss Joan," answered Doctor Bushnell, as he cut a dressing for the wound in the cook's face. "She must have fallen. It is nothing serious; do not let it agitate you."

Wiggly Price had looked up quickly at the name of "Joan," for this was the first time that he had seen her, the stepsister who was so much in love with Kirklan Gilmore. She was not aware of his scrutiny, so he had ample opportunity to study her closely. His experience at reporting had given him a sort of instinctive ability to gauge the human emotions, and he had a feeling that there was more than horror in the girl's dark eyes, and he read it with one brief word—fear.

This look of fear was not dissipated by the physician's assurance that Mrs. Bogart's injury was superficial. It remained, a peculiar, almost indescribable expression.

"Your mother, Miss Joan, is resting quietly after the shock?" murmured Doctor Bushnell, stanching the flow of blood in the unconscious woman's cheek. "I will see her again presently."

"Y-yes," Joan Sheridan said faintly; "mother is sleeping, and Bates has told me that Mr. Sarbella had been placed under arrest."

"That's true," nodded the doctor, "but it looks now that he will be released very shortly. You were right when you were so sure that Sarbella was innocent, and I have a new respect for a woman's intuition. I think you'd better go back to your room, please."

But the doctor's reassuring words seemed to have other than a soothing effect upon Joan; if possible, her face became a shade more pale. Certainly she gave a violent start, and that smoldering light of fear leaped into a wild light of terror.

"You mean—" The shaking whisper that came from her lips was hardly audible.

"Please, Joan, please!" exclaimed the doctor. "This is no time for questions. I've a fainting woman on my hands, and a new suspect entirely, a crook who got in by the window. The gun was his. No more questions now."

A gasp that seemed to be at the same time amazement and relief came from the girl; a look of bewilderment showed in her face. Her hands, so tightly clenched at her sides, relaxed; swiftly she turned and disappeared around the bend in the hall.

Wiggly Price's ears twitched violently, for he, unlike the others—and he, too, would have doubtless overlooked it but for the black hairpin and the gossip Etta Griggs had given him—had observed her agitation when told that Sarbella had practically been removed as a suspect, and her surprise and the relaxing tenseness when she learned of the other.

Did this mean that she had knowledge of the crime, which, for reasons of her own, she had kept to herself? With this Wiggly linked still another question: Why had Joan Sheridan been so positive of Victor Sarbella's innocence? For Wiggly was of the opinion that "woman's intuition" is something greatly exaggerated. The answer to the latter question was in itself unimportant; for that matter, so had Kirklan Gilmore been certain, to the point of vigorous protest, that the artist had not fired the fatal shot.

Wiggly made up his mind then and there that, while Constable Griggs was searching for Don Haskins, he would be searching for the answer to Joan Sheridan's puzzling behavior. He was certain there must be something behind it, a vital something that would have an important bearing on the crime.

Doctor Bushnell had completed dressing Mrs. Bogart's wound, having delayed restoratives until this was done. Now he was chafing her wrists briskly, and the woman was showing signs of coming to her senses. With startling suddenness her eyes flew open, and she sat erect; since her first conscious thought was a return to the moment of her swoon, a fresh cry of terror burst from her throat. It trailed off into a gurgle, as she realized that she was not now alone.

"It's all right, Mrs. Bogart," the physician told her soothingly. "You've had a nasty fall and cut yourself a little on those broken jars; but it's nothing to worry about."

"That man!" cried Mrs. Bogart. "Where—where did he go? It's Heaven's own blessing that he didn't murder me in my tracks. He was peering out at me, and everything went dizzy black in front of me. I—"

"Her head ain't right yet," grunted Constable Griggs. Mrs. Bogart, letting her heavy fingers touch gingerly to her bandaged face, heard the local officer's skeptical remark and bridled in indignation.

"I tell you I seen him!" she shrilled, pointing to the door which closed off the third-floor stairs. "I seen him behind there. He was holdin' the door shut on me. I was takin' these jars up to the storeroom. I seen him—lookin' out at me through the crack. He's there now, if he didn't run out. I tell you I seen him!"

All four of the men exchanged quick, startled, almost incredulous glances. The same thought had leaped into all their minds. Sergeant Tish, staring at the closed door, mechanically hitched his gun holster within easier reach.

"Do you think it's possible, men, that she did see a man, and that he is —" began Doctor Bushnell.

"Yes, it must be Haskins!" cried Wiggly. "Haskins is still in the house! We dashed out into the hall when she screamed. The man's had no chance of escape."

Sergeant Tish pursed his lips, frowned, and shook his head. "I can't believe it," he muttered. "I can't believe Haskins would be such a boob, hiding on the scene of the crime all these hours after the murder has been committed. It's ridiculous."

Constable Ham Griggs decided he had been in the background long enough; events had been developing too fast for him to keep pace with them, but here was a situation that he could cope with. It required no deductions, only action. He took a decisive step forward, dragging forth a somewhat ancient forty-five-caliber revolver, which he gave a dramatic flourish.

"Stand back!" he roared. "I'm the officer in charge here, and I'm goin' up there to get my man!"

# CHAPTER 23

## THE TRAPPED RAT

With the breath wheezing noisily through his parted lips, which were twisted back so that his clenched teeth were bared, Don Haskins leaned tensely against the wall of the storeroom on the third floor of the Gilmore house. Grim and desperate terror held him in its grip.

"They've got me—they've got me now!" he groaned. "Caught like a rat in a trap!"

Half the night and all of the morning he had tried in vain to slip out of the house—somewhere, anywhere. Each effort had been frustrated by the danger of discovery; at each attempt there had been voices or footsteps in the hall, or floating warningly up the stairs. Then the coming of daylight had made the contemplated dash all the more hazardous.

He had about made up his mind to wait for another coming of darkness, when he had heard the arrival of a car, and, peering down from the narrow dormer window, he had seen the arrival of Detective Sergeant Tish. The coming of Tish naturally filled him with wild terror, for that could mean but one thing—the New York detective had trailed him to Greenacres!

So, after several minutes of tortured indecision, he had crept down the inclosed stairs, determined to make a break for it.

He could not put up a fight, for he had no weapon. While he had crouched at the foot of the stairs, ears straining in an effort to catch any sound of warning from the other side of the panel, Mrs. Bogart had turned the knob, and Haskins had seized it from the inside, holding the door fast. Then she had yanked it again, the eyes of the two met through the narrow crack, and the woman had screamed.

For Don Haskins there had been but one choice, that was to hurry back to the storeroom and wait. There was no bolt on the door, but he barricaded it with a packing box filled with non-descript odds and ends, such as people relegate to the garret. There was no means of escape except the stairs; the dormer window mocked him with its deep, unbroken drop downward. And no weapon; even the clutter of stuff that half filled the storeroom offered him nothing that would serve as a cudgel. So, helpless, defenseless, muttering curses between his locked teeth, he waited. He wondered why it was so long, why the New York copper did not come pounding up the stairs to get him. His eyes were upon the door, his gaze intent upon the knob—watching for it to turn. And then he got an idea!

The knob was held in place by a screw, and, for lack of a screw driver, he went to the task with his finger nail. The screw was set fast, and the nail tore down to the quick, but he did not notice the twinge of pain, merely attacked the screw with the thumb nail of the other hand. At last it turned, and the heavy metal knob was free.

Haskins, that his shoes might make no alarming sound upon the bare boards of the storeroom, was in his stockings. Hastily he tore one of his socks free from his foot, dropped the doorknob into it and he had a deadly slung shot that he could swing with telling effect. Not much of a weapon, perhaps, but vastly better than no weapon at all. He put on both shoes, the one over a bare foot, and again waited with tense, twitching nervousness.

It must have been another five minutes—to Haskins the minutes dragged into the length of hours—before he heard a voice raised to a bellow and the tramp of heavy feet upon the stairs. He flattened his body even closer to the wall, at a point where he would be behind the door when it opened, as he took a tighter grip about the weighted sock.

There may have been some doubts as to Constable Griggs' nimbleness of mind, but there could be no doubt as to his personal courage, as, yards ahead of Sergeant Tish, he dashed, two and three steps at a time, to the third floor.

"Come on outta there an' surrender!" roared Ham Griggs. "Dead or alive, Haskins—that goes for you!"

But Don Haskins did not come out to surrender. He made not the slightest sound. Griggs again shouted, but still there was no response, and he began to share Tish's doubts of the wanted man being in the house. Perhaps Mrs. Bogart's story had been purely a figment of the imagination.

Without, however, relaxing the vigilant position of his gun, he reached forward and tried the door. It moved back a little, and he met the obstruction of the barricading packing box. The constable applied the pressure of his shoulder, and his free hand cautiously cocked the hammer of the revolver. The door was forced back another few inches.

The barred door, of course, was proof that the storeroom was occupied; he paused a moment to peer through the narrow opening. No signs of Haskins.

"He's here," he yelled down the stairs to Tish, who was looking up from the bottom. "He's got the door blocked. I'm goin' in, and I'm goin' in a-shootin'." Again his body battered against the door.

146

Don Haskins, his mouth parted into a terrible grimace, swung back his arm. As the constable's head and shoulders appeared at the edge of the door, the sock, the metal knob stuffed wickedly in the toe, described a swift arc and caught Griggs a heavy blow on the skull.

With a grunt he pitched forward to the floor in a senseless heap; the convulsion of his body pulled the trigger of the revolver, and its roaring, angry voice thundered through the upper part of the house. The gun slid across the boards and bumped against the leg of the discarded couch.

Haskins dropped his improvised weapon and leaped for the gun; his body had scarcely straightened when Sergeant Tish came pounding and panting up the steps, drawn automatic in his hand. As Haskins whirled, he again faced this Nemesis who had trapped him at Eighth Avenue Annie's. No word was spoken; both knew it was one or the other.

Haskins fired first, but only by the difference of a split second; the two shots rang out almost as one. Sergeant Tish's shoulder became suddenly numb, a searing numbness, as hot lead bored the flesh. His arm dropped limply helpless to his side, and a sickening nausea paled the chubby round-ness of his cheeks.

The other man reeled on his feet and steadied himself against the wall. A gasping gurgle, that trailed off into a curse, burst through his hideously parted lips, and his left hand, pressing to his waist, became red with a trickle of crimson.

But Haskins did not fire again; there was no need. Sergeant Tish's fingers had lost all their strength, and the automatic clumped to the floor. He could offer no resistance when Haskins stumbled forward, cleared the body of the unconscious constable, and went plunging down the stairs. In the doorway at the foot of the steps Wiggly Price and Doctor Bushnell were staring upward. Haskins lifted the revolver menacingly.

"Get outta my way!" he gritted. "I'll kill the first man that tries to stop me."

It would have been a foolhardy thing to have opposed the flight of this armed, desperate man, wanted for murder, trying to beat the electric chair. Doctor Bushnell, clutching Wiggly Price's arm, made haste to get out of Haskins' path. Mrs. Bogart screamed shrilly and dashed wildly for the first door. She hurled herself into the room and braced her body against the panel.

Haskins, as he reached the second floor, was reeling like a drunken man. His left hand, still clutching his body near the top of his trousers was hot and sticky with his own blood. He reached the top of the second stairway which led down to the first floor—and what? Even in his desperately chaotic state of mind, he knew that the odds were against him. But any-thing was better than the chair, and it was that—or this. He felt his strength

147

swiftly ebbing from his body, slipping away from him through that hot, burning hole in his abdomen.

Downstairs, Bates, the butler, had heard the double shot and for a moment was incapable of movement. It was only with supreme effort that he got his frail old legs in motion and propelled himself toward the stairs. Halfway up he faced Haskins, who held weavingly to the bannister rail.

"Out—out of my way!" ordered Haskins, but his voice was thick, hoarsely unsteady. The revolver wabbled with the lurching of his body. Before Bates, petrified with terror at the menace of the pointing gun, could obey, the wounded man at the top of the stairs sagged forward and went crashing down, sliding, bumping, clawing, and his body came to a halt on the first landing at Bates' feet. He had just enough strength to lift himself weakly to his elbow.

"That dirty dick—got me—good!" he muttered. "I—I hope I croaked—him. Curse the cops! The cops and the skirts—to hell with both of 'em!" He coughed chokingly. "I'm dyin'," he screeched. "I'm bleedin' to death—inside."

His distorted mouth was flecked with red.

148

# CHAPTER 24

## HASKINS KEEPS HIS SECRET

Stunned and sick from the paralyzing impact of Haskins' bullet, Sergeant Tish did not realize that his own shot had found an even more vital mark; he had failed to see the trickle of crimson that welled from between the wanted man's fingers, as the latter had pressed his hand hard against his body. In a daze the New York detective only realized that the desperate fugitive was escaping from him a second time, and that his flight must be stopped. As his thoughts cleared a little, it occurred to him that Haskins might try to leave in the police car out in front of the house, but he would have a hard job of that, for the plain-clothes man had the key to the ignition switch in his pocket.

The local constable still lay in a huddled, grotesque heap on the floor, and he had not moved. Despite his own haste to pursue Haskins—his injury would not stop that—Tish leaned over Ham Griggs, puzzled that there was no evidence of a terrible, lethal wound. He had taken it for granted that Haskins must have had another weapon in addition to the one left beside the body of the murdered Helen Gilmore, and that he had shot down Griggs, as the latter had burst in upon him in the attempted capture. All he could find was a purpling swelling at the edge of Griggs' temple; and then he saw the improvised weapon, the strangest that had ever come to his notice—the sock weighted with the doorknob.

"Huh!" said Sergeant Tish, with a grunt that was more than half a groan. He saw what had happened. "Haskins beaned 'im with that thing, handed him a knock-out, and then took his gun away from him." He bent still a little lower and perceived that the constable's breathing was reassuringly regular. "Don't look like he was goin' to croak."

As Don Haskins collapsed and went crashing down the stairs, Wiggly Price and Doctor Bushnell stood gaping at each other, both struggling with indecision as to which direction they would turn as their first move to follow this breathless race of happenings. What had happened upstairs they did not know, only that to their ears had come the ominous sound of three pistol shots, and that neither Constable Griggs nor Sergeant Tish had come down.

"What's happened to the two officers?" cried Doctor Bushnell. "Perhaps —" Before he could finish the sentence, Tish appeared at the head of the inclosed stairway, his right arm dangling limply, a trickle of blood seeping down beneath the edge of his coat sleeve, twisting into a fantastic crimson design about his wrist and the back of his hand.

"What's happened up there?" shouted the physician. "Heavens, man, you're wounded! Griggs—"

Tish had retrieved the automatic and held it in his left hand rather awkwardly, but determined to use it if he could.

"The constable is knocked cold," he said, as he came down the steps. "You'd better look after him, doctor. Haskins has—"

Wiggly Price had rushed to the head of the other stairs, from where he could see Don Haskins sprawled upon the first landing, gasping for breath and mopping the foam from his mouth with the back of his hand. The revolver had slid several steps down and was safely out of the man's reach.

"Here he is, sergeant!" shouted the newspaper man. "He nicked you, but you got him worse than that."

Again Doctor Bushnell struggled with indecision. Three men wounded! Which of them should have first call upon his professional services? Don Haskins' choking wail, coming from down the front stairs, decided him.

"I'm dyin'!" he croaked. "I say I'm dyin'." And with the next breath he muttered a vicious curse upon "the cops." But, before the doctor could move out of his tracks, Joan Sheridan had again come flying from the east wing of the house and clutched his arm. At the moment of her appearance she saw Tish.

"Those shots—what do they mean?" she panted. "What—what has happened now?"

"We have caught the murderer," answered Doctor Bushnell, gently pushing her away. "The crook who killed Kirklan's wife was in hiding on the third floor." Another groan came from Haskins. "There was some shooting; the man's desperately wounded. I am going to see now. Go back to your room, Joan; you've had enough horror."

But the girl crept to the top of the stairs after him and stared down with a shudder.

"I—I can't understand!" she whispered. "They say that man killed her. I —I can't understand!" she whispered. "They say that man killed her. I can't understand!"

Had Wiggly Price been privileged to hear those whispered words of Joan's it would have added fresh fuel to his smoldering suspicion that she knew more about the death of Helen Gilmore than she was willing to tell.

The newspaper man had hurried down the stairs and, elbowing the butler out of the way, bent over Haskins. A moment later Doctor Bushnell had joined him, Tish close behind. The doctor shook his head gravely, as he saw the bloodstained saliva about Haskins' lips.

"Internal hemorrhage," he murmured. "I don't think there's much chance for him."

As if to verify this diagnosis, Haskins gave a gasping cough, and the crimson foam became a trickle.

"Ain'tcha gonna call a priest?" he murmured. "I'm dyin', I tell you—dyin'."

"Keep him alive, doc, until I get a full confession out of him," urged Sergeant Tish. "Haskins, come through; make a clean breast of—"

"No questions for a moment," broke in the physician. "Let him be quiet until I see what can be done for him. No matter what he's done, he's entitled to the best a doctor can give him. It's barely possible that an immediate operation—"

Don Haskins made a half-sobbing, half-growling protest.

"Nix on the—operation stuff. It wouldn't do me no good—anyhow; I tell you that I'm bleedin' to death—inside of me."

Doctor Bushnell jerked his head toward Wiggly.

"Help me with him," he ordered. "We'll have to get him somewhere, so that I can see what can be done for him." And to the butler: "Bates, up the stairs quick—get my bag. It's on the floor in the hall—near the other stairs. And, Bates, where can we take this man?"

"There are but two guest rooms, sir; one Mr. Sarbella occupied, and the other—the body has been placed there."

"Then it will have to be Sarbella's room," declared the doctor. "Help me up with him, Mr. Price. Careful, Haskins; the more exertion the more the bleeding and the slimmer your chances."

Sergeant Tish's bullet-punctured shoulder, now that the numbness of the thudding impact was passing, throbbed with an excruciating agony, but he clamped his teeth together, having no intention of making a demand upon Doctor Bushnell's professional services until a statement was had from the possibly dying prisoner. He could offer no assistance, but he followed back up the stairs, as Bushnell and the newspaper reporter supported Haskins to the second floor and along the hall to the guest room which had been Sarbella's.

Joan Sheridan tarried indecisively another moment or so and then she returned to her own room, her mind in no way cleared of the bewilderment. She longed for explanations, but knew this was no time to ask questions.

In the guest room Haskins was placed upon the bed where, as his first act in an effort to save the mans' life, Doctor Bushnell quickly prepared an internal astringent, a drug calculated to check the inward bleeding. Then he examined the wound with the aid of a probe; Haskins' slowing pulse warned the physician that life was ebbing, and that there was no hope.

"The nearest hospital is fifteen miles away, and the trip would be fatal," he said. "And I have never specialized in surgery. I have tried to check the internal blood flow, but there is nothing else I can do. All that I can suggest is to call Doctor Hollis, who is a surgeon. If the man is still alive when Hollis gets here—"

"It—it ain't no use," gasped Don Haskins. "I'm gonna croak, and I know I'm gonna croak."

"Yes, Haskins, it looks that way," nodded Doctor Bushnell; "if you've got any statement to make you'd better make it now. Anyhow I'll telephone Doctor Hollis and then look after Ham Griggs. Unconscious, didn't you say, Sergeant Tish? Lord, the house has suddenly become a hospital! What about your own injury?"

Tish shook his head. "I can wait—until Haskins has talked," he said. "You'd better look after the constable first, anyhow. It may be worse than it seemed to me."

Don Haskins was breathing heavily, his eyes closed, his hands clenched. As the doctor left the room, Tish leaned forward, but became dizzily faint and had to seek the support of a chair.

"You might as well talk, Haskins," he said. "What made you shoot Gilmore's wife?"

The prisoner's lips twisted. "You're gonna give me the rap for that?" he muttered weakly. "Tryin' to hang two croaks onto me—and I never did either one of 'em." His eyes opened slowly. "Dago Mike—did he tell the cops that I did for the watchman—that loft job in the Bronx?"

Tish nodded. "Yes, that's what he told the inspector," he answered.

"It's a lie," said Haskins, but without any great emotion of indignation; perhaps, being so sure that he was dying, he did not care, or it might have been that he did not have the strength left for vehemence. Still, again, it was possible that it sounded so flat and colorless, this denial, because it lacked the ring of truth. "Dago Mike done it. I knowed he'd squeal; he always was a dirty rat. I was a fool to go into a job with that—that scum. Yeah, Dago Mike was the one that did the watchman."

Tish winced with a fresh throb of pain from his shoulder. "Why did you shoot Gilmore's wife?" he repeated.

Haskins turned his head, let his mouth twist into a harsh smile, and, lifting his hand slowly, wiped his lips with the back of his hand. There was again a little blood.

"Gilmore's wife?" he retorted in a hoarse whisper. "She was—my wife!"

Wiggly Price started forward with an exclamation of amazement, and his ears danced with excitement.

"W-what?" he gasped. "Y-your wife? You mean that? Great heavens, Tish, I believe he's telling the truth!"

The New York detective gestured for silence with his uninjured arm.

"Shut up!" he commanded tersely.

"Yeah, that's—that's what she was—my wife," went on Don Haskins in a whisper, which, as he continued to talk, was at times hardly audible. "She done bigamy when she married—Gilmore. She—she never got no divorce —from me.

"I'm gonna talk, see. What I'm tellin' you is strictly on the level. I know I'm goin'—fast; there ain't no use for me to—cover up. Curse the skirts! If it wasn't—for her—" His voice trailed off in a choking excitement, his eyes closed momentarily, and the two eagerly listening men were afraid that it was all over with him, but Haskins looked at them again.

"I—I guess she thought she'd shook me—after I busted up a mash she had on a guy named Sarbella; but I kept cases on her—got a line on her when I come back from Chi—parole from a long stretch at Joliet.

"Then I gets into that Bronx job jam, and I needs dough—bad. And quick. So I send for—for her, and she—" He had to stop again to wipe his mouth free of that trickle of blood which oozed upward from his punctured stomach.

"And she came to Eighth Avenue Annie's," supplied Tish. "She gave you some money. We know that much; go on, Haskins."

"She was comin' back—today—with a thousand iron men," proceeded the prisoner's weakening whisper. "Then Annie tipped off the cops. Curse the old hag! I dunno why Annie—"

"She did not," grunted Sergeant Tish; "I saw her buying some duds and trailed her. Annie didn't double cross you."

"When I lays you out—and beats it," went on Haskins, "I—I guess you know part of it, how I swipes a taxi an' blows out here?" Tish nodded. "I sneaks around the house an' spots—Helen's window, does a porch-climber stunt to the roof, gets into her room, an'—"

"And shot her—with my gun," prompted the detective. But, if Haskins was the murderer, he did not fall into this trap of suggestion.

"I'm givin' it to you—straight," his whisper went on. "I didn't croak her; I—I grabbed her, and she—got the gat—outta my pocket, but I didn't know that—then. We hears a door slam, an' we thinks it's Gilmore—in the —next room. She sneaks me into the hall and tells me to hide—third floor. Says she'll get me some dough and get me—away."

The man's words were so faint and came from his lips in such a jerky tumble that both Tish and Wiggly Price had to lean close in order to hear

153

the rest of his story.

"When I gets up there—third floor, I knows it was her—took—the gun. I—I guess she was afraid I was gonna—use it—on her. She knowed she'd done me dirt. Curse her—she made a bum—outta me."

"I—I wants that gun, see! After a while I sneaks back down to—second floor—to make her—gimme the gat. As I gets to—to the foot of the stairs I hears a scream. It comes from—from her room. Then—then there's—a shot."

Both Tish and Wiggly looked skeptical at this, but neither of them spoke; both sensed that Don Haskins had something to add. They were right; he had. After another moment of silence, Haskins' lips moved again.

"The—the door—was open; the—the light was burnin'—inside, an' I seen—the one who did the job—comin' out—of the room."

Sergeant Tish snorted derisively.

"Haskins," he flung out, "you're lying! Are you going to face your Maker with that lie on your conscience? That stuff's the bunk. You killed her, and you might as well come through."

"Wait a minute, sergeant," whispered Wiggly; "ask him whom he saw coming out of the room. There's a chance that he may be telling us the truth!"

Tish hesitated a moment, stirred in his chair, winced with the pain of the movement, and then accepted the suggestion.

"There's just one way that you can prove that you are giving us straight goods, Haskins," he said, "and that's to tell us who came out of the room."

Don Haskins closed his eyes again, and a queer, crooked, mirthless grimace caught up the corners of his mouth, a grimace all the more horrible because a fresh trickle of crimson seeped across his lips and trickled down his unshaven chin. Whether he had begun his story with the intention of ending it at this most unsatisfactory point, or whether the abrupt termination was a matter of sudden decision, can never be known.

"She—she was—no good," he told them in an almost inaudible whisper. "She—she made a bum outta me when—when she gimme the go-by. She made that Sarbella kid do a Dutch, and she handed Gilmore—a mean wallop. She got—what was comin' to her. If I wasn't gonna croak—I'd have to talk to save—my own self; but I ain't gonna make no trouble—for nobody —on account—killin' her. That's all you get—from me."

"He's lying!" gritted Tish. "Sure he's lying. He killed her."

But Wiggly Price was not so sure. If Haskins, as it seemed, knew he was dying, why should he lie? There was one possibility why he should; it might have occurred to him that he still had a chance to cheat death, and he had cunningly concocted this yarn out of the whole cloth.

154

Thoughts and theories leaped through Wiggly's mind. If Haskins' story, improbable as it sounded, were true, the Greenacres mystery had been returned to its first status, and suspicion returned even more strongly to Victor Sarbella. Guilt lay between the artist and Joan Sheridan. Again the newspaper man thought of the girl's agitation when told that suspicion had turned away from Sarbella, her relief and yet bewilderment when she had heard that circumstances pointed to Haskins, the crook; and he thought, too, of the black hairpin.

"You're lying, Haskins," Tish said again; "but what gets me is that you didn't make a break for it after the shooting."

The wounded man stirred slightly. "I—I tried—to make—my getaway," he whispered, "but there was two guys comin' up the front stairs, an' I hadda dodge back—to—the attic."

"Haskins," burst out Wiggly, "the person you saw coming out of that room—was it a man or a woman?"

But Don Haskins shook his head feebly. He made no other response. A little later, while Tish still plied insistent and exasperated questions, the man's body twitched and relaxed; then a gush of crimson poured from his mouth.

"He's dying!" cried Wiggly and made a leap toward the door to summon Doctor Bushnell.

It was too late. Haskins' eyes had opened and were fixed glassily upon the ceiling. He was dying with his last, stubborn silence unbroken; and the Gilmore tragedy was yet to be solved.

155

# CHAPTER 25

## THE SKEPTICISM OF SERGEANT TISH

The doctor had found Constable Griggs' injury worse than he had anticipated, for Haskins had struck a vicious blow with the doorknob wickedly concealed within the toe of his sock; there was a bad skull fracture that threatened fatal results. With Bates to help him, Doctor Bushnell had placed Ham Griggs upon the discarded couch and had just completed a painstaking examination, when Wiggly Price came pounding up the third floor stairs to the storeroom.

"Quick, doc!" panted the newspaper man. "Haskins is dying; he's got another hemorrhage—a worse one. I'm afraid he's a goner."

The doctor motioned to the butler.

"You stay here with the constable, Bates," he ordered. "I'll be back in a moment; we've got to get this man to the hospital. He's dangerously hurt, Price; a bad skull fracture." As he spoke, he was following the reporter back down the stairs. "I'm not surprised about Haskins. But there was nothing more than I could do for him, and Griggs needed me, too."

"The other doctor, the surgeon, you telephoned for—"

"Is operating at a hospital in New York this morning; I was unable to reach him. But, for that matter, I do not believe any human agency could have saved Haskins. Perhaps, after all, it's better this way; circumstances are doing what the State would doubtless have done—exacted his life in payment."

They had reached the door of the guest room. Sergeant Tish still sat in his chair beside the bed; he turned slowly, painfully.

"You're too late," he said.

Doctor Bushnell stepped forward, was silent for moment; then he inclined his head.

"Yes," he agreed. "I'm too late, but it doesn't matter; even an operation was a forlorn hope. I could not have kept him alive; nothing could have done that, I think." He stared down at the dead man's contorted features. "An evil face," he murmured. "An evil end for an evil life. Did he make a confession, sergeant?"

"No, confound his stubbornness!" growled Sergeant Tish. "He gave us a wild kind of yarn that explained his connection with the Gilmore woman, his hold on her, and how he got into the house, but denied that he did the shooting. Of course he was lying."

Doctor Bushnell nodded. "He killed her—certainly," he agreed. "The way he knocked out Griggs and shot you is proof that he was a cold-blooded killer. What was the hold that he had over the dead woman?"

"She was Haskins' wife—his legal wife."

The physician gasped and, thinking of the beautiful Helen Gilmore, stared down at the hideous face of the dead criminal, with a look of amazement that bordered upon incredulity.

"What—the wife of that man? It seems absurd, absolutely preposterous! I find it next to impossible to believe it. Then, when she married Kirklan, she—"

"Committed bigamy," finished Sergeant Tish with a jerk of his head that sent another stab of pain through his wounded shoulder. "That's it, doctor; and that is what gave him a hold on her—why he was able to have her visit him at Eighth Avenue Annie's day before yesterday, give him money and agree to give him still more; that was why he fled to her for protection and was hiding when I stumbled onto him. I guess that part of it is true, all right.

"Perhaps not so amazing as it would seem. Haskins was not always the bum he is now. They used to call him Nifty Don in his palmy days; he's hit the skids since then. He blames her for slipping; she threw him over, as I got it. I wish you'd take a look at this shoulder of mine, doc; the wound is throbbing like a sixty-horse-power engine."

Doctor Bushnell murmured a hasty apology for neglecting him so long.

"I'll have a look at that right now, Sergeant Tish. Three emergency cases all at one time is a big order for a doctor. Price, will you get my kit from the third floor? I'm hoping there's enough gauze and bandages to do."

"The constable come around all right?" asked Tish, as the newspaper man hurried from the room.

"A bad skull fracture, sergeant, where Haskins struck him a terrific blow on the side of the head. I'm taking him to the hospital just as quickly as I've got you patched up a bit. You, too, if there is need."

"Don't think it'll be necessary, doc. Lord, what a wild morning it's been!" He gritted his teeth, as the physician slipped down the coat sleeve and began ripping away the shirt. "What's happened to Gilmore? Strange that he didn't show up with all the racket."

"Probably asleep under the influence of the opiate that I gave him to re-lax his strain," answered Doctor Bushnell. "He's one of those high-strung, emotional fellows, and I couldn't risk too much nervous tension with him.

157

He was on the verge of a collapse. Poor devil! He's a good sort; doesn't deserve what that woman has done to him."

Wiggly returned with the doctor's kit, and Bushnell began to work swiftly; the wound in the detective's shoulder had bled but little. The bullet, he found, had struck the collar bone at a deflecting angle, plowing for a brief distance along the top of the clavicle, where it was imbedded just beneath the skin.

"You're a lucky man, Sergeant Tish," grunted the doctor. "If that had been a little lower there would have been the very devil to pay. The worst danger is that the bone has been cracked, and I do not think it has been. This treatment, of course, is only temporary; I'll look after you again later."

It was the work of but a few minutes to make a shallow incision which removed the bullet, cauterize the wound, and apply dressings.

"I shall take Griggs to the hospital in my car," said Bushnell, as he finished. "The butler can go along with me. We'll be back within an hour or so—just as soon as I can manage it. I suppose Sarbella will have to stay in jail until Griggs recovers consciousness and releases him."

Wiggly broke a considerable silence.

"It's my notion," he said, "that Sarbella had better stay right where he is until—well, until the case has been cleared up completely."

The doctor stared in surprise. "What do you mean by that?" he exclaimed. "Not that there's any doubt but Haskins killed the woman?"

"Not the slightest doubt that Haskins did it," Tish declared in a positive tone. "I don't take any stock in his story—that is, the part of it in which he denied doing the shooting. I suppose the rest of it is straight enough."

Doctor Bushnell looked reprovingly at the newspaper man. "I must say," he said severely, "that you are a most perverse young man. When the weight of all the evidence was strictly against Sarbella, you were trying to prove his innocence. Yet now, when the discovery and capture of this desperate criminal—the legal husband of the dead woman—makes it practically certain that Haskins was the murderer, you suddenly change front and —"

"Perhaps it's because I've got more faith in the truth of Haskins' story than Sergeant Tish has," broke in Wiggly Price. "In my mind the case against Sarbella is stronger than ever—circumstantially. But, with what we've got, I don't think for a minute that a jury would ever convict him. Haskins' account of things does explain how Sarbella, or"—he hesitated cautiously—"or some other person might have got possession of the gun."

"Or some other person!" exclaimed the doctor impatiently. "Tut, Price, don't be such an utter ass. I've something more important to do than listen to a new crop of empty theories. What other person, pray, have you in mind?"

Wiggly felt that any mention of Joan Sheridan would arouse the physician's antagonism; moreover it would serve no purpose. So he chose the wise course of answering the question only with a shrug of the shoulders.

"The constable is a heavy man, and the butler old and rather feeble," he said, abruptly switching the subject; "perhaps I'd better help you get him downstairs and into your car."

"Yes; please," grunted Doctor Bushnell.

Tish trailed along behind the two and waited on the second floor, while the physician and Wiggly went to the storeroom to carry down the unconscious Ham Griggs.

"He hasn't moved a muscle since you left, Doctor Bushnell," reported the butler. "Except that I can see him breathing I'd think he was dead."

The doctor issued brief, terse instructions, and he and Wiggly formed a human packsaddle by grasping each other's wrists. In this way, their heavy burden between them, they made their way down from the third floor, while Bates hurried off to get a supply of pillows for padding the tonneau of the doctor's car.

"I was going to suggest that you come along," Bushnell suggested; but Wiggly shook his head.

"No, I'd like to stay here," he answered. "Bates will do as well as I for your trip."

"Oh, I see," the physician said shortly, "you want to gather some new theories about the tragedy. You're making a fool of yourself, Price; the case, thank Heaven, is solved."

"Hope so, doctor, but that remains to be seen."

"Certainly it's solved!" exclaimed Bushnell with asperity. "As deputy coroner I shall convene a jury and hold an inquest as quickly as possible—this afternoon. I'll bring the district attorney back with me when I return from the hospital. The verdict will be a mere matter of formality."

"Yes," agreed Wiggly, "a mere matter of formality, unless we turn up something new."

The butler came hurrying out of the house with the pillows; the doctor took them from him and arranged them supportingly behind the unconscious constable's shoulders.

"Get your hat, Bates," he instructed; "you'll have to go along."

Three or four minutes later the physician's machine, Bushnell at the wheel and Bates in the rear seat with the insensible Griggs, rolled down the white-graveled driveway, and Wiggly returned to the house, wondering a little what had happened to Tip Gregory, reporter for the rival paper, *The Transcript*. Probably Tip, rebuffed at Greenacres, had gone to the village in search of information.

Sergeant Tish had come down from the second floor and had established himself in one of the library's roomy chairs, making himself as comfortable as his twinging shoulder would permit. His roundish face was still gray with the throbbing pain, but he endured it with fortitude.

"Well, young man," he grunted, "you've got a darn good story, and you ought to be satisfied. Seems to me that it's good enough to suit your paper without your trying to add anything imaginative."

"Meaning," replied Wiggly, "that you'd have me quit thinking. Nope, I stick to my hunch that Haskins' story was what he said it was—strictly on the level."

"Bunk!" snorted Tish.

"Let's talk it over, sergeant," Wiggly urged earnestly as, hands rammed deep into his pockets, he strode up and down the room, his ears twitching slightly. "Does it seem reasonable to you that Haskins would have left the automatic behind him after the shooting?"

"Humph!" the New York detective grunted non-committally.

"That gun," went on the newspaper man, "was his one friend, the only hope that he had if he were cornered. Besides, leaving the gun behind served no purpose—no purpose whatever. In fact, if he had the brains to reason it out, he would have known that there was a chance—a serious chance—of the automatic being identified as your gun. It's the common thing to trace a gun by its serial number."

"He might have dropped the gun accidentally and didn't have a chance to get his hands on it again."

"Oh, I say, sergeant, that's too thin!" exclaimed Wiggly. "It's taking too much for granted to presume that the gun accidentally fell in a position directly beneath the murdered woman's hand. No, that was done with the deliberate intention of having her death appear suicide."

"It's a good point, and it's reasonable," admitted Tish, "but it doesn't prove anything. I got to admit it does seem a little queer that Haskins would have left the gun behind."

"And it hooks up with Haskins' story about missing the gun, realizing that the Gilmore woman had lifted it out of his pocket, and his determination to risk a trip downstairs again in an effort to get it back."

"Humph!" Tish said again.

"When you identified the gun as yours—the one that Haskins took away from you when he knocked you out at Eighth Avenue Annie's yesterday— it did seem impossible that Sarbella, or anyone else, could have done the shooting. But let us suppose that Haskins' dying statement was true. The Gilmore woman had the gun; maybe she took it because she was afraid of her legal husband."

160

"Whatcha mean—'or anyone else?'" growled Tish. "You keep hinting at something you haven't let me in on. If it wasn't Haskins or Sarbella— Aw, you talk like a fool!"

Wiggly hesitated for a moment. "Tish," he said slowly, "I don't know that I'm exactly holding any aces, but I'm going to lay all my cards on the table and let you have a look at 'em. We know why Sarbella might have killed the woman."

"Motive ain't strong enough," broke in the detective with a shake of the head. "His kid brother lost his head over her and killed himself; that's all."

"Ordinarily I'd agree with you, but when we think of Sarbella's motive we've got to think of a race that is credited with a passion for personal vengeance. The Latins are hot-blooded, and their blood does not cool quickly like ours. They nurse a grudge for years.

"Let us suppose that Sarbella went to the Gilmore woman's room, not with the intention of killing her, but to tell her that, unless she made a full confession to her husband, he would tell Gilmore, himself. The gun was there—the gun that she had taken away from Haskins—and the man's hatred for this bronze-haired vampire who caused the suicide of his brother and the ultimate death of their mother, mastered him."

"Suppose anything you darn please," grunted Tish. "It's easy enough to cook up stuff, but making it hold water is something else. Yeah, I'll say it is."

"But there's something else," persisted Wiggly. "You've missed the hidden undercurrent that I've sensed. I tell you, Tish, there's something beneath the surface of things in this house."

"Meaning just what?" the detective asked skeptically.

"Did you notice Gilmore's stepsister—Joan Sheridan her name is—when she came out into the hall after the cook fainted?"

Tish eyed the newspaper man half curiously, half disgustedly.

"I saw her," he answered.

"Yes, you saw her, but did you see the expressions of her face? Did you notice how excited she became—"

"Say, I guess any woman would be excited, after what had happened, to hear a woman screaming like that cook did, and her face all bloody on top of it."

"When the doctor told her that Sarbella had been removed from suspicion, and that some one else had done the shooting," Wiggly went on, "well, I saw it, Tish; and I saw, too, what a look of relief came into her face when Bushnell told her that it was Haskins, the crook. The human emotions seldom lie, Tish, and, take it from me, that Sheridan girl knows a lot more about this thing than she is willing to tell."

"Rave on!" growled Sergeant Tish. "I'd given you credit for having a balance wheel, but that's nut stuff you're pulling now."

"Wait a minute," Wiggly pressed on, not discouraged by the other's derision. "Maybe you remember that Haskins refused to answer me when I asked him if it was a man or a woman he saw coming out of the Gilmore woman's room after he heard the shot."

"I can answer it, even if Haskins didn't; it was a man come out of the room, and it was Haskins himself. Whatcha trying to do now—hang it onto the Sheridan girl? Think it would make a better story for you, huh? Aw, forget it! Why would she have done it?" The question came in a triumphant tone.

"Oh, I've got you an answer for that, Tish," Wiggly replied. "So you demand a motive; all right, I'll furnish that, too. The strongest and most unreasoning of motives, the most deadly—jealousy!"

"Huh?"

"Joan Sheridan is in love with her stepbrother. I got that from the constable's daughter this morning."

"A woman's gossip!" snorted Tish. "I wouldn't go two cents on no kind of talk like that."

"And verified it by the butler," Wiggly added doggedly. "The constable's daughter is a great little gabber, and I wouldn't take her unsupported word; so I felt out Bates, and he admitted that the household had rather hoped for a match between Gilmore and Miss Sheridan. Yes, she's in love with her stepbrother; used to help him with his work and that sort of thing. The butler told me that it was a great shock to Miss Sheridan when she returned home from Europe and found that he had married during her absence.

"There's another little point; it might not seem so much, but I can imagine how it must have added to the blow. Miss Sheridan also returned home to find this strange woman—Gilmore's bride—had taken possession of her own room, a room that she had occupied for years and had formed a deep attachment for. I gather that a very strained situation resulted; even the servants took a dislike to the new Mrs. Gilmore.

"Man, I tell you there's something under the surface; I tell you that we've only scratched the surface, so to speak, of the Gilmore mystery. If Miss Sheridan would talk, we might learn something interesting." He tossed up his hands in a helpless gesture. "It would be silly to try and quiz her until we've got something to face her with; that would only spoil whatever chances we may have of getting to the bottom of it."

Sergeant Tish frowned and puffed out his plump cheeks; he was thinking things over now; then he shook his head.

"Don't take much stock in it," he declared.

162

"Jealousy is a primitive passion," argued Wiggly. "I'd consider it a stronger motive than revenge. Between Sarbella and the girl—"

"No," Tish corrected himself, "I don't take any stock in it at all. Haskins did the murder; Haskins is dead, and the case is closed. Don't bother me with any more of this stuff."

"There's one more thing that I haven't told you," said the newspaper man. "You remember the color of the murdered woman's hair?"

"Sort of a dull gold, isn't it?" grunted Tish, interested in spite of himself. "What's the color of her hair got to do with it?"

"Bronze is the right color, Tish; naturally she uses bronze hairpins, as I verified by a look at her dressing table. And yet on the floor beside the chaise longue I found a black hairpin, and Miss Sheridan's hair is dark."

Sergeant Tish puffed out his cheeks, looking up slowly. For a full minute he debated this information before he stirred.

"Women are always dropping hairpins outta their heads; might have been a servant, or Miss Sheridan, for that matter, paying a perfectly innocent visit to the room." Yet the detective's tone was deliberate, thoughtful.

"Remember the Hitchcock murder—solved by a black mourning pin?"

Moving cautiously in an effort to keep any painful strain from his shoulder muscles, Tish stood to his feet.

"Mind you," he warned, "I don't say that I think you're within a hundred miles of being right, but it'll do no harm to go upstairs and have another look around."

In the light of Tish's previously derisive skepticism, Wiggly felt that he had achieved something of a victory.

163

# CHAPTER 26

## BITS OF TALLOW

Presently Tish and Wiggly Price were once more within the room where Helen Gilmore had met death, again seeking from the mute furnishings some vital clew that previous examinations might have overlooked. The newspaper man was all eagerness, but the interest of the detective had already cooled. There was the window with Haskins' finger prints; he had the sort of mind that readily accepts the obvious, and his police experience had taught him that, nine chances to ten, the obvious is the true.

It was a little hard to think of this cheerful bed-chamber as a place of dark deeds. The north windows looked out upon the wide and shimmering bosom of the Hudson; a sailboat clipped daintily over the water, and in its wake the sunlight made the ripples scintillate like diamonds. Across the Tappan Zee the stern ruggedness of the New Jersey Palisades was softened with a verdant touch and splash of summer greenness.

"The answer to it all is here," said Wiggly. "There must be something more for us than just a woman's hairpin."

"Sure," grunted Tish; "my gun and Haskins' finger prints on the glass." He had returned even more positively to the conviction that he had been right in the first place.

"Ah, but what we're after now, Tish, is a clew that will outweigh the finger prints and the gun. There must be something more than that; there's got to be."

"That stuff about there always being a clew is the bunk," said Tish. "I've seen dozens of cases where there wasn't a thing for us cops to go on. But this is different. All the evidence points straight at Haskins. What else have you got? A hairpin and an imagination!"

Wiggly was not discouraged; beginning at the side of the room, he began to walk slowly, bent nearly double, his eyes searching, searching, while Tish watched him in a half-amused, half-contemptuous silence. Again the reporter came upon the shattered pieces of the broken vase which lay on the rug near the little mahogany table, but he had already rejected these fragments as things of no importance; proof, if anything, that some one, probably the murderer, had struck against the table, crashing the vase to the floor. Perhaps it was to his discredit as an investigator that it did not occur to him as strange that the vase should have been broken into as many pieces.

Near the table, however, he did find something that he had overlooked until now; it was a bit of whitish substance which, as he picked it up from where it had been crushed flat into the rug, was moderately soft between his fingers. He frowned over it, puzzled.

"Tallow!" he exclaimed. "The sort of tallow they make candles of."

"Huh!" grunted Tish.

"People seldom use tallow candles these days, except for those decorative candlesticks." His gaze roved swiftly about the room. "No candlestick in this room, either. This piece is too chunky to be candle drip; besides, why should any one have been walking around with a lighted candle last night? If the lights had been out of commission, some one would surely have mentioned it. Wouldn't you consider this just a little queer, Tish?"

"If you're asking me to speak my mind, I'd be more apt to say that you're a little queer, always jumping at little things that don't amount to anything. What if it is a piece of tallow? That don't prove anything—any more than a hairpin does."

Speculatively Wiggly turned the find over in his hand; it was grained with black specks. He looked to the floor again and, some three or four feet away, saw another bit of it.

"No children in the house," he mused. "Children might explain it; when I was a kid I used to take a candle and mold it into odd sorts of shapes—a juvenile attempt at sculpture—human heads, animals, and the like. Yes, Tish, this is queer—darned queer!" Completely baffled in his effort to account for the presence of the tallow, he put it into his pocket along with the black hairpin.

"Something else to think about, anyhow," he told himself and continued his literally inch-by-inch survey of the room. It was at the far end of the chamber that, almost completely hidden in the thick nap of the rug, he found another piece of the broken vase, this one little more than a sliver, and still another bit of the tallow.

"Tish!" he fairly shouted. "Come here! Here's a little mystery all in itself."

"What now?"

Wiggly exhibited the fragment of porcelain and pointed dramatically to the spot on the rug where he had discovered it.

"We've been presuming all along, Tish," he said almost breathlessly, "that the vase was broken when some one bumped into the table. It's a dozen feet from the table to this spot; it isn't reasonable to think that one of the pieces could have shattered for such a distance. As a matter of fact, Tish, there's something that I've been a blockhead not to think of before. This rug is pretty thick; it's only three feet from the top of the table to the floor, and yet that vase is broken into a hundred and one pieces. And here's a bit of it twelve feet away!"

"Humph!" grunted Tish.

"What do you make of it anyhow?"

"Maybe the Gilmore woman threw it at Haskins," suggested the detective, puffing out his cheeks and frowning; "maybe she saw what was coming, picked up the vase, and flung it at his head—something like that, huh?"

"Y-yes," Wiggly admitted hesitatingly; "that might explain it being broken into so many pieces, but that doesn't explain the tallow. I've got a feeling that those are the two things that are going to add up to four."

"Oh, forget the tallow!" Tish muttered peevishly. "What's a little tallow got to do with a murder—or a smashed vase, for that matter? You better stick to digging up news and let this Sherlock business alone."

Wiggly shook his head stubbornly.

"It's a puzzle, Tish, but I'm going to stick until these peculiar little things you scoff at are explained." He again took up his search, but further results were nil. Tish was growing impatient.

"I'm going back downstairs," he announced.

"Wonder where this door leads to?" murmured the reporter, as he reached for the knob. It did not yield to his touch, but the key was in the lock; a moment later he was looking within Kirklan Gilmore's sleeping chamber.

"Ah!" he mused. "She had the door locked against her husband. Wonder if that means there was discord in the new love nest?"

Sergeant Tish snorted derisively. "Next," he said with withering sarcasm, "you'll be trying to hang it onto the husband—and him downstairs when the shot was fired."

"Oh, not at all," Wiggly answered without resentment; "that was just an aside." He entered the room, gave it a brief survey, and then, satisfied that it had nothing to offer him, returned, closing the door and relocking it behind him. "Nothing in there that could interest us, Tish. The net result so far seems to be one black hairpin and a few pieces of tallow candle—perhaps a broken vase. I'm not so sure but that you've given a pretty logical explanation of the vase." He sighed in discouragement. "Not much to go on, eh? Wish I could figure out the tallow thing."

"Forget it," advised Tish.

"If we could only get Miss Sheridan to talk. Wish I had the authority to put her through a sprout of questions!"

166

Tish tenderly massaged the wrist of his injured arm; the bandages interfered with his circulation.

"Well, you haven't got the authority; neither have I. And I wouldn't waste my time quizzing her, if I had. So far as I'm concerned, the case is solved. Haskins did the killing. I've messed around here and let you play at the detective business long enough; me for one of those comfy chairs down in the library. Guess I'll stick around for the inquest. Coming down?"

Wiggly hesitated for a moment and then nodded. "Yes, I suppose I might as well," he agreed; "I think I've exhausted the possibilities here."

The two men went downstairs and into the library, Tish to take what comfort he could in one of the easy-chairs, and the newspaper man to speculate with discouraging futility on the puzzle of the candle tallow. He felt as if he had told the New York detective sergeant that the next move was to question Joan Sheridan. While he had no authority in the matter, he was several times on the verge of taking this course into his own hands.

Doctor Bushnell, he felt very sure, would resent any hint that the girl had a criminal knowledge of the murder; the physician would be prejudiced in her favor and wave aside the suggestion indignantly. It would be his natural inclination to consider Haskins guilty and brush aside any other theory. A cross-examination of Miss Sheridan, in the doctor's hands, was liable to be a perfunctory and negligible proceeding.

"Well, young un, got it figured out yet?" grunted Tish, breaking a considerable silence.

"Not yet," admitted Wiggly, "but I haven't given it up. I'm still struggling with it."

Again silence.

"Where's Gilmore?" asked Tish presently. "I haven't had eyes on the man since I've been here. Wasn't in his room when you opened that door, huh?"

"The doctor put him to bed somewhere here on the ground floor—gave him a shot of dope, I believe, to quiet him. I saw him last night; he was pretty well cut up over it, naturally. He'll get another jolt between the eyes when he's told that the woman wasn't legally married to him. It's pretty tough on a chap, losing illusions of the woman you're in love with."

"Uh-huh," grunted Tish. "A pretty woman sure can stir up a lot of hell for a man—when she's the wrong sort."

Wiggly turned in his chair, as there came to his ears the sound of a step on the stairs outside the archway dividing the library from the reception hall, the tap of a woman's high-heeled shoes.

"Perhaps—" he murmured and leaped to his feet; he was thinking it might be Joan Sheridan, and that he could manufacture some excuse to get her in conversation. His hopeful guess was right; it was Joan. She came slowly down the stairs, her face white and drawn. As the newspaper man, although she had no knowledge of his profession, appeared before her, she paused.

"I am looking for Doctor Bushnell," she murmured; "I am anxious to know——" Her voice trailed off.

"Doctor Bushnell has taken the constable to the hospital," he explained, "but, if there is anything I can do, I am at your service." He stepped aside with a gesture that she was to come into the library and, turning his head, gave Tish an entreating look. Now that the opportunity had presented itself he decided to play a colossal game of bluffing.

"Miss Sheridan, this is Detective Sergeant Tish of the New York police department. Sergeant Tish has been wounded—in the shooting on the third floor, you know."

"I—I am afraid I don't know exactly what has happened; everything has been such a terrible, excited jumble."

"One would hardly think so many things could happen in a quiet country place like this," said Wiggly.

Joan shuddered.

"It's been horrible! The man—the wounded man I saw on the stairs—" Her eyes were upon Tish; perhaps not so much upon Tish as his bandaged shoulder, where brown stains had seeped through the bandages.

"Haskins is dead, ma'am," Tish answered promptly, which was precisely one of the things Wiggly had not wanted him to say—not just yet. "I plugged him when he winged me with the constable's gun, up in the storeroom."

"Doctor Bushnell told me," Joan went on tremulously, "that it was this man who—who killed Kirklan's wife."

Sergeant Tish caught Wiggly's pleading signal, hesitated a moment, and then temporized.

"W-well," he answered slowly, "I guess there's what you'd call a division of opinion on that. Our newspaper friend don't think so." Wiggly could have choked him. Why did he have to tell her that he was a reporter! And why couldn't Tish have given him a square show? Under his breath he cursed the headquarters man's stubbornness.

"Oh!" exclaimed Joan. "So he's a newspaper reporter. I thought he must be a detective, too."

"Give 'im credit," grunted Tish; "he's trying hard enough to be one." He chuckled at his little joke.

"This—this man," pressed Joan Sheridan, now ignoring Wiggly entirely, "what was he doing in the house—in the storeroom? Was he a—a burglar?"

"As a matter of fact, Miss Sheridan, Haskins was the woman's husband."

Joan gasped.

"You don't mean—you can't mean Helen?"

"That's it, ma'am; seems that she had not taken the trouble to get herself a divorce before she married Gilmore." Briefly he recounted Haskins' trouble with the New York police, his criminal record, his flight from Eighth Avenue Annie's with the automatic, his coming to Greenacres, and his method of gaining entrance to the house.

Joan, leaning forward tensely, listened with wide eyes and parted lips.

"It was the gun—the gun that this criminal took away from you in New York that killed Helen?" she demanded breathlessly. Tish nodded.

"Then," she rushed on, her voice sinking to a whisper, "there—there doesn't seem to be much doubt that the man—Haskins—her—her legal husband—killed her? Did he say anything before he died?"

Wiggly Price leaped forward and stood in front of her, lest Tish spoil whatever chance might be left.

"Let me ask you something," he snapped out. "What made you so positive, hours before anyone else in the house knew that such a person as Haskins existed, that Victor Sarbella was innocent of the murder?"

Joan naturally was startled by this sudden verbal attack; all the blood had drained from her already pale face, leaving her features ghastly. Her eyes met his for a moment and then lowered.

"Why—why, what a strange question!" she exclaimed, but there was a noticeable nervous catch in her voice. "I—I never doubted Mr. Sarbella's innocence."

"I know you didn't, but what I want to know is—why?"

Joan's head went still lower, but Wiggly could see that her lips were quivering.

"I—I just knew it."

"Intuition, eh?"

"Call it anything you like."

"Was it intuition or knowledge?" Wiggly demanded sharply. The girl gave a suppressed start, which Sergeant Tish missed entirely; in fact, Tish had not quite recovered from his surprise at the way the newspaper man had plunged in with these rapid-fire questions of his. Wiggly had a thrill of elation; his hunch had been right, and the girl knew something.

His hand slid into his pocket, and his fingers closed about the bit of tallow that he had found on the floor of Helen Gilmore's bedroom.

"Look at this!" he commanded. Joan's head raised at the compelling tone, but her gaze, as she stared at the misshapen, somewhat soiled lump of white, was merely blankly inquiring. It was quite clear, even to the suspicious reporter, that this meant nothing to her. Again his hand went to his pocket.

"And look at this!" he ordered again, opening his fingers, revealing the black hairpin in his palm. "Look at it closely, Miss Sheridan, and tell if it doesn't belong to you."

"How—how could I know that?" she stammered. "All hairpins are so much alike. What—what right have you to ask me all these questions in that tone?" She turned appealingly to Sergeant Tish. "Has this newspaper reporter a right to ask me these questions?"

"I guess that's a reporter's main business, asking questions," grunted Tish, with a slow grin; quite evidently he wasn't taking Wiggly's cross-examination with any seriousness. "Might as well answer 'em, Miss Sheridan; no harm in that."

"This hairpin," went on Wiggly, "was found on the floor beside Helen Gilmore's chaise longue. She didn't use black hairpins, and you do. Do you deny, Miss Sheridan, that you were in the woman's sleeping room last night?"

For a moment, the barest instant, Joan hesitated. "Yes," she answered slowly, "I do deny it."

"Evidently you do not know," Wiggly went on mercilessly, resorting to a trick in an effort to force the truth from her, "that just before Haskins died he made a statement. He told us that Helen managed to get the automatic out of his pocket before she sent him into hiding on the third floor. He was in the storeroom when he realized that she had got the gun away from him. He came back down the stairs with the intention of forcing her to return it to him. He was in the hall when he heard the scream and the shot.

"The door was open, the light was burning inside, and Haskins saw the person who came out of that room!" This much, of course, was true, and for his purpose he did not consider it an unfair advantage, this failure to add that Haskins had refused to tell more.

Joan Sheridan's hands were frozen tightly about the arms of the chair; her eyes met Wiggly's with a hunted, terrified look. She realized what he meant—that he was virtually accusing her of the murder. But she was a quick-witted girl, Joan Sheridan; she knew that Sergeant Tish's attitude would not have been so jovially casual if he too had suspected her of the shooting. She mastered herself wonderfully.

"Why don't you proceed and say exactly what you mean?" she asked. "What you mean is that you think I—"

"Didn't you?" whipped out Wiggly, leaning slightly forward until their eyes were level. This time her gaze did not falter; it met his without flinching.

"No!" she answered firmly. "I deny everything you have said and intimated. If you have finished with your inquisition—"

Price, realizing that his strategy had failed, offered no objection, as she moved to leave the room. But when her steps had receded up the stairs, he turned angrily upon Tish.

"A nice mess you made of things!" he exclaimed hotly. "Why did you have to tell her that I am a newspaper man?"

"Well, ain't you?"

"You didn't give me a square shake. You queered any chance that I might have had to make her talk. You belittled me, and that took all the wind out of my sails. If you'd backed me up a little, we'd have had her dead to rights. If we could have made her believe that it was she whom Haskins saw coming out of the room after the shot was fired—"

"Aw, forget it," growled Tish; "she didn't croak the woman any more than you did."

"Probably not premeditatively, but there's one thing sure in my mind, and you'll never convince me any different: Either Joan Sheridan did the shooting, or she knows who did—and she knows it wasn't Haskins. She was on the edge of a breakdown, but you braced her right up. And you're called a detective!"

Sergeant Tish's face flushed. "See here, I'm not going to have any newspaper scribbler talk that way to me! If I'd have let you have your way, you'd have made a fool out of me as well as yourself. Hairpins, tallow! Bah! I guess you think you are a detective—a real detective. That's the way with you newspaper guys—always hunting for a chance to make the police wrong, trying to make monkeys of the police department. You make me sick!"

Wiggly's ears moved violently.

"You wait and see!" he retorted. "Sneer at hairpins and tallow, but I know I'm on the right trail, and I'm going to stick on this job until I've followed it to the end."

171

# CHAPTER 27

## WIGGLY REMAINS UNCONVINCED

For all of his asserted confidence, which bordered upon boasting, Wiggly Price realized that he had a hard nut to crack. Swinging out of the library and Sergeant Tish's presence, he went out to the porch and sat down to indulge himself in logic, speculation, guessing. He took the piece of tallow from his pocket again, staring at it fixedly; his belief that it had some vital part in the mystery had become an obsession; but there was one thing about it that discouraged him—Joan Sheridan had shown no perturbation when he had produced it before her eyes.

Following a simple bit of logical reasoning, if the bit of tallow were so important as he insistently imagined, and if the girl had done the shooting, it was extremely strange that she had shown no signs of agitation when faced with this evidence. He had been favorably impressed with the girl's face; she seemed to be a sane, well-balanced young person. Certainly, he argued, it was difficult to believe that she would have committed the murder after cold premeditation; but might she not have yielded to a suddenly and insanely jealous impulse, suddenly overwhelmed by the proximity of the automatic pistol?

No matter who did the murder, Wiggly reasoned, it had not been a premeditated crime; the slayer had not gone to Helen Gilmore's room with a weapon. The weapon was already there. These cogitations, of course, took it for granted that Haskins' dying statement had been entirely truthful; the reporter might have agreed with Tish that the whole yarn was a lie, except that he could not imagine a desperate man like Haskins deliberately leaving the gun behind. With the death of the only person who knew of his presence in the house, Haskins had nothing to gain by cloaking the crime under the guise of suicide.

That Joan Sheridan knew more than she had told, Wiggly was flatly certain; he had studied every changing expression of her face and he had seen the emotions which Tish had missed. Either she had committed the crime, or else she knew who did.

Presuming her innocence, whom was she protecting with her silence? Sarbella? That did not seem logical. Why should she go to such great lengths to protect Sarbella? Yet, other than Sarbella, Joan, and Haskins, there had been but one other person above the first floor when the shot was fired, and that was the other Mrs. Gilmore, Joan's mother.

"Ah!" thought Wiggly with a tingle of excitement, as his mind canvassed this possibility. "There is the person that the girl would protect, her mother. And the mother has kept closely to her room; the doctor had to look after her. Now what could have been her motive?"

That was a puzzler, particularly so since he had not so much as put eyes on the woman. Perhaps—this was guessing merely—the older Mrs. Gilmore had been mistress of Greenacres so long that she resented the appearance of an interloper; possibly she had taken the frenzied notion that she was to be dispossessed from this house which had been her home.

Both Bates and Kirklan Gilmore, downstairs in the butler's pantry when the scream and the shot had sounded through the quiet house, had been positive that they had got up the stairs before any one would have had a chance to come down; even Haskins had verified that. Their coming had been so swift as to cut off his chance of escape. Yes, decided Wiggly, counting Haskins out of it, there remained just three possible suspects. Joan, Sarbella, and the elder Mrs. Gilmore.

But the piece of tallow—he was not getting the answer to that. He was still considering it when Doctor Bushnell's automobile turned in at the Greenacres driveway. The doctor was returning from the hospital with the butler. A moment later the physician's touring car came to a pause near the porch, and Wiggly got quickly to his feet.

"How about Constable Griggs?" he asked.

"He'll make the grade, but it was a close call for him," answered Doctor Bushnell. "Mighty bad fracture. He'll have to spend a week or better in the hospital. I've explained the whole situation, and he's given me the jail keys and his permission to release Sarbella, which I shall do immediately. Has the district attorney arrived yet?"

"Haven't seen him," replied Wiggly, eager for an opening that he might have a frank talk with the deputy coroner.

"I telephoned him from the hospital and explained the situation in detail. He agreed with me that there seemed to be no doubt that Haskins killed the woman; said he'd come right over. I'll drum up enough men for the coroner's jury when I get to the village and release Sarbella. Whew! I'll bet it's a load off of his mind; it certainly looked bad for that fellow— mighty bad."

Bates had gone on into the house; the doctor had not got out of the car, his purpose in stopping evidently being merely to let out the butler. His hand was upon the gear lever, ready to start his car in motion again, but Wiggly put detaining fingers on his arm.

"Just a moment, Doctor Bushnell," he urged earnestly. "I know you've made up your mind that Haskins did the shooting, and that, since Haskins is dead, the case is virtually closed."

"Certainly it is," nodded the physician. "I thought about it all the way on the drive to the hospital and back. The evidence against Haskins is all that any reasonable man would ask. Practically a matter of legal formality, the inquest."

"I'm going to ask that you listen to me, with an open mind," Wiggly insisted. "I want to talk with you about the case in utmost seriousness; I feel that you're on the verge of making a grave blunder. I've found something —"

"Not more hairpins?" broke in the doctor with a faint smile.

"Doctor, I'm no novice in contact with crime; and, while I'm not nursing any notion that I'm a born detective, I've got eyes in my head and a logical sort of thinking apparatus. Without trying to toot my own horn, I might add that I've helped my paper solve a puzzle or so, after the police had fallen down on the job. I'm not saying that to boast; just want you to take me seriously."

Doctor Bushnell gave him a quick, sharp glance. "I'll listen, as we drive to the village," he said. "Hop in."

Wiggly hopped in, and, as the car got into motion, so did his tongue. Absolute conviction that he was right enabled him to give a forceful presentation of his theories, and his short, punchy sentences were punctuated by frequent twitchings of his ears.

He began by repeating in substance Haskins' dying statement and emphasizing the improbability of Haskins leaving the gun behind, the utter uselessness of Haskins covering up the murder beneath the guise of suicide. From there he switched to the piece of tallow, saving any mention of Joan Sheridan until the last. The doctor, listening patiently, gave him a fair hearing; but it is a difficult job to convince a man who has already made up his mind to the contrary.

"Now we come down to the nub of things," Wiggly went on; swiftly he voiced his suspicions concerning Joan and his reasons for them. He told of his effort to cross-examine the girl and the results.

Doctor Bushnell had an uneasy feeling, as he himself recalled Joan's perturbation of the previous night, but he brushed these thoughts aside.

"Do you realize," he demanded sternly, "that you are intimating that Joan Sheridan might have— Oh, it's absurd, preposterous! I refuse even to consider such a ridiculous notion. Why, I've known Joan all her life; a sweeter, finer young woman never lived."

174

"Did you happen to know that she's in love with Gilmore?" Wiggly demanded, and at this suggestion of a motive the doctor's eyes snapped angrily.

"So that's what you base all this wild talk on, eh? That reduces your reasoning to further absurdity."

"I'm not accusing her of the shooting, doctor, but I'm absolutely certain that she's hiding something; if not to protect herself, then to protect some one else. Her agitation—"

"Humph!" broke in Doctor Bushnell. "What sort of a woman wouldn't be agitated with all that's happened at Greenacres during the past few hours. Whom would she be protecting? Answer me that!"

"It would have to be some one who was on the second floor when the shot was fired. Tell me something—does Gilmore or his stepmother own Greenacres?"

"Gilmore does," the doctor answered. "His stepmother's share of the estate was in cash and other realty, but I'm afraid she managed it poorly."

"Ah!" murmured Wiggly. "Then she was virtually dependent upon her stepson. If things had become so unpleasant for her at Greenacres after the arrival of the house's new mistress that she could not stay—"

The physician's indignation became more pronounced.

"Gad, what a villainous imagination you've got!" he exploded. "You mean now, I suppose, that Mrs. Gilmore did the shooting, and that Joan is shielding her? Young man, I've lost all patience with such nonsense. I refuse to listen to these ravings any longer. Any one, except a hare-brained idiot, would know that Haskins did the shooting. No more of this twaddle; I simply won't listen to you!"

"Then you won't help me with a further investigation?"

"I shall certainly have no hand in such foolishness," answered Doctor Bushnell with a tone of absolute finality. "Talk to the district attorney, if you insist, but I warn you that he'll take no stock in it."

"Probably not," Wiggly agreed gloomily, "but just the same I know I'm right."

They had reached the village, and the doctor's car came to a halt in front of Borough Hall.

"I'll release Sarbella and then get busy drumming up my men for the coroner's jury," said Bushnell. "You've got a sensational enough story for your paper, as it is; forget that silly rubbish you've been talking to me."

Wiggly made no response, but followed the physician from the machine into the village building and downstairs into the basement, where Victor Sarbella was a prisoner. At the sound of their approach, Sarbella came to the door of the narrow cage and peered out between the rusting steel bars, but he uttered no word of protest, of outraged innocence; only stared in a stony, narrow-eyed silence.

"I've the best of news for you, Mr. Sarbella!" Doctor Bushnell exclaimed heartily. "I've come to let you out."

The prisoner's head jerked up, his fingers tightened their grip about the bars of the cell door, his lips parted, and his eyes brightened with the look of relief that flashed across his face.

"You mean," he asked slowly, "that I am to be released unconditionally —that I have been removed from suspicion?"

The doctor, with the constable's keys, was struggling with the lock that would unfasten the bolts; the mechanism was badly in need of oiling, and it was giving him trouble.

"Yes, unconditionally," he answered. "We find that we have done you an injustice, although you must admit that we were within our rights, everything considered. The murderer of the Gilmore woman— Oh, curse this lock!"

Sarbella pressed his body closer to the bars. "Yes?" he demanded with an eager impatience. "The murderer—go on, man!"

The lock finally yielded, enabling the physician to turn the handle that slid the bolts, and the door opened. Victor Sarbella was a free man.

"Tell me," he commanded again. "Who—" The newspaper reporter sensed his grave concern, his anxiety—and wondered.

"Luckily for you," answered Doctor Bushnell, "the slayer was still in the house—a criminal who, it developed, was the woman's undivorced husband."

"Thank Heaven!" breathed Sarbella, and it was apparent that this news was a great relief to him.

Briefly the doctor related the facts.

"What a blessedly fortunate ending!" murmured the artist. "I was afraid of other things—something more terrible."

"I'm driving back to Greenacres after I get together a jury for the inquest," went on the physician. "I'm anxious to get it over with as quickly as possible, for my private practice has to wait until this official business is disposed of, and my patients are liable to lose their patience." He chuckled a little at his own pun. "You may ride back to Greenacres with me, if you choose."

"Thanks," nodded Sarbella, "I will."

The three men made their way out of the basement cell room and to the street, where the doctor said that they could wait in his car, if they liked. A moment later he was hurrying along the village thoroughfare in quest of his jurors, picking up practically the first citizens that he encountered. Sarbella got into the rear of the touring car, and Wiggly Price sat beside him.

176

"You seem to be well out of a bad situation," said the newspaper man.

The released suspect nodded soberly. "Yes," he agreed, "a bad situation —an overwhelming situation. Circumstantial evidence can be a damning thing. Perhaps I owe something to you; your attitude, when you came to the cell about the cigarette—"

"You do not owe your release to me, Sarbella; it was the appearance of Sergeant Tish, his identification of the gun and the presence of Haskins in the house." Wiggly paused for a moment with his eyes on the other's face. "You were greatly relieved when you heard the doctor's explanation of the tragedy?"

Victor Sarbella inclined his head.

"I was!" he exclaimed fervently. "Knowing my own innocence, I am afraid that I was as much inclined to suspect other people as other people to suspect me. I am afraid that I even suspected my friend Gilmore."

"Why Gilmore?" asked Wiggly. "He had a perfect alibi—downstairs when the shot was fired."

"Yes, I know," murmured Sarbella, "but the poor chap was so over-wrought, so beside himself, so obsessed with the suspicion that there had been an—ah—affair between me and—and his wife—but let us not talk of that."

"I wonder," pressed Wiggly, but careful to make his tone carelessly casual, "if you also suspected Miss Sheridan?"

"Eh?" exclaimed Sarbella, turning quickly, and then he laughed briefly. "Yes, I think I even suspected her. Her attitude it was—ah—very strange, it seemed to me. Only excitement, of course, as we know the facts now; but at the time—well, I hardly knew what to think."

Wiggly's ears twitched slightly. Further confirmation of his theory! Yet it convinced no one except himself.

"I condemn myself for harboring any such suspicions," went on Sarbella musingly, "but it was strange. She was up, had not retired, and yet she had not heard the scream or the shot."

"What!" exclaimed Wiggly; this was something new to him. He had not known that. "You mean that she was up and dressed?"

Sarbella shot him a quick, curious glance, saw his eagerness, and was warned to sudden silence.

"Let us talk of something else," he said. "Am I to understand that there are still any doubts in your mind—"

"Haskins made a dying statement in which he denied the murder," said Wiggly; "he said, however, that he did see the murderer coming out of the room after the shot was fired."

Sarbella gave no guilty start, such as might have been expected, if Haskins' story was true, and it had been himself that Haskins had seen coming

177

out of Helen Gilmore's room.

"What could you expect but lies from the lips of such a man?" the artist asked. "Thank Heaven that the ending is as it is. This man, this Haskins, must have been the husband who went to my poor brother with the story that unbalanced his reason and sent him to his death. Poor Andrea! The hand of Fate has avenged him! There is a God of retribution!"

Wiggly Price made one more effort. His fingers went to his pocket for that puzzling piece of tallow.

"Had another look around that room this morning," he said. "On the floor I found several pieces of this."

Victor Sarbella turned and glanced at the white, black-flecked, shapeless lump, but he betrayed no more visible signs of emotion than had Joan Sheridan.

"What is it?" he asked, frowning. "What of it?"

"Nothing!" grunted Wiggly Price, as his arm raised in a disgustedly impulsive gesture to toss it into the street. Even his own persistent faith in this as a vital clew was being badly shaken. Yet his fingers closed about the bit of tallow, and he returned it to his pocket again. His mouth tightened.

"Nothing—so far," he added. He was one of those chaps who just naturally can't quit.

Sarbella gave him a curious glance, shrugged his shoulders, and dismissed both the man and the bit of tallow as of no further importance; then he lapsed into a moody sort of silence. A moment later Doctor Bushnell returned to the car; it had taken him no time at all to drum his jury for the inquest.

"All right," he announced, "we'll be getting back and having things over with. Shouldn't take much longer than an hour: Presley, our local garage man, will bring the jurors out in a bus, and they'll be no great distance behind us."

He took the wheel, started the motor, and the three men were on their way back to Greenacres. Wiggly sat stiffly in the seat beside Sarbella, trying in vain to drive his brain over the hurdles. Time with him was short, for, as the doctor had just said, in another hour or so it would be over. The law would have finished with the Gilmore affair and write the easiest, most obvious ending to the dramatic business of the past night, charging the whole tragic account to Don Haskins and, through his death, mark the whole deed as "Paid."

Once the verdict of the coroner's jury was in, Wiggly knew, it would be next to the impossible to have the case reopened again. He had just about sixty minutes longer to prove he was right, and that the rest of them were wrong.

# CHAPTER 28

## THE BLACK SMUDGE

Along the ribbon-smooth road Doctor Bushnell shot the car at a lively clip; one couldn't blame him, of course, for thinking of his private practice, and one of his patients had been telephoning for him all morning. He would have been the last man to hurry the Gilmore case to a legal finish, if he had thought there was anything to be gained by prolonging the investigation; but he considered that the affair had been solved to all reasonable satisfaction.

In less than five minutes they arrived at Greenacres, and hardly had the three men stepped from the machine to the porch of the house when Kirklan Gilmore, evidently having seen them from a window, came rushing out, both hands stretched out toward the artist. There were tears in his eyes, and his voice was husky, trembling with emotion.

"Thank God, Victor!" he cried. "I've just heard the whole inside of things from a man, the New York detective, that you're cleared, absolutely cleared! You don't know what a relief it has been to me, although I never did think, even when things were the blackest, that you did it."

"And I appreciate your loyalty, Kirklan," answered Sarbella. The hands of the two men remained clasped.

"Forgive me, Victor, for thinking last night that you—that you and Helen—"

"That there had been an—ah—affair between your wife and me," finished Sarbella. "Yes, I was afraid that my silence would put dark thoughts into your head, but—"

"Why didn't you tell me?" broke in Gilmore, and a peculiar expression convulsed his features. "Why didn't you tell me last night, out in the study, that she was the woman over whom your brother—"

Sarbella shook his head.

"No! I could not in honor do that," he protested. "You were my friend, and the woman was your wife. My lips were sealed. She was your wife; you loved her."

179

Kirklan Gilmore's face was still white, haggardly drawn, but he was no longer the broken wreck of a man, tottering upon the brink of a mental collapse, that he had been some hours before. He seemed to have recovered from the first over-powering shock of horror; Doctor Bushnell's course in placing him under the influence of a sedative had apparently been a most wise one.

At Sarbella's words his lips twitched piteously, but he managed to keep control of himself.

"No," he said slowly, huskily, "I was in love with—with the woman I thought her to be—in love with an ideal, a creation of my own imagination. The woman I thought her to be did not exist—except in my own infatuated fancies. And she was not my wife. She— Oh, what a nightmare it's been—what a nightmare!"

Doctor Bushnell stepped swiftly to his side and, taking his arm, urged him toward the house.

"Keep a grip on yourself, Kirklan," he murmured in a kindly, paternal tone. "It's been a pretty terrible business, old man, but that thing we mortals call fate has cut a lot of the strings to the tangle for you. It is better that things are as they are; it saves a vast number of troublesome complications. It saves—well, trucking a lot of mire through the courts."

Gilmore compressed his lips and lowered his head. "Yes," he agreed dully, "you're right about that; it saves the courts."

"Buck up, Kirklan! As you say, the woman you thought her to be did not exist."

"Ah," murmured Victor Sarbella, "but losing an ideal is one of the hardest things in life."

The novelist, leaning a little on the doctor's friendly arm, made his way slowly into the house. Sarbella and Wiggly Price followed.

"Have all the legal details been satisfied?" asked Gilmore, as he lowered himself into a chair. "There is, of course, no question but that—"

"But that Haskins killed her," finished Doctor Bushnell. "Absolutely none, Kirklan. There remains now only the inquest—a double inquest in this case. One jury will suffice for both; the verdict, of course, is a foregone conclusion."

There fell a brief silence, Gilmore's eyes staring straight in front of him, with a dull, vacant expression. No doubt he was thinking of the bronze-haired, beautiful woman who lay upstairs, cold in death—the woman who might have been.

"Everything has become quite clear to me," he said slowly, more as if speaking to himself. "She was making a visit to this Haskins in New York day before yesterday, when Atchinson saw her on the street. She must have gone there in answer to a letter that my butler tells me she received that morning."

"Atchinson?" Doctor Bushnell asked inquiringly.

"My publisher," Gilmore replied. "Since she was employed by the publishing firm before our marriage, Atchinson knew her quite well. He said it was she, but I thought he must be mistaken. She had told me that she was going to motor into the country. I wonder how it would have all come out if the man, Haskins, had not been trapped in the storeroom?"

No one responded to that musing question. Withdrawn unobtrusively into one corner, Wiggly had again taken the lump of tallow from his pocket and was meditatively rubbing his fingers over it. Suddenly his attention centered upon those black specks that he had taken for granted were dirt, caused, perhaps, by a soiled shoe sole pressing down on it, as it had lain upon the floor of the room upstairs; he saw now that those dark, almost pin-point discolorations were imbedded into the substance. This, however, increased rather than solved the puzzle.

"The district attorney has come, hasn't he?" asked Doctor Bushnell. "I took it for granted that it was his car I saw at the side of the driveway, as we came up."

Kirklan Gilmore nodded absently. "Yes," he said, "a young fellow—the assistant district attorney, I believe. Lasker, I think his name is. He's upstairs looking around with that detective fellow, Sergeant Fish."

"Tish," corrected the physician. "Quite a game sort, Tish; it was he who shot Haskins."

Again Gilmore nodded. "So he told me," he said.

"I think I'll go upstairs," added the physician. "It won't be long now until the men who are to serve on the jury arrive." He glanced at Wiggly with a patronizing sort of smile. "Are you coming up with me to look for more —more hairpins, young man?"

The newspaper man smiled grimly.

"I'll go up with you," he said, "but it's not hairpins that I'm mainly interested in right now; it's this confounded piece of tallow." He turned his eyes toward the novelist and thought he saw a sudden tightening of Gilmore's muscles, a suppressed start. He was not so sure about it. "Tell me, Mr. Gilmore, were candles used frequently in the house here?"

Gilmore did not reply for a moment. "Candles?" he murmured. "Why, my dear sir, what a peculiar question. I don't believe I understand."

Doctor Bushnell, moving toward the stairway, paused with a brief, discounting laugh.

"Our enthusiastic newspaper friend, Kirklan," he explained, "thinks we haven't begun to get at the bottom of things. He's found a few pieces of tallow candle on the floor of the room upstairs; he's trying to attach some importance to it—just because he doesn't hit upon a ready explanation to it, I suppose. I'm afraid we've humored him a little too much, in gratitude for the first assistance that he gave us in identifying your wife."

Gilmore was frowning slightly.

"And I'm afraid that I can't help him explain his little mystery, doctor," he said. "So far as I can recall, there aren't any candlesticks in Helen's room; nor in my room, which is adjoining. Still"—he paused for a moment —"it does occur to me, gentlemen, that the third floor has never been wired for electricity; the storeroom is so seldom visited. If Haskins had wanted to have a light up there, a candle would have afforded about the only possible illumination for him."

"Ah!" exclaimed the doctor. "See, Price, there's the explanation for you! The woman must have got Haskins a candle, and he carried it down with him when he shot her. He probably mashed it underfoot and—"

"No, that will hardly do," Wiggly interrupted with a quick negative jerk of his head. "In the first place, I can't believe that Haskins would have been fool enough to have taken a light with him to the storeroom; too much chance of the illuminated window attracting attention. Secondly, this tallow was broken into a good many small pieces; the trodding of a foot on a candle wouldn't do that; it would only have mashed it, and it wouldn't have scattered it several places about the room."

Doctor Bushnell shrugged his shoulders. "Oh, what matter!" he exclaimed impatiently. "Whatever explanation there is would probably be absurdly simple."

Before the physician could gain the stairs, Sergeant Tish and the assistant district attorney were coming down. The latter was a youngish, blond fellow, with rimless spectacles glistening in front of pale-blue eyes; one could see that he appreciated the gravity of the situation and the importance of his own official position, and that, beneath his outward pretense of grim poise, he was a rather nervous and inexperienced young man.

One look at young Lasker told Wiggly how futile it would be to approach him with any theory calculated to upset the accepted situation; the lawyer's words confirmed this impression.

"Ah, Doctor Bushnell!" he exclaimed, frowning his best official frown and clearing his throat several times. "I have just been over the ground with Sergeant Tish, who has been kind enough to lay all of the facts before me—in quite a comprehensive manner. I have canvassed the evidence thoroughly. I quite agree with you, doctor, that but one sensible hypothesis can be drawn. I would even call it more than an hypothesis. The evidence is quite clear-cut and incontrovertible. Sergeant Tish's markmanship has— fortunately for him, however—cheated the electric chair of its grim function. There can be no question of Haskins' guilt; absolutely no question."

182

"In spite of hairpins, tallow, and such stuff," grunted Tish, with a grin at Wiggly, evidently taking a keen delight in belittling him. The young assistant district attorney glanced at the newspaper man and lifted his hands in a gesture of depreciation.

"So this is the journalist you were telling me about. If positive evidence were lacking, my dear sir, it might be very well to bear these things in mind, but in a clear-cut case of this kind such minor trifles become entirely irrelevant and immaterial. Any other theory than that of Haskins' guilt is absolutely untenable. I am willing, Doctor Bushnell, that the inquest shall proceed with the evidence in hand."

"I think I hear Presley's bus coming along the road now," nodded the doctor. "He's bringing the men from the village."

From outside there came the sound of the lumbering, noisy conveyance, bearing the coroner's jury. All attention at the moment was focused in this direction, and Wiggly, without a word to any one—he was playing an absolutely lone hand now—made for the stairs. No one registered any objection to his taking another visit to the second floor, but halfway up he turned and saw Kirklan Gilmore's eyes fixed upon him in a sort of set, expressionless stare. Was it expressionless? Wiggly had a feeling that the blank look might be concealing a degree of—well, perhaps of wary apprehension.

"Humph!" Wiggly said under his breath. "Gilmore was downstairs when his wife was killed; he couldn't have had a hand in it, and yet, dash it all, I did get a reflex from him when it came to mentioning the tallow. And he was pretty prompt in trying to find an explanation for the stuff being in the room. I wonder—" But what he wondered was too vague even for his thoughts. Passing on up the steps to the head of the stairs, he let himself into the murdered woman's bed-chamber.

"I don't know what I can expect to find more than I have," he told himself discouragingly, "but the old line in the copy book used to tell me: 'If at first you don't succeed, try, try again.' Here goes for another try. Gilmore was startled when I mentioned tallow candles. Why?"

Obviously that question could never be answered until he found out for himself what part the tallow had played in the tragedy, until he had explained its mysterious presence in the room. He walked about the room slowly several times and then dropped to hands and knees, crawling back and forth, his eyes close to the rug, picking up all of the tallow that he could find. Presently he had quite a little accumulation of the stuff, gathered from a surprisingly wide radius.

The palm of his hand was pricked by a sharp surface hidden from view in the nap of the rug—another fragment of the broken vase. The vase hadn't impressed him greatly; for that was one thing that could be explained. As Tish had suggested, if it hadn't been tipped from the table, Helen Gilmore might have flung it at the murderer in a desperate effort at self-defense.

Yet, as he was about to toss aside the fragment of porcelain, his jaw sagged, and a startled exclamation came from his parted lips, for there clung to what had once been the inside of the vase, a small particle of tallow!

"Gosh!" breathed Wiggly, his ears twitching violently. "The tallow was inside of the vase when it was broken! The two go together; I'd never thought of that. By George, I've been missing something!"

The shattered porcelain vase had, in light of this discovery, taken on a real importance within Wiggly's mind. Hastily he began crawling on hands and knees about the room, retrieving every piece of it that he could find. When he had got together all of it he could find, he placed all the pieces on the table, with the tallow in a separate pile and, drawing up a chair, sat down and began to study it. Still no inspirational solution flashed through his mind; he began at nowhere and ended at the same place. Times without number he handled the pieces, absently sorting and resorting them, and at last, with a hopeless sigh of defeat, he realized that an explanation was beyond his powers of either deduction or imagination; he was simply beating his head against a stone wall.

"Its no use!" he muttered under his breath. "Possibly I'm wrong after all! Possibly—"

Outside the closed door in the hall he heard voices. Bates had come upstairs to call Joan Sheridan and her mother to attend the proceedings down in the library. Wiggly wondered if they would ask him to testify; probably not. Doctor Bushnell and the assistant district attorney would not want him upsetting things and confusing the accepted explanation by flinging his unproven theories at the jury.

For a moment or so the newspaper man debated.

"I know I've no authority to do it, and I will probably get thrown out on my ear, if I'm caught at it; but I've got a notion to have one more try."

Leaving the piece of broken vase and the lumps of tallow on the table where he had been studying them with so little result, he turned toward the door, slipping quietly into the hall. The sound of voices came up the open stairway; Doctor Bushnell, in his capacity as deputy coroner, was swearing in the jury.

Wiggly made for the wing of the house where he knew Joan Sheridan's room to be. He had never rid himself of the notion that she knew something about the murder that she would never tell unless it was forced from her unwilling lips; and the only force to which she would respond would be evidence.

Her room was unlocked. He let himself in with the unconscious stealthiness that overtakes a man who finds himself entering unbidden places. Closing the door gently behind him, the reporter straightway went about the business in hand, which was to determine whether or not the room might not reveal something that would incriminate Joan Sheridan.

First, he went to the girl's dressing table; the top of it, except for some silver-backed toilet articles, was barren; but in the right-hand drawer he did find hairpins. Quickly he compared them with the one in his pocket; they were of the same size, color, and pattern. As alike as the proverbial two peas in a pod; yet that in itself was slim proof, for, as Joan herself had said, all hairpins are so much alike. He had to have more than that—a great deal more than that.

Wiggly was closing the drawer when he noted for the first time the black smudge on his finger—a smallish streak which flecked free from the skin, as he rubbed at it with the ball of his thumb.

"Hello!" he exclaimed under his breath. "What's that? Where did I get it?" With a curious and puzzled frown he stared at the dark spot on his finger, as he continued to fleck off the black, grainy particles. He lifted his hand to his nose and sniffed, and, as he caught the faint, but unmistakable, odor, his ears fairly did a dance at the sides of his head.

"Great guns," he whispered. "It's powder—burned gunpowder! Where did I get that?" His bulging eyes swept the dressing table and the only articles that he had touched since coming into Helen Gilmore's room. And then he thought of the candle tallow and the black specks that had mocked him with their enigma. Slowly, through a fog of bewilderment and incredulity, there pierced a dawning light of understanding. He had solved the murder!

# CHAPTER 29

## "LET THE GUILTY MAN SPEAK!"

The young assistant district attorney and Doctor Bushnell had indeed reduced the double inquest to a cut-and-dried formality, and the proceeding was heading swiftly toward its anticipated conclusion. Extra chairs had been brought into the library, and it was here that the hearing was in progress.

In his capacity as deputy coroner, Bushnell presided at a small table, and near him, at his right, was the young attorney, blinking with official severity from behind his rimless glasses; at the doctor's left was the witness chair which faced the jury. The latter were an assorted lot of village types—Mr. Judson, the ordinarily genial grocer, with his fat, stubby fingers locked tightly in front of his ample middle; Henry Blackburn, a local fire-insurance agent, who was tall, lean and hatchet faced; Jim Striker, local manager of the telephone company; and so on down the list.

There had been no move to bar any one from hearing the testimony of the other witnesses. Behind the jury chairs Joan Sheridan murmured soothingly in an effort to calm her mother's muffled, hysterical sobbing; a little apart sat Kirklan Gilmore, slumped deep into a chair, chin on his chest and his eyes half closed; but he was listening carefully; not a syllable was escaping him. Victor Sarbella was seated nearest the door; his dark eyes were roving restlessly about the room.

Sergeant Tish had been the first witness, identifying the gun which had killed Helen Gilmore and recounting, for the benefit of the jury, how it had got to Greenacres. Doctor Bushnell previously had given an outline of the facts, as he had found them.

Bates, the butler, followed Tish and did not forget to color his account of the happenings with a none-too-modest tribute to his own shrewd deductions that it had been murder and not suicide. He was proud of that little achievement. He told how he had been fast asleep when the ringing of the doorbell had awakened him, and he had got up to admit Gilmore, who had been out at the studio and had forgotten his keys; he described how he had been in the butler's pantry; that he had just finished making Gilmore a

186

toddy, which the latter was drinking, when both of them had heard the scream, closely followed by the shot.

Joan Sheridan suppressed a shiver, but no one noticed that.

"After that, Bates?" urged Doctor Bushnell.

"Mr. Gilmore and I hurried upstairs. When we was about halfway up we heard a door slam shut—Haskins when he scooted back up to the attic, I guess. The door to the younger Mrs. Gilmore's room was open, and the light was burning. I went in first, and there she was—all covered with blood, the gun on the floor beside the couch. It looked like suicide, but I knew it wasn't, because she wouldn't have screamed before shooting herself. She might have screamed after she did it, but the shot was fired after she screamed. More than that; the door was open, and, like I said, people don't shoot themselves with the door open."

"A very good deduction, Bates," nodded the doctor.

"Yes, sir; I rather thought so myself," agreed Bates.

Other questions and answers followed, and the entire ground was covered swiftly, but thoroughly. The jurors were then asked if they wished to interrogate the witness. None of them did, and Bates was excused.

"Miss Sheridan, merely as a matter of formality, will you please take the witness chair?" murmured Doctor Bushnell, and Joan, her face becoming a shade more pale with the ordeal, got slowly to her feet and walked to the front of the room. Kirklan Gilmore's body tensed, and his hand clenched, but he did not lift his eyes.

"I want you to understand," the doctor told her gently, after taking her oath as a witness, "that this is a mere formality. You will please tell us, in your own words, just what you know about the tragedy."

Joan Sheridan was plainly nervous; her fingers, resting in her lap, were twisting about each other, and for a moment she did not answer.

"There is nothing—nothing that I can tell," she answered in a strained, muffled voice.

"As I understand—in fact, from what you told me—you did not hear the fatal shot."

Joan's voice became a little clearer, as she answered: "No, I did not hear the fatal shot."

"I might explain to the jury," added the doctor, "that Miss Sheridan's room is in another part of the house."

From outside the library came the sound of hurrying feet, as Wiggly Price came down the stairs, two steps at a time. Just outside the library he paused, screened behind the portières. Across his arm was a woman's silk dressing gown, and in his hand was a handkerchief, caught up at the corners and sagging with the weight of the broken vase and the particles of candle tallow.

"Just the psychological moment!" he said under his breath. "It's made to order."

"And there is nothing more that you can add, Miss Sheridan?" asked Doctor Bushnell.

"There is nothing more that I can say," she answered.

"That will be all," murmured the doctor.

Wiggly Price entered the room, billowing aside the portières, as he swept past them, and his ears were wiggling for all they were worth. The silk dressing gown across his arm added to the dramatic effect of his entrance.

"Just a moment, Miss Sheridan!" he exclaimed. "What you really mean is that there is nothing more you want to say. But I am very much afraid that you will have to say something, whether you want to or not."

Doctor Bushnell leaped angrily to his feet, his eyes snapping.

"What do you mean by this, Price?" he shouted. "I forbid—"

"I demand," broke in Wiggly, "that Miss Sheridan be forced to explain several things, including why she tried to clean spots from the sleeve of this dressing gown that she was wearing last night." Joan had started to her feet, but sank limply back in her chair, a moan upon her lips.

"Look at her face!" cried Wiggly. "Isn't that proof enough for you? Don't look at me—look at her!"

Joan's face was chalk white, and she swayed in her chair and would have fallen, had not the assistant district attorney leaped forward to support her.

"Look at this dressing gown!" went on Wiggly in a rush of words. "Look at the sleeve, here. I just took it out of her closet a minute ago; the odor of a cleaning fluid, chloroform, can still be detected. And it didn't take out the spots. She didn't know that cold water was the best thing to remove bloodstains." He swung upon Joan. "Do you deny, Miss Sheridan, that these are bloodstains? Do you deny that you attempted to remove them after the murder?"

Joan's mother screamed shrilly. "It's a lie!" she moaned. "It's a lie. He's trying to make it appear that my little girl—" A merciful unconsciousness gathered her in.

Doctor Bushnell, dazed to a point of speechlessness, stared from the accusing newspaper man to Joan. There could be no denying the wild terror that gripped her.

"If she does deny it," went on Wiggly, "a chemical analysis will establish that it is blood—human blood."

Doctor Bushnell at last found voice. "Joan," he cried, "do you understand what this means? This man is virtually accusing you of murder. In Heaven's name, say something!"

But Joan Sheridan, her lips twitching, shook her head. "I—I didn't—do it!" she whispered. "I didn't do it, but I have nothing to say—absolutely nothing to say."

"But, you've got to say something!" the doctor urged desperately. "Silence like this—"

Again she shook her head. "I've nothing to say," she repeated.

In the excitement that had accompanied this sudden and amazing turn of things, all attention had been centered upon the quivering, ashen-faced girl in the witness chair, and no one—unless, perhaps, it was Wiggly Price from the corner of his eye—had observed Kirklan Gilmore. The novelist had leaped to his feet and clutched at the back of his chair with palsied fingers. Tears were streaming down his cheeks.

"Great God!" he whispered. "That she would make a sacrifice like that!" His voice raised. "Tell them!" he commanded hoarsely. "Tell them, Joan—the truth!"

Joan sobbed wildly, uncontrollably. "Oh, Kirk!" she moaned. "Kirk—don't! In Heaven's name—don't!"

"Since Joan will not talk," said Kirklan Gilmore, "I will."

Wiggly Price dropped his handkerchief to the table, and the loosened corners fell back, revealing the little pile of broken porcelain and the bits of tallow.

"Let the guilty man speak!" he said. "If he does not—the evidence is here."

# CHAPTER 30

## WIGGLY MAKES A WAGER

The room was tensely silent, as Kirklan Gilmore made his way slowly to the front of the room and, with a shaking hand, took the glass of water that rested upon the coroner's table. He gulped a drink nervously. He put the glass down clumsily.

"It's impossible—utterly impossible!" Doctor Bushnell muttered helplessly. "Gilmore was downstairs—Bates was with him—when the shot was fired on the second floor. I can't understand—"

Kirklan Gilmore did not sit down, but stood there, leaning heavily against the table, facing the coroner's jury.

"The truth," he said huskily, "would have been best in the first place; the truth is always best. I suppose any chance that I may have had is gone now. Yes, I—I killed her—with that gun." He pointed to the broken bits on Wiggly's handkerchief. "The evidence is there. I felt that it was coming when—when this reporter started talking—about the tallow."

"Suffering cats!" This interruption came from Sergeant Tish, who gave Wiggly Price an uncanny look of reluctant admiration.

"It began," went on Gilmore in a heavy, toneless voice, "on Monday, when Helen went to New York to meet Haskins, her—her husband." He winced, as he said that. "That night she wanted money to pay the blackmail of the man's silence. She lied to me, and I knew that she lied, but she would not tell me the truth.

"The next day Sarbella came, and I saw—we all saw—that there was something—something that terrified her. I got Sarbella out to the studio, tried to force him to tell. I suspected a—a love affair. I was mad with jealousy. He gave me his word that he had never so much as seen her before, but I thought that was a gentleman's lie. It was true.

"That night—last night only, but it seems an eternity—I stayed for a long time out at the studio, tortured by those black thoughts. It was after eleven o'clock when I came back to the house. Everybody had retired. I went upstairs to my room. It was next to Helen's. I was trying to compose

190

myself before I went in to her to demand the truth. I had no weapon; there was no thought of violence.

"The connecting door between our rooms was locked—from her side, but through the panel I thought I heard hushed voices. I thought—what could I think other than that Sarbella might be in there with her? Somehow I hesitated, and it must have been while I debated, trying to think, that she got Haskins out and to the third floor.

"And then I went in to her. She was sitting in a chair, facing the door. I didn't see the gun; it was on the floor at her feet. My mind was in such a daze that I hardly think I can make it clear just how it happened. I think I told her that there had been a man in her room, that I had heard them talking.

"I know that I was wild looking, disheveled, haggard. I had not slept at all the night before. Perhaps she thought I meant to kill her. Anyhow, she leaned over and picked up the gun swiftly. That was the first time I had noticed it.

"'Go away,' she told me. But I did not go away; I had come for the truth, the truth from her own lips. I told her to put down the gun, and when she did not, I did a very foolish thing; I attempted to take it from her by force. I couldn't control myself.

"That was when it happened—in the struggle for the gun. It was her own hand that pulled the trigger. I swear before Heaven that is true." He paused a moment, breathing heavily.

"The muzzle must have been pressed close to her body," he went on; "that was why there was scarcely any explosion; her body muffled the shot. She collapsed, and I put her on the couch. She did not move or speak. That is how it happened."

The young assistant district attorney gulped, as if he were choking, and Doctor Bushnell stared in dazed bewilderment.

"But there—there was a shot!" he gasped. "A shot—and her scream. I can't understand—"

"He hasn't finished his story, doctor," said Wiggly Price. "He hasn't told you how he worked the clever scheme of covering up the shooting, trying to make it appear suicide." He pointed to the bits of porcelain and the tallow. "There's the answer to that. He took the black porcelain vase as his alibi, put gunpowder into it and tamped it in with candle tallow, made a sort of firecracker. The wick of the candle, from which he stripped the tallow, was his fuse. He lighted it and went out of the house again, pretending that he'd forgotten his keys and had been locked out; that was an excuse to get the butler up and to have a witness to his alibi. Bates could truthfully swear that he was downstairs when the explosion sounded.

"Those black specks in the tallow that have been worrying me all morning, were burned gunpowder. Don't think I'd have obtained the answer to it, though, if I hadn't handled the pieces of the vase, and a black smudge—burned powder again—came free on my fingers.

"After that it was clear; the murderer was some one who wasn't on the second floor; that could mean only one person—Gilmore himself."

Lasker, the assistant district attorney, leaped to his feet.

"But in that case," he demanded, "what about the scream and Joan Sheridan's silk dressing gown and the bloodstains?"

"I fancy," answered Wiggly, "that it was Miss Sheridan who screamed."

Bates, the butler, gave a violent start.

"It was!" he exclaimed. "I said at the time it sounded just like the time she had screamed when Mr. Kirklan was thrown by his horse."

Gilmore spoke again. "Yes," he said, "the shot that awakened the house was not a shot, but the explosion of the powder in the vase. When I thought Helen was dead, I was suddenly afraid.

"Who would believe that was the way it had happened? They would arrest me, send me to prison, and I was suddenly a coward. I—I don't know how I happened to think of what I did; it just came to me suddenly, every detail of it.

"In my own room, in a closet, was a box of shotgun shells that I had used for duck hunting last fall. It was a simple matter to remove the wads and take out the powder from two shells and pour it into the vase. I had to go downstairs for the candle. That is all; it would take ten minutes or so for the candle wick to burn down to the powder. I went out of the house, but returned almost immediately and rang the bell. Bates let me in; I—I had to detain him downstairs until the explosion.

"When the scream came, I was even more startled than Bates. I could not understand that. And then when we got to the top of the stairs a door slammed, and the door to her room was open. I had left it closed; also I had turned off the lights, and they were burning.

"You can imagine the torture I was in. I tried to make myself speak, but I was a coward. I was afraid of the consequences. I would have spoken, if the net had tightened about Sarbella; I want that understood, that I should not have let an innocent man suffer.

"Then Haskins in the house—dead—it seemed to make me safe, to solve the whole terrible situation. And it was not murder. Believe me or not, I have told the truth."

Joan Sheridan lifted her head. "Yes," she said, "he has told the truth. I had it from—from her own lips."

"What!" cried Gilmore. "You can't mean that she—she was still alive. Merciful Heaven, I let her die!"

192

"I was unable to sleep," Joan went on slowly. "I had started downstairs for a book. As I passed the door of her room I heard her moaning. I opened the door and went in. I switched on the lights, bent over her; that must have been when the hairpin fell from my hair, and I got the blood on my sleeve. She was dying. She gasped out that Kirklan had shot her by accident. And that was when I screamed. The vase exploded an instant later." Her head lifted. "I realize that I am under oath; Helen told me with her own lips that it was an accident."

Wiggly Price wondered if this were true, or a superb falsehood to save the man she loved.

"If it was an accident, why didn't you talk?" Wiggly countered.

"The vase, his effort to hide by a porcelain mask what had really happened," she answered.

"And that was why you were so sure that Sarbella was innocent?"

Joan nodded.

"But you stated on your oath," pressed Wiggly, "that you did not hear the shot."

"That was the technical truth," answered Joan. "It was not a shot."

There fell silence; Doctor Bushnell fussed nervously with some papers on the table, notes he had been taking of the testimony. The jurors, although still dazed by it all, looked toward him expectantly.

"Gentlemen," he said slowly, "you have heard the evidence and the—er —confession. You have heard Miss Sheridan's statement of the dying words from the Gilmore woman's lips. I might add, as the examining physician, that the nature of the wound makes it plausible that it could have been inflicted in such a struggle for possession of the pistol as Mr. Gilmore has described. Mind you, gentlemen, I am not trying to sway your verdict; I merely state that the nature of the wound makes it plausible. Are there any questions that you wish to ask of any witness?" There were no questions; perhaps the jury was still too aghast to think of any. "Very well, the witnesses will retire, while the coroner's jury considers the case."

When Wiggly Price stepped out to the porch he found himself beside Sergeant Tish.

"Well, Tish," he said. "I told you that I was going to do it, and I did."

Sergeant Tish grinned feebly. "I gotta hand it to you, you did," he admitted. "And to think it was Gilmore that did the croak! You didn't have *that* doped out. Ain't it funny now that he didn't watch his chance and make away with the evidence? Guess he thought it was so clever nobody would get wise. I wonder if the girl was lying about the Gilmore woman telling her it was an accident."

Wiggly pursed his lips and toyed with something in his hand, the black hairpin.

"I wonder, too," he murmured. "But, whether she was or not, Gilmore's story was straight, dead straight. It was an accident, but he got panic and tried to cover it up by—what did Miss Sheridan call it?—the porcelain mask."

"Aw, g'wan!" grunted Tish derisively.

"Tish, I'll lay you three wagers: First, that the coroner's jury brings in a verdict of death by accident; second, that the district attorney's office will never go behind that verdict and bring Gilmore to trial; third, that Gilmore and Joan Sheridan are married within a year."

Tish snorted, but did not accept; had he done so, Wiggly would have won the first two and lost the third. It was almost two years before the last prophecy was fulfilled.

www.ingramcontent.com/pod-product-compliance
Lightning Source LLC
Chambersburg PA
CBHW011445170626
46816CB00008B/2519